the memory garden

Praise for *The Memory Garden*

"Fans of Alice Hoffman and Sarah Addison Allen will find a new passion in this atmospheric, eerie, and utterly beautiful debut. Mary Rickert walked me through a witch's garden by moonlight, perfectly invoking a magic place where lies smell like salt, memories taste of ash and honey, and ghosts whisper their last secrets to a girl on the verge of womanhood. *The Memory Garden* is a mother–daughter love story, soaked with intrigue and seasoned with both regret and the most lovely kind of breathless hope. Don't miss this one."

—Joshilyn Jackson, *New York Times* bestselling author
of *Someone Else's Love Story*

"A potent brew of guilty secrets and tragic histories, but also of enduring friendship and love. Add a pinch of the botanical. Serve on a luminous night faintly reminiscent of a Midsummer Night's Eve. A totally charming, totally engaging story told by Rickert, a magus of the first order. Magic in every line."

—Karen Joy Fowler, author of *We Are All Completely
Beside Ourselves* and *The Jane Austen Book Club*

"Mary Rickert's debut novel is absolutely stunning. An emotionally complex story bridges the divide between the past and the present, between generations, and between age-old friendships compromised by a web of secrets and lies. Be prepared to fall under this novel's strange and sensuous spell."

—Christopher Barzak, author of *One for Sorrow*

the memory garden

MARY RICKERT

sourcebooks
landmark

Sourcebooks and the colophon are registered trademarks of Sourcebooks, Inc.

Published by Sourcebooks Landmark, an imprint of Sourcebooks, Inc.

P.O. Box 4410, Naperville, Illinois 60567-4410

(630) 961-3900

Fax: (630) 961-2168

www.sourcebooks.com

Library of Congress Cataloging-in-Publication data is on file with the publisher.

Printed and bound in the United States of America.

VP 10 9 8 7 6 5 4 3 2 1

For Marie Angkuw, Mary Leanord, Liz Musser

and

In loving memory of Sharon Tholl
1960–2009

PENNYROYAL *Growing less than two feet in height, its flowers are usually blue, though they also occur in pink or white varieties. It is useful for flatulence, headaches, nausea, constipation, nervous weakness, and as an abortifacient.*

⁓◌

O ver the years, shoes were often thrown at the old house brooding atop its slope on Muir Glenn Road. The sole occupant of the old Victorian showed no distress upon finding footwear strewn about, however; she merely studied the smelly things as though evaluating works of art before taking them inside where boots, sneakers, heels, and cleats were transformed into charming planters.

It was because of the shoe garden that the house became locally famous, though there had always been rumors about disturbing fertile elements in the soil. The large elm tree, for instance, was not only unaffected by the disease that killed so many in the sixties, but also thrived, branching dark shadows across the entire left side of the porch, which did not impede the vigor of blue heaven morning glory or moonflowers trained to crawl up the railings. The rose mallow flourished in their boots, as did the hollyhocks; the hostas' great leaves obscured the shoes they were planted in, the pennyroyal grew so vigorously in the lady's slipper it had to be divided several times, and the forget-me-not sweetly flowered blue above men's work shoes.

The rumors about the gardener grew along with the garden. She was a witch, wasn't it obvious? Consider, as evidence, the young women arriving at all hours, alone, in pairs, occasionally accompanied by a man. Who knows what went on there—black magic, séances, love spells, abortions? But if you happened to drive down the isolated road as a visitor approached the house, she lowered her head or sheltered her face behind her hat and gloved hands, once even hiding behind an umbrella, though the day was sunny, with no threat of rain. Eventually, the rumors of women coming to the house on Muir Glenn Road were replaced by the rumor of a baby left there, a foundling delivered by fairies, a wild child abandoned by wolves, a creature neither human nor beast, the product of a teenage romance, a little witch, a freak; but as the child grew she proved to be mostly normal, except for the strange habit she had of talking to herself, and who could blame her? What child wouldn't be driven to distraction raised in such circumstance?

Ravens perch on the gables of Muir Glenn, cawing at drivers who slow to look at the whimsical garden. Those who drive there do not always return; it is a dangerous road, especially after dark, when the moonflower blossoms white blooms as big as dinner plates, their perfume so sweet that on certain summer nights it is rumored that anyone within a twenty-mile radius is enchanted.

On those nights, women dream of walking up to the house in moonlight, the elm tree leaves whispering overhead, its branches groaning, the air perfumed with flowers dying. The great wooden door opens and the women enter, the door closing silently behind them, severing dreamed from dreamers, leaving the dreamers in the dark.

PUMPKIN *The round, edible fruit of a trailing vine, pumpkins are a symbol of fertility. Dead spirits are invoked by the pumpkin when faces are carved into it, and it is lit from within. The spiral of life is represented by the pumpkin; the harvest brings death, but the seeds bring birth.*

〜♦〜

In October, Nan does all the expected things. She sets the unlit jack-o'-lanterns on the porch, knowing they will be thrown to the ground, their pulpy flesh split, smiles broken, eyes torn; she fills the wooden bowl with bags of candy and turns the porch light on, though no one will come begging. "We live so far out in the country," she'll say to Bay, who sits with her legs crossed easily beneath her at the kitchen table. Nan wonders when the flexibility of youth left her so entirely that she must sit with her feet in the old clogs, planted firmly as a Quaker's, on the floor.

They eat the candy bars, gummy worms, and chocolate chip cookies by candlelight, talking awkwardly about the change of weather, Bay's school projects, the news from town, stopping in midsentence and midchew to listen to a car slow in front of the house, its occupants shouting something unintelligible, before speeding down the road.

"Why are they so stupid?" Bay asks. "Can't they see you're not evil?"

"Not everyone thinks witches are evil," Nan says.

Bay rolls her eyes and bites into a Butterfinger. "No one calls you a witch as a compliment."

Nan sighs. She should have set things right years ago when Bay came home from second grade in tears because a classmate accused her of living in a haunted house with an old witch, but Nan was so pleased with the benign accusation she only said, "What a silly child. Not everyone is smart like you are, Bay."

Nan thinks that if she could go back to that day she would change her response. What is the term they use lately? Teaching opportunity? Yes, she could have used that moment as a teaching opportunity had she not been so distracted by her relief that she lost focus. Sadly, this seems to be a theme in Nan's life, as if she's always suffered from an untreated astigmatism.

"Do you smell something burning?"

Frowning, Bay shakes her head.

Nan closes her eyes against the scent of Halloween bonfires, remembering herself as a little witch, running down the dark street with her friends, Mavis dressed as a ghost, Eve as a fairy, and Ruthie, her fat legs churning beneath the orange pumpkin costume, struggling to keep up.

"Nana? Nana?"

"Goodness, what is it, child?" Nan says, immediately regretting the harsh tone of her voice.

Bay shrugs one shoulder, a gesture Nan finds maddening though she can't say why.

"I just wanted to make sure you were okay."

"It's good you called me back," Nan says, trying to make things right. "I believe the fairies took me away for a while."

She pretends not to notice Bay sulk further into her chair, as though even here, in the privacy of their kitchen, Nan is an embarrassment.

Well, Bay is fourteen now, that age when the company of her own kind is greatly preferred over spending time with her old mother. In fact, Nan had expected Bay would have a Halloween party to attend this year. Nan was not adverse to the idea of spending the night removed from Bay's censorious gaze, with a glass or two of pumpkin wine (truth be told, not her favorite, but if not tonight, when?).

"What are you talking about?" Bay asked when Nan mentioned, in passing, her plans. "Are you trying to get rid of me?"

Well, of course not! Nan couldn't imagine. Why would she

want to do such a thing? Bay is the light of her life, the joy of her soul, the rose of her garden, the spice, the sweet, her heart, her great love story arrived at an age when Nan thought she would never have one. So what if the child has been difficult lately? She is a teenager, after all, and some difficulty is to be expected.

Now they sit at the small kitchen table, their faces flickering in the candlelight, pretending not to mind the silence that settles between them, the heavy loneliness of no longer knowing how to talk to each other.

Bay goes to bed first, her lips smeared with chocolate, wormy bits stuck between her teeth, sugar blossoming on her tongue. She does not, in fact, sleep, but sits at the edge of the bed, listening for her Nana's footsteps creaking up the stairs. Bay waits until she hears the distressing sound of Nan snoring before tiptoeing down the service stairs into the kitchen, still scented of candle wax and chocolate, to the front of the house, where she peers around the curtain to watch through the dark glass.

When she was younger, Bay never recognized the tricksters, but in recent years, she has. Some are no surprise at all: Chad Lyle, Darren Prost, even Kelly Madden, just the sort Bay would expect to cause trouble. Last year she thought Wade Enders was with them, though she couldn't be sure. It made no sense, after all. Wade wasn't a boy known for what he did in the dark, not then at least, though there are rumors about what he does now with Shelly. Bay can't help but wonder what it would be like to be kissed by Wade Enders.

It is so late when they arrive that Bay thinks even the moon has been swallowed by the night, though later she realizes this is the sort of thing her Nana would say, rather than admit to clouds. Bay is both disappointed and pleased that he is not with them. She wonders, as she watches Chad, Darren, Kelly, and some freshman whose name she doesn't remember, if Wade is with Shelly tonight, maybe parked down the road in Wood Hollow, the nearly deserted subdivision behind Bay's backyard, close enough that she could walk there, though her Nana has warned her against the nettles and poison ivy that grow wild in the forest. Bay is not allowed to go beyond the two weeping apple trees, their twisted limbs barely visible through the tall grass and overgrown lilacs. She has no interest in spying on Wade and Shelly anyway, fumbling for buttons, zippers, and lace, tearing into each other's costumes. Instead, she stands hidden behind the dark glass, watching vandals curse at the smashed pumpkin that explodes with the water balloons she stuffed there. By the time she crawls back into bed, Bay is content with her Halloween celebration.

Having tossed the pile of clothes from the bedroom chair to the floor, Nan wakes in an uncomfortable posture to the sound of little criminals beneath her bedroom window. She waits for them to depart, then listens to Bay tiptoe up the stairs, a tradition of sorts these past few years. Nan can't believe she fell asleep when she is supposed to keep watch as she has every Halloween since Bay's arrival, guarding against ghosts. She uncorks the wine and pours a glass, taken somewhat aback by the pungent, overripe scent of pumpkin. The taste is pleasantly sweet, and after a few sips she barely notices the odor, replaced as it is by the rosemary scent of memory.

Life is what you remember, Nan thinks, remembering the scent of dried leaves, apples, and smoke, recalling that long-ago Halloween of her youth, when Eve wore her pink-dyed First Communion dress. Layers of scalloped lace poufed around her skinny legs and arms; the fairy wings glimmered behind her face with its pointed chin and almond eyes spaced just a little too far from that button nose, giving her the pleasant appearance of a kitten. How happy Eve was, spinning down the dark street, waving her wand at the houses, the gardens, and the moon.

Mavis, however, was annoyed. She thought that the Amazing Mr. Black was stupid. "Who cares about dumb magic tricks?" she said, her hand on her white-robed hip.

"Oh, I don't know," Nan said. "I thought that thing with the rabbit was neat."

When Mavis rolled her eyes, the whites of them in the midst of her white-painted face gave her the look of a real ghost.

Nan wished she had not agreed to take this route. She promised her mother they would come straight home, but Mavis insisted they walk past the graveyard, making fun of Nan, Ruthie, and Eve when they said they didn't want to.

"Hey, wait for me!"

Nan frowned at Ruthie, with her flushed face beneath the green stem cap, almost a perfect circle, her cheeks bright red. *A pumpkin face on top of a pumpkin face,* Nan thought and bit her lip. "You got chocolate on you," she said, pointing to the corner of her own lips.

Ruthie's tongue explored the perimeter of her mouth until it touched the smear. She smiled and wiped her cheek with her finger, which she sucked before asking where Eve had gone to.

Though this was decades before the epidemic of missing children, Nan remembers the stab of fear. She remembers thinking, *I am going to be in such trouble,* before Mavis said, "There she is," her white-gloved finger pointing.

Eve was so far down the street she really did look like a fairy waving her wand, unaware she'd left the others behind.

They all saw the figure step out from the dark, looming over her, and then bending low, as though whispering in her ear. They saw her take half a step back. Was it a trick of the night or something else? When she turned toward them, it is as though the space between was an illusion; Eve's eyes in that moonlit face were wide and beseeching.

"Come on," Mavis said.

"Come on," Nan said to Ruthie, and they ran behind Mavis,

whose white sheet twisted around her legs but did not slow her pace. By the time they caught up, Eve had stepped aside, and Mavis was talking to the man, not a stranger at all, but Mr. Black himself.

"Oh, I doubt that," she said.

It was shocking, really, how bossy Mavis could be with some adults.

"Well, hello, little girl," Mr. Black said. "Maybe you can help me? I seem to be lost."

"Hey, you're Mr. Black!" Ruthie shouted, so loud Nan worried someone would come out of one of the houses lining the other side of the street to see what the noise was all about.

"One and the same." He bowed deeply.

Up close he was very tall, very thin, and missing a tooth Nan hadn't noticed when he was onstage. He was also older than she'd thought, his face lined with wrinkles, though his hair was quite dark.

"Where's your rabbit?" Ruthie asked.

"Oh, Bella? Bella? Well, she's not any ordinary rabbit, you know."

Mavis made a noise, a grumbly sort of cough, enough to cause them all to look at her, standing there with her hand on her hip.

"Look, mister," she said, "I doubt you know anyone from around here, and we're not supposed to talk to strangers."

"Well, that's where you're wrong," Mr. Black said.

The previous Halloween there had been a marionette show at the Legion Hall, and Nan thought Mr. Black looked a lot like one of the puppets. He even moved like one, as though his wrist, elbows, and head were pulled by strings when he turned to face her.

"Grace Winter."

"Witch Winter?" Ruthie said, again too loud. "She's Nan's neighbor."

"And Nan is…" Mr. Black looked around, though Nan had

the odd feeling this was some sort of game, that he already knew all their names, but how was that possible?

"She lives next door to me."

"She's not really a witch," Mavis said. "That's just something little kids think."

"We're going to sleep at Nan's house tonight," Ruthie volunteered, giving no indication if she realized Mavis just insulted her. "You can come with us."

Rolling her eyes at Ruthie, Nan noticed they were standing in front of the cemetery gate, with its black spikes pointing to heaven. Eve must have realized the same thing, for she had taken off again, running as though her wings were on fire. Ruthie made the sign of the cross over her pumpkin chest, which caught Mavis's attention. She frowned at the stone angels and dark tombstones, but continued at her usual pace. Nan walked beside Mr. Black, pretending she didn't care about the graveyard. It didn't take long. It was not a very big town, and there weren't that many dead people yet. Eve waited for them in front of Old Lady Richie's house, her rose garden in autumn thorns.

"You're a very fast little girl," Mr. Black said.

Eve turned away without answering, waving her wand as though creating the night.

"She's not mean," Ruthie whispered, "she's just sad 'cause her Mom is dying."

Mavis told Ruthie to shut up, while Eve continued to wave her wand in wide, slow arcs, like a weary fairy pointing at the moonlit houses, the cracked sidewalk, the dried leaves.

"Mr. Black?" Ruthie asked.

"Speak up. I can hardly hear you."

"Where do you get your power?"

Mr. Black laughed so hard and for so long that Eve turned to watch. Nan felt bad for Ruthie. It's just how she was. She asked stupid questions. When he finally stopped laughing, they continued on their way—Eve waving her wand, Mavis taking broad, unghostlike steps, Nan and Ruthie walking on either side of Mr. Black—until Nan noticed that Ruthie looked like she might cry and crossed over to hold her small hand, which was sticky and warm.

When they stopped in front of Nan's house, Mavis pointed her ghost finger at the one next door, the porch covered in dried vines and dead flowers, the carved pumpkins on every step flickering candlelight grins.

"She lives there," Mavis said.

Mr. Black bent until his face was so close Nan could smell his breath, which was surprisingly cotton candy. He lifted his hand in front of Ruthie's nose, his bony finger pointed straight up.

Nan followed the line from crooked nail to the moon. "You get your power from here," he said. She looked down just in time to see him touch Ruthie's lips with the tip of his finger, which made Nan feel funny, like she'd seen something bad.

Nan suspects her little-kid mind, full of Halloween excitement, makes her remember it like this, but she always pictures him standing and turning away, losing his human proportions like a figure drawn in black crayon on the silver night. She remembers watching him walk up the stairs to Miss Winter's house, almost disappeared sideways; the great door creaking open, a cackle of laughter from the other side, the enchantment broken by her mother's voice.

"Nan, what are you doing? Where have you girls been? Do you know how late it is?"

Nan was distracted for only a moment, but by the time she turned, Miss Winter's door was closing, creating a draft, which blew out every pumpkin grin, and splashes pumpkin wine on Nan's hand, startling her back to the present, sitting in the uncomfortable chair, blinking at the dark.

Nan inhales deeply, steeling herself against the pain of moving stiff bones to set the glass gently on the floor beside the open bottle. At seventy-eight, she is too old for sleeping in chairs, too old for raising a teenager, and certainly too old to be afraid of ghosts. But what can be done, she asks herself, as she has so many times before; what else can the guilty do but fear the retribution?

PINE *Pine, slow to decay, is a symbol of immortality. It is used to treat despondency, despair, and self-condemnation.*

⌒◯⌒

The worst day is her birthday. *Seventy-nine years*, Nan thinks on that cold December morning. *Not much time left.*

"What are you doing?" she mumbles, staring at her bedroom ceiling. "Get a hold of yourself." She glances at the digital clock's red numbers glowing through the clutter on her bedside table. Six fifteen. She needs to get up. Make sure Bay doesn't miss the bus.

Nan shivers against the cold as she throws off the blankets and quilts, awakening Nicholas in the process. Only as she slides her legs across the flannel sheets and sits up does she realize she smells something wonderful, which is most unusual for her birthday. A knock on the bedroom door, situated strangely low, as though made with the fist of a tiny creature, or perhaps someone's foot, startles her; she is sitting with her hand over her heart when the door swings open and Bay enters, carrying a tray of pancakes and coffee.

"Happy birthday, Nana," Bay says, grinning broadly.

Nan makes a big deal of clapping her hands in delight, though it is mostly pantomime and doesn't make any sound at all. Bay doesn't seem to notice. She walks slowly across the room. Nan moves to sit with her pillows against the cold, hard wall, pulling the blankets up around her lap. Nicholas, clearly annoyed by this break in routine, jumps to the floor and scurries out of the room, a flash of white.

"I hope you're hungry." Bay sets the tray on Nan's lap, then turns to flick on the bedside lamp, knocking over an empty mug in the process.

"Oh, I am," Nan lies, blinking against the bright. "This smells wonderful," she says, no longer locating the pancakes or coffee through the salty scent that permeates the air.

Bay, her red hair uncombed, still wearing her pajama pants and the lavender sweater someone gave Nan years ago, encourages her to eat, which she does.

Everything tastes like salt, but Nan continues swallowing against the gag reflex, smiling and complimenting the breakfast. She knows the meal is probably as delicious as she says it is. Bay is quite competent in the kitchen. Nan glances at her, sitting in the chair on top of the clothes tossed there, the once lovely sweater stretched over her knees. Bay doesn't know this is the worst day of Nan's life. Not a celebration, but a lament. She had not been very good at friendship, in the end, but she likes to believe she has been a good mother.

"You better get dressed," Nan says. "You don't want to miss the bus."

The room dims with Bay's sigh.

Nan has found that the best way to get through all the birthday eating is to pretend exuberance, shoveling food into her mouth like a person starved, just to get it over with as quickly as possible. She chews vigorously. Nan knows what Bay wants. She wants to stay home. It's been a struggle for years to get Bay to school, and lately it's gotten worse.

Nan is grateful she has chewing as an excuse for not speaking. Truth be told, she would love to have Bay's company to distract her, though maybe it would be better if she did not. The memories that arrive on this day are a crash of blood and hope so spectacular, they leave Nan breathless; what if Bay's presence is not enough to stave them off? She would be traumatized to find Nan clutching her heart and weeping.

Bay stands suddenly. She smiles, but it's a salty smile. Clearly the child is exasperated. She leans over to kiss Nan's forehead and says something about how much she loves pancakes. Of course Nan concurs.

"I better hurry," Bay says, and just like that, she is gone. Nan can hear her in the bedroom, opening drawers and not closing them. The girl is dressed in five minutes, calling good-bye, sounding like a pony running down the stairs. The house shakes when she slams the door. Nan lifts the heavy tray off her lap, sets it on the bed, shivering as she walks to the window, arriving just in time to watch the small orb bobbing through the dark.

It is only a moment, brief as a single breath, but Nan does something she hasn't done since she was seventeen. She makes a birthday wish, using Bay's flashlight as conduit. "Be happy," she says.

At the heavy sound of the bus coming around the corner, Bay turns the flashlight off, and Nan feels a dark terror. Wishes bring spirits out of their hiding places. Now, in an unguarded moment, she's opened the door that is impossible to close. "Please," she whispers into the cold room. "Leave her out of it." Somewhere in the distance she hears the voice singing happy birthday. "Just stop," she says, and it does.

HOLLYHOCK AND MALLOW *Hollyhock should not be confused with Mallow. Mallow is useful in cases of difficult or obstructed menstruation, especially good as an abortifacient; placing the fruit over a dead person's eyes will keep evil spirits from entering the body. Hollyhock root powdered or boiled in wine prevents miscarriage and kills worms in children.*

O n the morning of Bay's fifteenth birthday, Nan wakes to the pleasant scent of summer flowers and loamy earth. She eats a bowl of blueberries, savoring the sweet flavor unassaulted by the rosemary scent of memory or salty scent of lies, before going to the garden where she tends her hollyhocks, the old-fashioned single blossoms in shades of pale pink, blushed violet, and creamy white. Settling quickly on the menu for Bay's birthday dinner, Nan's mind wanders, as it does so often lately, but at least this time it goes in a pleasant direction.

Though Bay might have been born the night before her arrival, they celebrate her birthday on the July date when Nan found her, left in a box on the front porch, mistaken at first for a shoe donation until she heard the strange cry, even then expecting a kitten, not the baby who blinked tear-beaded lashes when Nan parted the odd draping like some kind of primal mosquito netting, though she recognized the caul immediately for what it was, the sign of a witch.

Nan peered down at the strange arrival as if expecting the newborn to disappear, which did not happen, of course. When she looked up, she scanned the front yard, its crowd of shoe flowers yawning open in July's mist, craning her neck to peer around the side of the house, leaning over the railing, careful not to squash the morning glory's blue throats. She walked, barefoot, past the two rocking chairs, to the other side of the porch, frowning at the elm tree, scanning the quiet S-curved road and the bank beyond lined with a blaze of tiger lilies and purple phlox.

Who knows how long she stood there, breathing in the minty scent of pennyroyal, before a strange sound interrupted her reverie? Nan returned to the abandoned baby just opening her little mouth to cry in protest. A bright sunbeam pierced the dawn to shine on the newborn as though anointed.

Nan squatted, feeling the resistance of her knees and the uncomfortable girdle of her belly, placing one hand under the soft, small head covered in downy red hair, one beneath the swaddled blanket. Their eyes locked, for just a moment, in a very adult manner before Nan brought the baby to her shoulder when she realized she could not easily rise to stand from this position, which caused a momentary panic. She could not risk wavering to a fall, not with this innocent creature depending on her, nor could she put the baby back into that sun-tortured box. Nan sat on her bottom, and once there, stayed for quite a while, watching the mist depart in wisps like night fairies frightened of the light, not realizing for some time that she had been singing to the child, a lullaby of sorts, from that poem by Yeats.

"For the world's more full of weeping than you can understand."

Goodness, why would she sing such a thing? Nan shook her head at herself. She was old. Well, not that old, only sixty-four, but certainly at an advanced age for realizing she could no longer do, or say, or sing whatever she pleased.

Nan discovered that by scooting across the porch she could place her feet on the step below and, holding the baby tight with one hand, using the other to pull on the railing, she rose to stand, by which time she was overheated, her hair damp against her forehead.

"Well," she said, as she turned back to the house and the cool rooms that waited there, "I haven't killed you yet, at least."

It was meant as a joke, but she immediately regretted saying it.

Over the years, Nan had received other strange donations. Mrs. Vergonian, for instance, always donated only one shoe of a pair. Nan wondered what she did with the other. Perhaps she'd started a secret shoe garden of her own. Some people seemed to confuse Nan with Goodwill, leaving boxes of clothes for children and men that Nan had no interest in. Somebody left bags of giant zucchinis on Nan's porch every fall, which she very much appreciated. For years someone had left homemade bread, still warm enough that it was sweating the plastic bag it was wrapped in. Nan was sorry when that tradition came to an end. One summer, someone left honey, and though the jar was sealed, bees clustered around the lid when Nan discovered it at the far corner of her porch. She took advantage of the situation and whispered her secrets to the swarm until, one by one, it became too much for them, and they flew off. Once there was a hand-knit sweater. It was a beautiful shade of lavender, too precious for Nan. She did not wear it, but tucked it into the bottom drawer of her dresser.

She was never sure what she'd find on her porch, the lovely gifts interspersed with bags of dog poop and nasty words written in chalk, or flowers torn from their shoes and thrown, which Nan found quite upsetting. No one had ever before left a baby. Nan decided it was probably a trick of some kind. A test.

She called the sheriff.

Sheriff Henry, who at first did not understand what Nan was telling him ("A what?" he'd shouted into the phone three times before shouting, "A baby?"), arrived within the hour to begin his "investigation," which amounted to poking his index finger gently into Bay's tummy, producing a much-older-than-her-hours smile.

Nan showed him everything—the box, the blanket, even

the caul, which in hindsight was a mistake; he remarked on the strange color and feel of it. When he asked Nan what it was, she explained how the baby had likely been born with it around her face. The sheriff made an expression as though he'd just gulped sour lemonade, then quickly changed the subject. He would find a place for the orphan, he said, to which Nan replied, in the legendary word burp of her life, "What are you talking about? Her place is right here."

The sheriff, who had arrived in Nan's kitchen, blinking against the light, his usually neat hair uncombed, was momentarily struck silent by Nan's suggestion that she keep the foundling, then mumbled something about paperwork, red tape, the annoying habits of his deputy, and what he called "the scourge" of gossip. (In spite of the odd rumors that circulated about Nan, she had her advocates, and the sheriff's mother, though now dead, had been one of them; it is for this reason, Nan assumed, that he was so kind in his pessimism.) He did not know, however, that the social worker owed Nan a big favor.

Mrs. Hevore arrived the next day. Looking as if she bore no relation to the young woman Nan found a decade ago weeping in her garden, shoving hollyhock and mallow blossoms into her mouth, as though there were no difference between them. She toured the house without making reference to the trouble she'd once been in, or how Nan, who had already been retired for some time by then, helped. Nan needed to fill out an absurd amount of paperwork, but with Mrs. Hevore's peevish assistance, and with almost no one claiming the child or challenging Nan's right to parent her (no need to dwell on that dark matter now) the adoption was completed.

The whole thing happened with shocking efficiency, which, Nan later learned, was attributed by the locals to something unnamed, but certainly of an occult nature that she had done to hex the system. Soon after, she was confronted by the terrible things being said. Of course she suspected there were rumors, how could there not be? A baby left on the porch in a box! It was the most sensational thing to happen since 1965, when the local high school basketball team had a terrible accident and two of the boys were killed. What Nan didn't anticipate (which in hindsight she realized was shockingly naive—she knew small-town judgment, after all) was the breadth of cruelty that so easily embraced the innocent newborn.

But that was long ago, Nan thinks, picking a hollyhock blossom for the kitchen windowsill. Fifteen years! Surely no one would be so cruel as to fault Bay for the circumstances of her birth! Yet what else can Nan conclude from the distressing state of Bay's social life? She is spending her birthday with her best, and apparently only, friend, Thalia, a perfectly nice girl who stares at Nan too much. The girls have spent a lazy morning, first upstairs in Bay's bedroom, and now on the quilt beneath the elm.

Pretending to fuss over her herbs, Nan realizes with a start that Thalia has caught her spying. Thalia waves while Bay frowns; she has told Nan several times that she looks silly wearing the wreath of walnut leaves, but Nan won't part with it. After all, it keeps the flies away, and that is the point. As Nan picks mint for the frosting, she thinks how all those years when she mourned motherhood, she had never guessed at the anguish of the position.

They call Bay wolf child because, they say, she was raised by wolves before she was left on Nan's porch wrapped in a blanket, in a box with lace draped over it to keep the mosquitoes out.

"Like that makes any sense," Bay says. "How could wolves wrap a blanket? They don't even have fingers."

Bay knows she should probably stop; Thalia has her own

problems, after all, but sometimes Bay just needs to talk, even if it is her birthday, the supposedly happiest day of her life.

Sitting at the edge of the quilt, Bay glances at Thalia to see why she's so uncharacteristically silent, and discovers her waving at Nan, who stands in the middle of the shoe garden, wearing that stupid wreath. This is the kind of thing Bay is talking about. How can she ever expect the kids at school to treat her like she's normal? Her Nana ducks her head, shuffling along the side of the house, carrying her basket filled with herbs and cut flowers, looking just like the witch everyone says she is.

"I'm not going back."

"Back where?" Thalia asks.

"School."

"What? Where are you going?"

Bay shakes her head. She has no idea where this came from. It just came out, a word burp, her Nana calls them, but now that it's been said she realizes how much she wants it to be true.

"What about—"

"Don't say anything to her. She doesn't know." Bay lays back on the quilt, squinting against the sun streaming through the green leaves of the old elm tree to the blue sky beyond. Her whole life, it seems, she's wanted to be only here. Would her Nana consider home schooling? Or will Bay have to think of something else? She doesn't have the answer, but one thing she knows is that saying she isn't going back to school makes her feel immediately different. Lighter. As if she's suddenly holding a giant bouquet of balloons, like in that movie. Like she could float away at any minute. Like anything could happen. She hopes for anything good.

⌒

The birthday feast is a great success. The menu consists of herb-roasted chicken, cream cheese mashed potatoes (Nan makes extra of these, knowing how much both girls love them), and boiled beets. She serves good red wine, chosen for its smoldering taste, hoping it will ruin both girls for the cheap affection of high school boys.

The girls smile and make eyes at each other when the wine is poured, but it quickly becomes apparent that they prefer the lemon water. They eat in the dining room, off china set on the lace tablecloth, the white taper candles lit, the chandelier dimmed. In spite of the still air of a July night, the sheers billow around the open windows, bringing with them the scent of lavender, basil, and something else Nan can't quite identify, something musky, damp, slightly unpleasant, like a sweater left in the rain, or a dead animal in the garden.

The girls are at the perfect age and of the perfect temperament to appreciate the celebration. Nan wonders if this is the last time they will do so. Oh, she is melancholy tonight, but this is Bay's fifteenth birthday, so who knows? Thinking of her own abandoned friendships, Nan drinks the wine that only she seems to appreciate.

"You don't have to eat those," Bay says.

Thalia has been shoving beets around her plate like a dreaded homework assignment. Nan smiles kindly, meaning to reassure the girl that of course she doesn't have to eat them if she doesn't want to, at which point Thalia spears a large slice of beet with her fork, opens her mouth wide, and chomps quite vigorously, staring at Nan as if challenging her to a beet-eating duel. Instead, Nan cuts the cake without ceremony, placing large slices on pink crystal plates.

"When do we light the birthday candles and sing?" Thalia asks.

"Not until dark," Bay says. "Outside."

"It's supposed to rain."

Nan knows this is true, but both she and Thalia turn to Bay, who shakes her head and says it's not going to, so Nan sees no reason to change their plans.

While they eat the chocolate cake, Nan notices that what little wine the girls had has blossomed blotched roses onto their cheeks. She thinks her own face must be aflame, for she has not refilled either girl's glass, yet the bottle is almost empty, and besides, she feels light now, as if suspended above the room, escaped from the cage of her old body.

"Nana? Are you all right?"

Nan opens her mouth, prepared to say something important about friendships and time; instead, she burps. This prompts such a horrified expression from Bay that Nan can't help but giggle, putting a damper on the lovely evening. Bay announces, with a distant, slightly disgusted tone, that she and Thalia are going into the parlor to watch movies. For some reason, Nan finds this funny. She pretends to concentrate on her plate as the girls pass, glancing up just long enough to note the studied way Bay ignores her and the soft smile Thalia graces her with, which Nan appreciates. Once the girls leave, Nan's humor subsides. She sits at the table, trying not to remember her eighteenth birthday. When her mother sliced the cake, red velvet and Nan's favorite, she could only think of blood.

Nan stands to clear the dishes, and the room wavers. She has had too much to drink, yet how lovely it is to feel released from the ache of bones and body. The table is half-cleared when the girls come out to help. They don't need to, it's Bay's birthday, but they work while chatting happily about the vampire movie they're watching.

After the dishes are done, Bay kisses Nan on the cheek and thanks her for a wonderful dinner. The girls go back to their movie. Nan sits on a rocker on the front porch, waiting for the dark, which comes so suddenly; she must have fallen asleep during its arrival. She is confused, trying to remember where she is and why, thinking she is the birthday girl, before recollecting. That's when she notices the smell, the overwhelming scent of honeysuckle. "Eve?" she says, but there is no answer.

Nan shakes her head, rousing herself to place the tea lights in a circle of flat rocks in the backyard, fifteen of them, just the beginning of the spiral of life. When Nan tells the girls it is time, they appear near sleep, their eyes half-closed, their cheeks bright, but they quickly rally, in the way of the young.

It is a starry night, surprisingly cool for July. Bay lights the candles while Nan and Thalia sing. The three of them sit watching the flames in silence until Nan decides to go back to the house. "You girls stay out here as long as you like. Just don't leave the yard." Raised on terrible, true tales of kidnapped children, the girls agree.

Nan would like nothing better than to crawl into her narrow bed, but instead she pulls the chair, with its uneven cushion of tossed clothes, to the window overlooking the front of the house.

It was a nice birthday, wasn't it? She thinks it was. Bay seems happy, yet Nan cannot shake the feeling that creeps over her, of trouble coming. She peers into the dark until her eyes burn, determined to stay focused, though she knows better than to think all danger can be seen.

Bay and Thalia have been best friends since kindergarten, when they were paired up as line buddies, standing shoulder to shoulder every time the class went anywhere: to lunch, recess, the library, field trips to the cheese factory and the post office. Over the years, they've both changed; Bay is taller than Thalia now, and Thalia can draw anything, a talent Bay does not possess. One thing that has remained constant through all the years is Thalia's ability to keep the conversation going. Hours may pass, sometimes entire days, especially when she is so busy during the school year, but Thalia always resumes their conversation as though they had only been briefly interrupted.

"So, where were we," Thalia says. "Oh, that's right, vampire or werewolf? You know they make it look like one is the obvious choice, but when you really think about it, a vampire is always a vampire, and a werewolf is only horrible when there's a full moon. So..."

Much later, after measuring the benefits of a real boy against a fantastic one, the tea lights burned low, they agree they are tired. Thalia says they should blow out the candles before they go inside. "We don't blow them out," Bay says. "That would be like blowing out the years of my life." Thalia opens her mouth to say something but instead drapes her arm over Bay's shoulder as they walk up the grassy slope.

After Thalia falls asleep, Bay lies in the dark, thinking about the day. She doesn't know anyone who celebrates birthdays the way they do. Even in the middle of winter, they set tea lights in snow for her Nana's birthday, making an impressive spiral of fire that Bay likes to watch from the warm kitchen. She rolls to her side, rearranges her pillow. It would be nice to fall asleep the way Thalia does, in midsentence, but Bay has never been an easy sleeper. It was a nice birthday, a really nice party, but she can't shake the feeling of dissatisfaction that settles over her.

Bay's whole life she's felt like there's a deep secret she hasn't been told. Years ago, she tried to talk to her Nana about it, but she acted so distressed, spooning heaping teaspoons of cinnamon into her yogurt as though she were having some kind of a fit, saying over and over again, "Whatever could you mean? I never hid that you're adopted," Bay hasn't brought it up since.

She rolls to her back and stares up at the ceiling. *Maybe that's all it is*, she thinks. Maybe the feeling she gets, that there is some great secret to her life, is just because she has never met her birth mother. "Are you thinking about me tonight?" Bay whispers into the dark, then clenches her lips. She is fifteen now. She needs to get over this terrible habit she has of talking to herself. If there is some secret to her life, other than being adopted, well, "it's time to know."

"Time," Thalia mumbles. "Time for what?"

"Nothing. You're dreaming," Bay says, wincing at the words.

It's the sort of thing her Nana says when Bay wakes up in the middle of the night. Thinking of Nan's short figure in the dark, her shadow face framed by the silver glow of hair hanging down, makes Bay sad. It's not that she wants anyone else for a mother; she just wants to know where she came from.

But no, that's not really it either. Bay is suddenly wide awake and filled with the need to look out her window. She moves carefully, she doesn't want to wake Thalia, but the squeaky floorboards are impossible to avoid. Thalia mumbles in her sleep and rolls to her side. Bay stands very still, like when they were kids and used to play statue at school, one of the few games she was good at.

When Thalia's breathing returns to the deep rhythm of slumber, Bay leans close to the open window, inhaling the fresh scent of summer, looking at her small circle of candles below. Thinking of her Nana's impressive spiral of light each December, Bay presses her fingers against the windowsill to lean closer.

It isn't that I want to know where I come from, she thinks, *but that I want to know where I'm going.*

That's her wish. She makes it over her candles, even though she's never made a birthday wish before.

"We don't do that sort of thing," her Nana said, years ago, when Bay came home from school, asking about it.

Well, who knows, Bay thinks, sending her wish into each flickering flame. *Maybe I do. Maybe I make wishes on birthdays, and maybe next year I'll blow out my candles, and maybe I'll be here, and maybe I won't.*

"What are you doing?" Thalia mumbles. "It's the middle of the night."

Bay opens her mouth to tell Thalia she's dreaming again but instead runs lightly across the floor to kneel on the bed and whisper into the dark, talking about everything she's just realized, until she is interrupted by Thalia's soft snoring. *Maybe I'll move away*, Bay thinks. *Not like a runaway; I'll find a job at a camp somewhere.* Her Nana has mentioned how she had a job like that when she was eighteen. Of course Bay is only fifteen and summer is almost over, but who knows—there must be camps during the school year, and fifteen isn't that young. Bay suspects she has been babied all her life; it is time she asserts herself. She can't believe how excited she feels. *Maybe I'm someone who can stay up all night,* she thinks. *Maybe I'm a night person.* And that's the last thing she remembers thinking when she wakes up early the next day and wonders if maybe she is a morning person, after all.

LAVENDER *Associated with love and fertility, lavender works as a protection against evil and is thought to help bridge the gap to the spirit world. The sweet scent of lavender is conducive to a long life.*

⌒◦

O n the night of Bay's fifteenth birthday, Nan falls asleep in the chair in front of the window——a disturbed, achy sleep from which she wakes at dawn, shivering in the damp air, to the sound of morning birds, with a headache. *I have let this drag on far too long*, she thinks as she crawls into bed. Bay is fifteen now. Fifteen! It is time Nan tell her everything. Well, not everything, of course, only the pertinent information. Hopefully, it isn't too late. Yes, today is the day, Nan decides, which does nothing to soothe her headache. She finally falls asleep, but it is a fitful slumber from which she is thoroughly awoken when Nicholas jumps on her chest and mews.

Though it is July, Nan cannot shake the ache from her bones, or the terrible feeling that accompanies it; as if she'd spent the night walking too far, or doing calisthenics, as though she were no longer a person with a body, but a spirit trapped in one. She tries all morning to cast off the disturbed state, even as Bay and Thalia pick lavender flowers from their stalks for the homemade soap.

When the sound of the honking horn signals Mrs. Desarti's arrival, Nan wipes her hands on her apron as she follows the girls outside. She briefly considers not letting Bay go to the river, but that would only cause a big upset. Besides, Nan needs time to prepare herself, and there is the matter of the soap to attend to as well. Bay leans out the window, waving wildly as Mrs. Desarti taps the horn in quick salute.

Once she is sure they are gone and not returning for some forgotten item, Nan takes the bowl of carefully harvested lavender outside, sprinkling it around the house, tossing the leftover into the forest. She picks up the spent tea lights, clutching all fifteen discs against her stomach, hurrying inside to fill them with water. She looks about the sunny kitchen at the remnants of the lavender shucking, bits of purple everywhere like confetti. She decides not to sweep up. It looks so pretty on the floor, the counter and table.

Reminding herself to stay focused, Nan goes upstairs to her bedroom, to the small closet there, shoving coats and dresses aside as she pushes to the back, too hot and close. *Like a casket*, she thinks, immediately scolding herself for her morbidity. She removes the pile of old sweaters and quilts from the box they hide, which she opens, immediately flooded by the scent of lavender.

Nan pulls out a large block of soap wrapped in brown paper, closes the lid, piles the sweaters and quilts, careful to cover the box entirely, nearly tripping over Nicholas as she backs out. She apologizes to the cat, who responds by commencing with a tongue bath.

When Nan returns to the kitchen, she is as exhausted as the time she really did make soap all those years ago, which, for some reason, Bay latched on to as one of her favorite traditions. Though today is the day for telling Bay almost everything, it certainly doesn't have to include this transgression. The whole soapmaking business is minor and does not require a confession. Nan searches through the cleaning supplies in the basket under the sink (a place Bay never explores) for the blue bottle, which she spritzes about the room, then checks the stove-top clock (Nan has no tolerance at all for large clocks hanging on walls, with their constant reminder of time passing) and sees that it is late enough for a glass of wine, though truth be told, it always is.

She is shuffling toward the kitchen table when the phone

rings, startling her with its loud trill; she yelps, clutching glass and bottle while she considers not answering, but the unsettled feeling she's had of trouble coming decides her. She sets the wine and glass down and hurries to the small, crowded computer table where the phone sits.

"Hello?"

"Nan? Nan Singer? This is Sheriff Henry."

"What is it? What's happened?"

"I wonder if this is a good time to—"

"Is Bay all right? Tell me."

"Oh, this isn't that kind of call."

"Well, what kind of call is it?"

"A warning? I was just going to stop by but—"

Nan finds that she has pulled the receiver off her ear and is staring at it as though it just stung her. She can't think. She has to think.

"Mz. Singer?"

"No," Nan says. She clicks the phone off and listens to the dead silence until the dial tone finally buzzes, sounding dreadfully loud.

When the phone rings again, Nan doesn't answer, of course. She pours a glass of merlot from the previously uncorked bottle, surprised and irritated to discover only enough left for a single glass. Could Bay be drinking? On top of everything, is there also this?

Nan gulps the wine the way she used to gulp the cherry cough medicine her mother foisted on her when she was a kid, though actually the wine is quite good. *Time's up*, she thinks. Hasn't she been tired for so long? Tired of all these secrets? Just plain tired? She sets the empty glass on the table and closes her eyes, waking at the sound of the screen door slamming shut. Before Nan can even open her mouth, Bay says, with an unmistakable quiver in her voice, "It smells great in here! Why do I always miss the soapmaking?"

Tell her, Nan thinks. *Just get it over with. Tell her what you did and tell her what you are and what she is and be done with it.* "Oh, it's just a big mess. You're here for the best part."

"Well, next time"—Bay's voice sounds as tremulous as water—"I want to be here for the actual soapmaking."

"Did you have a good time at the river, dear?"

"Oh, yes," Bay says, though Nan smells the lie. "Something funny happened though."

"Funny?"

"Not funny. Weird. Nothing. But Mrs. Desarti made me promise to tell you. She's going to call later."

Nan keeps her voice level. "What happened?"

"Nothing bad."

Is it the unusual darkness of Bay's damp hair that makes her countenance so ghostly?

"Don't be mad, okay?"

"Why would I be angry? Is Thalia all right?"

Bay nods.

"Mrs. Desarti?"

"She's going to call you."

Nan starts to speak, but Bay, flitting about the kitchen like a moth at a light, continues. "It's just stupid. One minute I was underwater, and the next it felt like someone was pulling me by the ankles. Duckweed, that's what Mrs. Desarti said it was. Anyway, the next thing I know, this guy from school is pulling me, really hard. He even had to go up for air a few times before he got me out. Nana, are you all right?"

"Who? Who did this?"

Bay sighs. "His name is Wade. He's in my class."

It does not escape Nan's attention how Bay blushes as though the boy's name alone is enough to make her bloom in a way Nan finds most alarming. "Well, that certainly was very nice of him, but I'm sure you would have been fine."

"I was not fine, Nana! I was drowning, and he…he…"

"You were never in danger."

Bay, leaning against the counter, shrugs in that maddening way she has, with just one shoulder, staring at the floor as though she had something to be ashamed of.

"Bay, did something else happen? Is there more?"

"Everyone was there. Everyone from school. Everyone!"

Nan sighs. She picks up the wine bottle and turns it over her glass, hoping to discover an unharvested drop; she waits, apparently longer than she should, for suddenly Bay stamps her foot. It is a small stamp, not like the great foot stomping of her grade school years; its return almost makes Nan smile.

"You don't understand, Nana. I'm not going back there. I can never see those people again!"

Nan sets the bottle gently on the table. She concentrates on the brightly painted chicken salt and pepper shakers. They were on the table the night of her eighteenth birthday, when she had to pretend everything was normal, though nothing was, and they were on this very table when she had that trouble after Bay's arrival; they are here now, years later. Who would have guessed that the constant watcher at every worst event, the icon of her life, would be these silly chickens? *Tell her*, Nan thinks. She takes a deep breath and inhales the near scent of wine, the perfume of lavender, the mineral odor of water.

"Well, to begin with," Nan says, "you were never in danger."

Bay lifts her head to glare with wide eyes, her jaw slack. Nan has seen this look before, this teenage look, and she does not enjoy it.

"You don't understand," Bay says. "I'm going to bed."

"Bed?" Nan squints at the stove-top clock, too small to read from where she sits, though clearly it's not even dark out. "What's wrong with you?"

"I'm tired, okay? We were up late, and I'm tired, and I almost died, even if you don't care, and…" Bay breaks off midsentence, turning so swiftly to run up the stairs that Nan is sprayed with a few drops of river water.

Nan sighs at the sound of the bedroom door slamming shut. Of course Bay doesn't understand. She doesn't know she was born with a caul, and she doesn't know that because of this fortune, she has no need to fear drowning. She doesn't know because Nan never told her, though even if Bay were not in possession of her particular talent, Nan thinks it unlikely there was any real danger. Why, Bay herself said everyone was there, which of course is an exaggeration, but how many people does it take to pull a girl out of the tangle of duckweed?

Unless…Nan is momentarily frozen, paused in the middle of a thought she does not want to complete, holding a breath she does not want to let go. Unless…unless it wasn't duckweed after all.

"How horrible are you?" Nan hisses. "Leave her out of it."

She immediately realizes her mistake. The plea serves her ghosts more than herself. After all, what is the point of revenge but to hurt her most completely, and what could do that more than by hurting Bay? Nan shakes her head but doesn't speak further. What does she know about such matters? She's just an old woman with secrets, and one is this: Nan is almost powerless. Maybe once she could have been something, before she became a woman afraid of making the wrong choice. Whatever powers Nan had have been quite depleted, her strength reduced to whimsy: a shoe garden, a walnut-leaf wreath, a basic understanding of herbs and cycles, garden magic, a sensitive nose. Possibly (Nan can't be sure) enough store of untapped potential to keep the sheriff away long enough to get her affairs in order.

Nan walks slowly up the stairs, trying to still the thumping in her head. Can everything be happening at once? Apparently, yes. And as so often happens when Nan considers time's diminishing supply, her thoughts turn to Eve. She remembers Eve's fingers reaching out to seek purchase where there was none, the gentle snowfall, large white flakes drifting onto the cracked sidewalks. Nan places her hands over her heart. "You need to get a hold of yourself," she whispers in the dim, warm space, and her mind makes a leap, the way it's been doing lately, to Bay standing in the kitchen, blushing when she said the boy's name; her rescuer, her prince.

Nan snorts as she shuffles into her bedroom, which smells quite strongly of lavender. She opens the top dresser drawer, pushing aside cotton underwear and socks, until her fingers brush the narrow box, which she lifts with a flutter of blue silk scarf she doesn't remember owning. She considers the box for a moment with its cover of floral script and watercolor posies, then wraps the scarf around her neck. It's a comfort as she walks to Bay's room.

When Bay was a little kid, her Nana used to take her to the river. Not as often as Bay would have liked; she would have gone every day once she discovered the wild world there—the dangerous bloodroot, buttercups (which Bay never tired of holding under her Nana's chin to see if she liked butter) and all that green: the grass, the leafy trees, the weeping willows with their long branches draped like hair. Her Nana called them "the three old women." Even now Bay thinks of them that way, as old women standing at the banks of the river, watching over her.

That's what she used to think, at least.

Bay lies on her bed beneath the slanted ceiling, remembering floating on her back, looking up at the green sky. Of course it's not really green, but she always thinks of it that way when she's there, staring up through the overhanging branches, her ears half in the water, muffling all noise except the sound of her own breath. Bay closes her eyes, trying to pretend she is floating, and she almost is, when the knock brings her back to her room with the low ceiling, the lumpy mattress, the clammy feel of the suit she still wears beneath her clothes.

"Not now," Bay says, but she doesn't say it loudly, because actually, she's not sure. Lately she feels torn like this, like she wants her Nana to come and she wants her to go and Bay can't decide which she wants more.

It doesn't matter. Nan shuffles into the room for some reason wearing a scarf draped around her neck even though it's the middle of summer.

"I'm taking a nap," Bay says.

"There's something I haven't told you."

Bay pushes onto her elbows to sit up.

"You have an inheritance."

She knew it! Didn't she know it? Didn't she know there was some wonderful secret to her life?

"Not money, dear." Nan laughs. "Something more precious."

Who said anything about money? Bay reaches out to take the long, thin box. What can it be? What can it mean? She holds it gently, as though it were not made of cardboard, but glass, reading the swirled pink letters: "Rosewater Handkerchiefs." This better not be one of her Nana's jokes.

"Before you open it, I should explain. Remember how I said you were left on the porch in a box draped with lace?"

"To keep the mosquitoes off me."

"It wasn't lace."

Bay used to like the story, the way her Nana told it, of finding her on the porch "like something delivered by the moon." When Bay was young, she imagined the moon sinking through the night sky to bring her home, though now she knows it's just a stupid story. She glances up at her Nana, her gray hair like a hornet's nest around her face.

"Go ahead, open it."

Bay removes the lid, for a moment disappointed by the pink tissue; the excitement returns as she parts the soft paper. *What can it be? What is it?* she thinks, lifting from its nest some kind of animal-skin balloon, an ugly, flattened thing.

Bay once went through a very short period of eating dirt. Who knows why? Little kids do things like that. But the feeling she has now, looking at this ugly thing, is as though she just swallowed a pile of dirt. It sits in her gut like mud.

"Careful," her Nana says, "it's fragile. You mustn't tear it. That would change everything."

Bay holds it up in front of her face, pretending to inspect it as a way to hide her disappointment. She peers through the dried, fleshy mess at her Nana, who is blurred, like someone reflected in water. With a shudder, Bay lets it fall back to the box, flooded by the memory of being pulled under, as though the river intended to keep her.

"Bay, I told you to be careful. You can't just go tossing it around like that. If it gets torn, your whole life will be different. I know it doesn't look like much now, but the morning you arrived, it was quite lovely. I knew right away what it was."

Bay can't decide if she wants to roll her eyes or throw the weird thing across the room. She tosses the box toward the foot of the bed, which causes her Nana to gasp and lunge as though it were explosive.

"Aren't you listening? Am I speaking Urdu? This isn't something to be careless with. This is your life. You need to understand. This is important. No matter what happens, you are going to be all right."

Bay wishes she could start over, go back in time to this morning. She wishes she would have stayed home and finally learned how to make the lavender soap. In fact, Bay wishes she could go back to last night to make a different wish over her candles. She hadn't thought it would really work. What had she been thinking? Why wish for the future? It always comes, and here she is, about a million times sadder than just a day ago.

"Are you listening? Have you heard anything I said?"

Bay nods, though why, she has no idea. Her Nana always knows when she is lying.

"It's called a caul, Bay, and you were born wrapped with it around your head and face. I assume. Well, with recent developments, I'm actually quite certain."

"A cowl?"

"Caul, a caul. C-A-U-L. I don't know if she, your birth mother that is, knew what it was. I've always wondered if she did. It's nothing to be afraid of; in fact, it's quite a good thing."

"I don't understand," Bay says, though she thinks she might. It's too terrible to consider, really. All this time she's had this secret place to go to in her mind, the solace of believing her birth mother is normal. It never even occurred to Bay that her birth mother could be weirder than Nan. Bay realizes this has been incredibly stupid. After all, what normal person leaves a baby in a box on a stranger's porch?

"To be born with a caul is extremely fortunate. The person born with a caul has no fear of drowning."

"You don't think—"

"Wait, Bay. Let me finish. You can't drown. It's impossible. You didn't need some boy to save your life."

Bay can't believe this is happening. Her Nana stands there, petting that scarf, looking like she's just presented Bay with something wonderful.

"Also, you are possessed of a talent for predicting weather, which, Bay, I'm sure you've observed, you do have a flair for."

Bay remembers the way Mrs. Nellers, her kindergarten teacher, looked at her as though she'd wet her pants, which she had not, when she said she smelled lightning. Thalia always asks if she'll need a sweater or umbrella, or if they'll have a snow day or not. Even Mrs. Desarti recently pulled out her iPad to check possible dates for her niece's outdoor wedding next summer. Bay just shook her head and said she had no idea what the weather would be in a year. It's not like she can tell the future. So what if she can look at a blue sky and know a storm's approaching? So what if she can smell snow before it falls, and so what if she didn't drown?

Well, not so what about that, but is she really supposed to believe that this ugly thing, this caul, is what saved her, when it was actually Wade Enders?

"You also have a talent for healing."

Is this it? Bay thinks. *Is this the great secret of my life, an ugly thing kept in an old handkerchief box? Is my Nana really nuts?*

"All talent comes with challenges, Bay, but at times like this, you will find yourself held up by your talents. Not everyone is so fortunate. If something should happen, I'm not saying it will, but if it did, you have all you need to survive."

"I don't want to be a doctor."

"Who said anything about being a doctor? Oh, you mean the gift for healing? You don't have to be a doctor, Bay. There are many ways to heal. You can choose how you want to do it. These are gifts, not burdens."

"I'm going to be a chef. Maybe a lawyer. I haven't decided."

"Of course!" Nan says. "Be a lawyer, if that's what you want, though I can't imagine why you would. Or a chef. Heal with cakes! I, personally, have often found cake to be quite healing."

"Heal with cakes?" Bay says, not wanting to admit she sort of likes the idea. She can't take any of this seriously. Obviously her Nana is, well, maybe not nuts, but not realistic, that's for sure, even if some of her strange ideas do work. That stupid wreath she wears, for instance. Bay refuses to wear one, but she has noticed the way flies pass over Nan in the garden, and flies don't pass over anything. Bay herself has enjoyed the benefits of cramp bark, which provides her with relief during her period when nothing else does, and she enjoys the way they celebrate birthdays, lighting the tea candles and not blowing them out, but this is too much. Her Nana stands there with her head slightly tilted in that way she has, as if the world can be made to look right only at a slant. *What am I,* Bay thinks, *some kind of freak?* "Maybe I don't want to heal with cake."

Nan sighs. "Bay, you don't have to heal with cakes. It's a

talent. The healing, I mean. You don't have to do anything with your talents at all, though believe me, it doesn't make things easier. All talent comes with challenges. All life does."

"I get to choose?"

"You get to choose what you do with your talents. You do not get to choose what those talents are."

While Bay's been sitting on her bed, pretending everything is normal, the dark mass of disappointment in her gut has started to quiver in a terrible way, as though wasps have begun building a nest there, though of course they haven't. It's just an expression. It's not reality.

I almost died today, Bay thinks, shaking her head at her Nana. The wasps build so fast, so furiously, Bay is storming out of the room before she even makes up her mind to do so.

"Bay, wait, there's more."

More? Bay runs down the stairs, through the kitchen, and out the back door, into the lavender dusk.

Nan calls it the blue hour, this time in a summer day when the sky seems to fall, casting everything in its net. She looks at the yard below, watching Bay run to the small clearing behind the lilacs and pampas grass. The trail to Bay's special place was once so well-traveled there was a path leading to it. Nan used to leave little presents: a pretty stone, seashells, a marigold, a child's shoe. Occasionally, Bay found things Nan had no memory of leaving—a ribbon, a button, a scrap of lace.

Nan gasps at the painful realization. "Also, you will see ghosts," she whispers. How can she have been looking so carefully and not seen what was happening right before her eyes? Do other people see clearly? Somehow, Nan must explain everything. Where will she find the courage to do so?

There have been many moments, over the years, when Nan

has thought of calling Mavis and Ruthie, and each time she came to the conclusion it wasn't necessary. That first morning, fifteen years ago, when she opened her door and found a baby there, she vacillated between wanting to call and hoping they would not hear the sensational news. Nan worried about it quite a bit, actually, until she became preoccupied with feedings and diaper changing, all the burdens of being a new mother at an age when most women were enjoying the freedom of grandparenting. More than once Nan thought of calling for advice, solace, celebration, friendship, especially after the trouble with that boy, but then she'd remind herself of the secret they shared, as dangerous as the *Ithyphallus impudicus* she'd rooted out of a crack at the side of the house, the nasty fungus said to portend death, and quickly decided that one secret was enough between friends whose friendship had not survived it.

Nan clutches the box against her chest. The hallway is too warm, the way it gets in summer. She feels a little woozy, suddenly realizing she has only had wine for dinner. She decides to make chicken sandwiches. She and Bay can eat on the porch, sitting in the rockers, watching the fireflies.

She shuffles into her room, trying not to be distracted by the fluid nature of space after wine on an empty stomach. Pulling the stubbornly resistant dresser drawer, she almost drops the box, which gives her an idea. She could take care of Bay's trouble (and some of her own) by executing one great tear. Rip up the caul, and Bay will be in no danger of ever hearing the accusations of ghosts. Is that too much to ask? That Bay not suffer Nan's consequences? Isn't it enough already, the things people say, and the things they will say when Sheriff Henry arrests Nan for murder? She shivers at the terrible word. With a resolute tug, the drawer finally opens, and Nan returns the box to its usual spot. It wouldn't be right to interfere in Bay's life on such a profound level. Truth be told, Nan sadly admits, her attraction to the solution might have been mostly for her own benefit. Nan enjoys the glide of silk as she pulls the scarf off to drop it into the drawer, which closes so easily, she entertains the fleeting idea that the dresser has blessed her choice.

Nan walks slowly down the back stairs into the kitchen, thinking how she needs help. A little wine would be a good start, or maybe just a diversion. Eyeing with disappointment the empty bottle, she sits before the computer. Is she trembling? Yes, she is. What if *this* is the wrong thing to do? What if she is seeing this all wrong now?

They are well past the Facebook generation, and women of Nan's age changed their last names when they married, but she quickly finds Mavis. At least Nan thinks it's her. There is a woman in Arizona selling antiques, but when Nan clicks on the bio page, she thinks for a moment she's mistaken.

Of course, even Mavis has aged, her once-beautiful dark hair now dyed a frightening black, but it's her, all right, her lips bright red with her signature lipstick. Though she is no longer beautiful in the traditional sense of the word, Mavis still looks like someone who doesn't mind causing trouble. It is almost enough to make Nan reconsider. At the bottom of the page there is contact information, an email address, a post box, and, incredibly, a good old-fashioned phone number. Nan calls before she loses her courage.

"Hello?"

She would recognize that voice anywhere; they used to call it a smoker's voice, deep and throaty.

"Nan?"

She considers hanging up, but instead finds herself nodding into the telephone, feeling, much to her surprise, happy. "How did you know?"

Mavis cackles. "Caller ID."

"Oh."

"What? You think I have some kind of superpower?"

Nan isn't sure how to respond. It is her hope that Mavis has retained some of the power of her youth.

"It's been more than sixty years."

"Oh? Has it been that long?"

"Cut the crap, Nan. You keep this up, I'll be dead before you get to the point."

"I have a daughter."

"You said you never would."

"She just turned fifteen."

"What? That's the age of my grandchildren."

"Oh, you know me, I always was ponderous." Mavis cackles, and Nan closes her eyes. The headache has returned with a vengeance. She can't believe she's doing this. She swore she'd never speak to Mavis again. "We're getting old."

"This is a revelation?"

"I was thinking we should get together."

"Ruthie too?"

"Yes," Nan says.

"Just like old times."

"Not really," Nan says, remembering Eve lying in the bed of blood. "I hope not."

LILAC *Lilacs are one of the most common trees in old cemeteries. The sweetly scented flowers are used to surround the dead when they lie in state, to mask the odor of decaying flesh.*

⌒◦

When Nan says they will be having guests, old friends staying overnight, Bay wonders what else she doesn't know about her Nana. "Why?" Bay asks, but Nan never settles on an answer. She makes vague references to an anniversary of some kind, yet later acts like she doesn't know what Bay is talking about. Another time Nan alludes to a ceremony, but when Bay presses for details, says that all the cleaning they're doing in preparation for her friends' arrival is a kind of ceremony in its own way. Bay has to focus on her Nana when she talks like this; she doesn't like it when Bay rolls her eyes. Once, when Nan is half-asleep in the rocker on the porch, she mumbles something about blood. Not for the first time, Bay wonders what Nan dreams about.

Now it's happening to Bay. She hasn't told her Nana or Thalia—she hasn't told anyone—but ever since that day at the river, Bay's been having nightmares. When she finally struggles to surface, she opens her eyes into another dream world: the shadowy figure of a woman standing at the foot of her bed.

But that's not all that bothers Bay these days. She worries about her Nana, suddenly weird about the phone, not letting Bay answer it, often allowing it to ring without answering it herself; or, one minute staring at Bay as though expecting her to morph into something frightening, and the next giving her big bear hugs. Thankfully, Nan does not bring up the subject of the caul again. Bay hates to think about it, born with that thing wrapped around her, like a caterpillar or some kind of insect, strange from the start.

She has mostly stopped checking her Facebook page. It was always bad anyway; she'd regretted almost immediately begging her Nana to let her join, but ever since the day at the river, it's gotten worse. Now they call her "the drowned girl," "water bug," and "witch."

"Well, 'cause, you know, witches can't drown," Thalia said.

Bay has not told Thalia about the caul. Thalia is Bay's only friend, and she doesn't want to lose her. Thalia has been acting different lately, strangely distant, busy when Bay phones. Yet, when Thalia invites Bay to go to the river again, she holds the phone against her heart until she thinks enough time has passed to make it seem she really did ask before she says her Nana won't let her go. They have a lot of work to do, preparing for the guests. Thalia actually believes Bay, which she finds strangely disturbing. Doesn't Thalia notice how Bay has changed? *I almost died*, Bay thinks. *Doesn't anyone care?*

Nan has been so preoccupied lately that Bay hasn't found the right time to discuss her plans for not returning to school. She'd like to have a solid idea of what she is going to do, but it's been hard to figure one out. She's made a few Internet searches, though that's not easy, since she doesn't have any privacy with the stupid computer in the kitchen. So far, all she's found are places for troubled children and drug addicts. Bay does feel troubled, but she's pretty sure that's not what they are talking about.

"If I started smoking crack or beat someone up, I'd have lots of options," she mumbles.

All this, combined with the days of cleaning, washing windows, dusting furniture, changing linens, and trimming loose strings off old towels is ruining Bay's life. They usually have such nice summers: planting flowers, reading under the elm tree, eating tomato sandwiches, watching fireflies, and sleeping on the porch! Besides all the distraction and disappointment of having such sublime activities replaced with housework, there is the added factor of the boy in the forest. If things were normal, Bay would tell her Nana about him, but there never seems to be a good reason to bring it up, and after a while, Bay realizes she enjoys keeping the mystery to herself, a secret she shares with no one; a pleasant secret for once.

The first time Bay saw him, she was gazing out her bedroom window at the unusual sky, that shade of light peculiar to some August evenings when time seems temporarily stuck, feeling like she might cry, though she couldn't imagine why, when she became aware of an odd movement among the lilacs. She leaned closer, expecting to see a bird or squirrel causing the stir, but what she saw instead made her step back.

Staring up at her from the midst of green was the pale face of a boy. Bay's heart fluttered in a most alarming way; she wondered if it was an attack of some kind. She leaned closer to the screen, smelling the heavy scent of flowers, the grass, the aroma of citronella. Was this boy created out of her longing, the way she used to have imaginary friends when she was little? Did he really just smile, revealing dimples she could see even at this distance? Was a boy staring up at the house like this the beginning of something good, or something terrible?

Bay ran to find her Nana, who was asleep in the parlor, a dust rag in her hand. By then, Bay thought maybe she'd imagined him; after all, she used to imagine seeing people all the time when she was little. Besides, her Nana looked so old that Bay decided not to disturb her. Instead, Bay went to peer out the kitchen window. Seeing no sign of him, she walked into the backyard where the strange light had already returned to ordinary dusk. She worked up all her courage to walk over to the lilacs. There was no sign of anyone having been there, no broken branches brushed aside by reckless hands, no footprints in the dirt. The only thing unusual was how the air smelled sweet, as though the lilacs were in bloom, when in fact, they were long dead.

The next time Bay saw him was in the clear light of day. She was reaching into the basket at her feet for a sheet to hang on the line when she thought she spied him out of the corner of her eye, but as soon as she turned, he was gone.

Bay began leaving sandwiches tucked among the shoes in the garden: tahini with orange marmalade, basil and tomato with vinegar dressing (she couldn't risk the mayonnaise, which everyone knows becomes poisonous in the sun), goat cheese with a black-olive tapenade, cheddar and mustard on a seven-grain bun. At first Nan encouraged the kitchen experimentation, but after a while, she began complaining about all the missing Tupperware. He never took the sandwiches anyway; they were blue with mold when Bay retrieved them. Annoyed that he'd wasted all that food, she decided she couldn't risk arousing her Nana's curiosity by tossing them in the compost bin. Bay threw them into the forest instead, something she regrets now that the yard has begun to smell sour.

After long hours of walnut-oil furniture polishing and vinegar-scented window washing, she is so miserable she thinks she almost could go back to the river, in spite of what awaits her there. Thalia doesn't ask again, though, and Bay wonders if her Nana said something strange to her.

Bay always thought a solitary nature was something she shared with Nan. Of course other adults have friends; Bay just can't shake the feeling that it doesn't really make sense that her Nana's old friends, who Bay has never heard of before, are suddenly coming to visit.

"Why?" she asks Nan, who is on her hands and knees, polishing floorboards in the dining room.

"We haven't seen each other in years. We thought now would be a good time."

Bay nods, pretending to understand, until she thinks maybe

she really does. She can't believe that she and Thalia would lose touch for sixty years, but if that did happen, well, of course they would want to get together again. Bay watches Nan in her brown dress and clogs, her gray hair in an untidy bun, the flesh on her arm shaking as she polishes.

"Let me do that."

But Nan says she likes polishing wood. "You know what would be a big help? Why don't you put together the menu?"

Is Nan trying to get Bay excited about the idea of healing with food? She frowns, trying to sort it all out. There's a chance she is being manipulated; on the other hand, Bay really does enjoy planning menus.

"What do they eat?"

"Oh, everything," Nan says, with a dismissive wave of her hand. "Mavis loves spicy food: hot peppers, garlic, cayenne, and chocolate. She loves chocolate. She loves chocolate so much that she used to send it to herself in pretty boxes with a gift card, and lucky for her, it had no effect on her figure. She loves red wine too. Don't worry. I have that taken care of. Ruthie, well, Ruthie has a hearty appetite. I don't think there's anything she doesn't like to eat. Which reminds me, we better make sure to put her in the story bedroom. The bed in there is good and solid."

All of a sudden they are living in a house with titled bed-rooms. The pink bedroom is Bay's old room, and it isn't pink at all, though the bedspread is. The story room has a bed, a small closet, and a desk, but it is mostly filled with Nan's books, old-fashioned hard covers with gold-trimmed pages and watercolor illustrations, which Bay was given the task of dusting. It took longer than it probably should have. She managed to confine herself to a paragraph or two for the most part, until she lost a whole afternoon to Hans Christian Andersen. She'd forgotten how sad the stories were, how much love was lost.

When the boy starts appearing in the garden, Bay wonders if

he is the wonderful thing she's been waiting for. Perhaps this is the beginning of a love story of her own, and if so, she wants it to be good. The boy keeps disappearing though, which makes a difficult start to any relationship. How can love grow with someone who doesn't even want to be seen?

Sprawled across her bed, Bay pages through the cookbooks, paper-clipping recipes. Mavis, the frightening-looking antique lady with the dyed black hair and bright red lips (Nan showed Bay the photo online), is due around nine the next morning. Ruthie, of the hearty appetite, will arrive just before lunch.

"I bet she planned it that way," Nan says. "Why don't we eat on the porch?"

Bay loves the idea and has already carried the card table up from the basement. She marks a page with a recipe for something called "chocolate lasagna" (there is a small amount of dark chocolate in the sauce), then pushes the stack of books aside. She stands to stretch, her fingers scraping the slanted ceiling as she walks to the window, inhaling the green scent of summer. All she has to do is get through the next day and a half with her Nana's friends, then things can get back to normal. After making such a production out of all the cleaning and preparation, Bay thinks it's strange that they're not staying longer, but her Nana says it's long enough.

"We want to see each other again," she says. "But there's no reason to go hog wild."

Bay spends all her spare time in her bedroom, staring out the window; hoping to spy the boy again, she spends a great deal of time staring at the shoe garden instead. Many people love it, even slowing on the curvy road to take photographs, while others think the old shoes, aged by sun and weather, mud-splattered, breaking open at the toes with roots boring out of them like worms, are an eyesore. She wonders what her Nana's friends will think.

Tiny white flowers rise like clouds from above a purple heel, a man's old work boot holds black-eyed Susans, an assortment of ladies' boots compose the hollyhock and mallow garden (though the flowers are beginning to look a little sad), the hostas have blossomed their strange, stalky white and purple flowers, the leaves covering the shoes that contain them, and the boy's feet are bare.

Bay raises her hand. She doesn't expect a response, not really—she's not even sure he's not just something leftover from her little-kid imagination—but after a moment, she sees a pale wave of light, like the reflection of sun on water, or a small bird taking flight, the boy, waving. Bay spins out of her room and down the stairs, through the kitchen and out the back door, which she lets slam shut behind her. "Sorry," she calls. Her Nana hates it when she slams the door.

It is a perfect summer day. The sky is cloudless blue, and the air is fresh, but the boy stands in the hostas as though rooted there, looking sorrowful.

"So, it's true," he says at Bay's approach.

"What's true?"

He shrugs.

An odd boy, Bay thinks, though she can't figure what it is about him that makes her think so. His hair maybe, dirty blond, cut long at the front, parted on the side. He flicks his head like a sparrow at a birdbath, though it does little good; the hair continues to fall in his eyes, which are watery blue and small. The sprinkle of freckles across his face doesn't make him look friendly, nor do his thin lips. Bay reconsiders. *This*, she thinks, *is probably not a love story.* "What's your name?"

He hesitates, as if doing some reconsidering himself, then shrugs. "Karl."

"So what's up?" Bay asks, and when he only looks at her quizzically, "Are you a runaway or something?"

"Don't tell her I'm here."

"Who?"

He juts his chin at the house. "The old lady. Or any of her friends."

"How do you know about them?"

"Kind of common knowledge, ain't it?"

Bay supposes this is true. Nan hired a college boy to transport her guests from the airport. She paid Stan to come clean out the gutters, which turned out to be a massive undertaking, neglected for years. Stan said there were trees growing up there, which Bay thought an exaggeration until he started tossing down saplings. *No wonder people think we're so weird,* Bay had thought, while her Nana had fretted about killing "the poor things."

Bay didn't know why they needed to do all this work for guests staying a single night. When Thalia sleeps over, the only preparation they make is to be sure there is toilet paper in both bathrooms. Up until this summer, Bay considered dusting a winter activity, like shoveling. In spite of the little forest produced by the gutter cleaning, Bay thinks her Nana is overdoing it.

"Hey! Hey, you!"

Bay frowns at the boy. "What?"

"You're one of them thinking girls, ain't you? I once knew a girl kinda like you."

Ever alert for information about anything that might be interpreted as familial reference, Bay's heart lurches. "You did?"

"She was always figuring stuff out. She couldn't let things alone, you know? She thought everything was, like, a problem."

"I don't think everything's a problem."

"Sure you do. You think I'm a problem."

Bay shakes her head.

"Yeah, you do. That's why you been leaving those weird sandwiches all over the place."

"I thought maybe you were hungry," Bay says, hurt by the unfavorable review.

"Well, anyhow, that ain't why I've been hanging around."

"Why are you?" Bay asks, thinking his answer will help her determine whether he is, in fact, a problem or not.

He shakes his head, as though Bay has just said something ridiculous. "I need shoes."

Of course! How obvious! "Wait right here." Bay is happy to have an excuse to leave. It gives her time to figure things out while she runs up the grassy slope to the house. What is it about Karl that makes her uncomfortable? Maybe he just seems strange because he's standing barefoot in her yard, hiding in the hostas. Bay closes the screen door carefully behind her, relieved Nan isn't in the kitchen.

When Nan gets a donation of shoes, she brings them into the basement where she modifies them with fancy laces, polish, colored markers, ribbons, and paint. Over the years, many shoes have come and gone, but for some reason, the old pair of boy's sneakers remains. Bay asked her Nana about them once, and she said they were "unsuitable," whatever that means. Over the years, Bay has seen them shoved into an old flowerpot, in a box of old magazines, on the shelf above the work table, and at the foot of the stairs. Currently, they are wedged between two piles of clothes set aside for Goodwill. Bay saw them just that morning when she was looking for the card table.

Or so she thought, because they are not there now. She spends quite a bit of time shoving things around, almost giving up, when she finds the sneakers neatly hanging from a peg behind the door. She wonders if they carry sentimental value that her Nana is reluctant to explain, but what could be sentimental about smelly old shoes?

Bay tiptoes through the kitchen, not wanting to arouse her Nana's curiosity. Though Bay has nothing to compare it to, she is certain Nan would not approve of her becoming friends with the runaway hiding in the forest.

But he is gone. Bay searches for him in much the same way she looked for the shoes, thinking perhaps she had not left him among the hostas with their stalky flowers, but near the lilacs, devoid of blossoms, bushy with green leaves, a great place for hiding, though he isn't there either.

"You could wait five minutes," she says, so annoyed she considers taking the sneakers back inside, but remembering the nettles in the forest, Bay sets the shoes on the ground, then catches herself waiting as though he might suddenly materialize in them like a ghost. The thought sends a shiver down her spine, even though Bay does not believe in ghosts, in spite of what her Nana, or Thalia, or anyone thinks. "After all," Bay says, "wouldn't I know if my own house was haunted?"

She walks up the hill, opens the back door, and enters the kitchen, murmuring to herself about the stupid things people say, so absorbed in her monologue she doesn't even notice that all the kitchen cupboards are open and her Nana is standing there, frowning.

"Where have you been? We have to go to the store. I don't know what recipes you've chosen. They'll be here soon."

"Nana, no one's coming until tomorrow. Everything's going to be fine."

Nan, her head slightly tilted, looks at Bay as though studying a problem, until she nods. "Yes, you're right. What was I thinking? I'm lost in space, I guess! Why don't we take the cookbooks out to the porch?"

Which is what they do, sitting in rockers in the shade, drinking sun tea and discussing the merits and deficits of various recipes. Nan says everything looks wonderful, but it's important to consider how much kitchen time is involved. "I haven't seen my friends in sixty years. I don't want to be cooking all day."

They choose the chocolate lasagna, which can be assembled in the morning and baked off for dinner. They discuss what snacks to have available (fruit, good store-bought cookies, bread and jam for toast, also some of those chocolate toads Nan recently discovered), drinks (Coke, bottled water, red wine, prune juice, milk, coffee, and tea). Bay writes the shopping list, making several trips into the house to check ingredients against supplies. When she returns from her final check, having determined that they have plenty of olive oil, Nan is asleep. Bay watches closely to be sure.

She still remembers the day at kindergarten when Thalia said, "Your grandma's here." Bay was excited; she'd noticed that other kids had grandmas, and she wanted one too.

"Where's Grandma?" she asked Nan, waiting with the other mothers.

"I'm sorry, Bay," Nan said. "She died before you were even born."

Bay cried the whole way home. Nothing Nan said could comfort her. It was Bay's first experience with death. It didn't matter that she never knew her grandmother; she felt the loss as sharply as if she had, but that wasn't all Bay was crying about. Though she wouldn't have been able put it into words at such a young age, and even now hardly dares to think it, Bay became acutely aware that Nan was old enough to be a grandmother, and this knowledge arrived with the unfortunate realization that grandmothers die. Bay checks to make sure Nan is breathing.

As the car pulls up in the front of the house, a raven caws from its gabled perch, sounding mournful. Nan is still asleep, spittle drooling down her chin. Bay sits up, prepared to accept the shoe donation. The woman who emerges peers up at the house and pats her strangely solid-looking, penny-colored hair, then mumbles to herself as she searches through her purse, clasping it shut before she opens the car door, which emits an annoying beep. Nan is awake by the time the woman turns with a trium-phant expression, keys in hand, measuring the house with small eyes set close to her narrow nose.

"Oh!" Nan gasps.

The woman, apparently still not having seen them in the rocking chairs, heaves a great sigh as she opens the car door to return to the driver's seat. Nan perches on the edge of the rocker as the car windows rise; that done, the visitor emerges once more.

"It can't be," Nan says even as she stands in such a rush that Nicholas, who had been lazing at her feet, runs down the stairs, followed closely by Nan, who stuns Bay by running (more or less) to the stranger, who lets out a yelp, opening her arms wide.

"Ruthie, is it you?"

Nan is laughing, and Ruthie (for apparently it is she, and someone had the dates mixed up) appears to be crying. She and Nan are hugging and making all sorts of noise while Bay walks slowly to join them, not wanting to interrupt. The women hold each other at arm's length until, as though by mutual agreement, they part.

"You must be Bay."

She has rouge circles for cheeks, and a mouth smaller than the pink lipstick it is meant to bear. Her eyes, too close to her nose, are made less mean by their color, delphinium blue. She smells good, like a lemon.

"Bay, this is Ruthie."

Bay is surprised by the woman Nan described as of "healthy appetite," slated for the sturdiest bed in the house. She's tall, but skinny.

"You didn't drive all the way from the airport, did you?" Nan asks.

Ruthie raises her eyebrows, glances back at the car, shudders, and nods. "As they say, the early bird catches the beetle, right?"

Nan smiles.

"The thing of it is, I'm quite early." Ruthie opens her purse and fumbles through it, though when she closes it again, she is empty-handed, her pretty eyes extraordinarily wet.

Nan pats her friend's back, clucking softly. "There, there. Don't worry. Don't give it another thought."

Ruthie leans, as if to rest her head on Nan's distant shoulder.

"Come now; let's get out of the heat. We can get your luggage later."

Bay follows the two women walking arm in arm up the sidewalk, stepping around Nicholas lying in a patch of sun.

"The girl at the airport thought I was an idiot."

"Oh, they have no idea," Nan says.

"Everyone else was quite nice and helped me work it out. I was halfway here before I realized how I would inconvenience you."

"Inconvenience? None at all."

"I could stay in a hotel."

"Don't be ridiculous." Nan lets the front door close, apparently unaware of Bay standing there, feeling like a stranger on her own porch. She is trying to decide what to do when another car pulls up and parks behind Ruthie's. Who could it be now? Bay enjoys the pleasant sensation of being part of a family where surprising things happen.

When the elderly woman steps out of the car, Bay immediately suspects it is Mavis, with her bright slash of red lipstick, though her hair is entirely different than it was in her picture. She peers up at the house, a sour look on her face as she comes clicking up the walk in gold sandals, a bright accompaniment to the orange dress and lime-colored jacket, stopping short at the foot of the stairs.

"You must be my Nana's friend—"

"Well, I'm not her pet rabbit," the woman rasps, her voice deep and smoky.

"I'm—"

"I know who you are. You're Cinnamon or Spice, or something like that. What are you staring at?"

Her hair, which is lavender and spiky short. "Nothing, I—"

"Bay, who are you talking to?" Nan holds the door ajar, peering around it like someone afraid of an intruder. "Mavis?"

"Well, you going to invite me in, or are you just going to stare at me like you can't believe the horror?"

"No. Of course. Come in. I'm sorry. You took me by surprise. Do you have luggage?"

"Of course I've got luggage. I've got one bag that has nothing in it but pills." She turns to Bay. "Why don't you make yourself useful and get my bags?"

Bay wonders how her Nana ever became entangled with Mavis. What had Nan said about her? Bay wishes she'd paid closer attention. When she opens the car door, she gasps. "Smells like a funeral in here," she mumbles, borrowing the phrase from Nan, who always says the scent of perfume reminds her of death.

Bay struggles with the two large red suitcases on the backseat; they are heavy and bulky and seem entirely too much for such a short visit. There is also a leather bag on the front seat, which Bay grudgingly admires. When she picks it up, she hears the clacking of plastic bottles inside.

Bay would never look in anyone's purse, no matter how unlikable that person might be, but this is the sort of bag with a single snap closure. By merely looking down, Bay can see that Mavis was not exaggerating about its contents. One whole bag filled with prescription medicine. "She must be really sick," Bay says, the notion softening her hard feelings.

After Bay sets the bags down in the foyer, she follows the sound of laughter and scent of smoke into the kitchen, where the screen door is propped open with a small pile of shoes. Bay recognizes Mavis's gold sandals and her Nana's clogs. She assumes the pair of white sneakers belongs to Ruthie, who is sitting at the kitchen table, a half-filled glass of lemon water before her. Mavis, who has taken her jacket off, revealing fleshy arms heavily bangled with bright-colored bracelets, sits on a kitchen chair pulled close to the door, trying to blow cigarette smoke into the yard, a saucer balanced on her lap for a makeshift ashtray. Her Nana stands by the counter, drinking from a wineglass, the open bottle at her elbow.

"And then, and then," Ruthie says, quite loudly, "she goes, 'We are not responsible for your senior moments.'"

"No."

"She didn't."

Ruthie nods. "She did. So I…"

Suddenly everyone is looking at Bay.

"Go on, Ruthie," Nan says. "You can say anything here."

"So I said a prayer for her." Ruthie bobs her head a few times, her small lips pursed.

"Well," says Nan, "a prayer?"

Mavis frowns at the coughing Bay and tamps her cigarette out into the saucer. "Goodness, Pepper," she says. "You are sensitive."

"What did you call her?"

Mavis shrugs. "Pepper?"

At this Nan and Ruthie burst out laughing, and after a moment, Bay joins them. It feels good to laugh. It feels especially good (in spite of her need for an entire bag of prescription medication), Bay thinks, to laugh at Mavis.

Everyone is laughing so hard that when Mavis speaks, in spite of her commanding tone, they don't hear what she says until she raises her voice, like a woman in community theater. "There seems to be a young man lurking about in your garden."

"No there's not," Bay says too quickly.

"A handsome lad," Mavis says.

Ruthie sets her glass on the table and walks with quick feet over to the open door, leaning above Mavis to look.

"Oh my, he is a good-looking one."

Bay pretends sudden and compelling interest in her fingernails.

"He's coming. Act real." Ruthie poses behind Mavis in a most unnatural way, her hands clasped behind her board-straight back.

"Mrs. Singer? I'm Howard. I thought I'd just stop by to confirm the airport transportation."

Howard? Bay looks up, thrilled that her secret about Karl is safe.

"Oh, Howard! Well, my goodness, you didn't have to drive all the way out here. Why didn't you call? Come in, come in."

When he steps into the kitchen, Bay feels herself go still. He is a very good-looking one, almost perfect but for the faint blush of a birthmark on his cheekbone. Nan introduces him to her friends, absentmindedly waving in the direction of Bay, quickly veering into a cheerful account of the early arrival of her guests, during which his demeanor changes from pleasant to sullen. When he tilts his head to listen to Nan, Bay realizes it's not a birthmark at all, but a bruise.

While Mavis and Ruthie were impressed with his looks, they seem quite uninterested now, absorbed in a separate conversation about their bunions. How could they? Don't they feel it? He walked into the kitchen and changed everything. Even the air is different! Bay can hardly breathe. The temperature has changed as well; it is suddenly hot. Even at this distance, Bay can feel the heat rising from his body.

"You have the shopping list, don't you?" Nan says.

They are all looking at her, apparently expecting some kind of response.

"Bay, Howard is going to take you and me to do our shopping. You don't mind, do you?"

Mind? Of course not. It would all be so perfect had not Mavis announced that there were a few things she needed as well, which reminded Ruthie of her toiletries confiscated by "those horrible security people." Howard says they don't have to make up stuff for him to do just because the people he was supposed to transport have already arrived, at which Mavis and Nan offer their wineglasses as proof of the need for a designated driver, while Ruthie says she simply cannot get behind the wheel of a car so soon after her harrowing trip from the airport, if ever again.

Bay reconsiders going along but can't deny herself his company. It doesn't matter that he doesn't seem the least bit curious about her. It doesn't even matter that she is squished between the lemon-scented Ruthie and Mavis, with her horrible death perfume, in the backseat of Howard's small car. It doesn't even matter when the three women start singing some song from an old TV show which, surprisingly and much to their delight, Howard sings along with. What matters is him.

So carried away is Bay by the sweetness in her heart that she finds herself nodding vigorously when Ruthie invites Howard to join them for dinner.

"Don't embarrass the boy," Mavis scolds. "I'm sure he has more interesting things to do than spend the evening with a bunch of old ladies."

And me, Bay thinks.

"Of course he does," Nan says. "He's already going out of his way as it is. He only stopped by to confirm the schedule for tomorrow, now we've got him taking us to the grocery store. I'm sure he has plans for the evening."

"Well, I just asked. He's a big boy. He can say no."

"You're putting him in an awkward position."

"Goodness, how awkward can it be? I mean, really, Mavis—"

"Actually, I think it would be nice," Howard says.

"What?"

"I think it would be nice."

"Has anyone ever told you that you sound just like Marlon Brando?"

"Yeah, I get that sometimes."

"You must have other plans."

"I don't. My parents moved here after I started college. I don't know anyone local. I think dinner would be nice. If you don't mind."

"Oh, not at all!" Ruthie says in her sing-song voice, while Nan says something about how his presence will make it even more of a party.

"We'd love to have you," Bay says too loudly and out of sync with the rest.

"Yes," Mavis drawls. "We couldn't be happier."

Bay casts a sideways glance at Mavis, who sits staring straight ahead, a slight smile playing at the corner of her red lips. Bay suspects she is being mocked. She folds her arms across her chest and leans, ever so slightly, closer to Ruthie. Bay has discovered that Ruthie smells like lemons, Mavis smells like death, and Nan smells the way she always does, like lavender, but Howard smells like melted brown sugar and butter, which Bay thinks just might be the best scent ever.

HONEYSUCKLE *Sometimes referred to as "Love Bind," the honeysuckle's flowers look like intertwined lovers. Its heady fragrance induces dreams of love and passion. Honeysuckle protects the garden from evil and is considered one of the most important herbs for releasing poisons from the body.*

⌒☉

Everything is going rather well, Nan thinks. There was a point there, in the car, when Bay seemed annoyed at Mavis, but Mavis at her best is annoying. Nan can't really worry about that now. Everyone has to learn how to cope with Mavis until they fall in love with her.

"Tell us what you are studying in school, Harvey," Mavis says, serving herself another piece of lasagna.

Earlier, after he moved Ruthie's and Mavis's rental cars from the street to the driveway behind the house, Howard helped Bay bring another card table up from the basement; the tables, pressed together and covered in white linen topped with the silver candelabra, make a pleasant setting on the front porch where the moonflower blossoms trail up the railings, luminescent in the candlelight. Nan is pleased that their sweet scent obliterates the stench she's noticed this summer arising from the backyard.

Howard wipes his mouth with the cloth napkin, smiling behind the flickering flames. "I'm majoring in biology."

"Oh, are you going to be a doctor?" Ruthie asks.

"Might be."

"These things don't happen by accident," Mavis says. "What is your intention?"

Howard looks taken aback. Nan worries the pleasant mood is ruined. Mavis has always been good at ruining things.

"This isn't a complicated question, Harold. Do you intend to be a doctor or not?"

"His name is Howard. Howard. Not Harold or Harvey. How hard is that to remember?" Bay asks.

Nan feels an odd combination of panic and pride at Bay's rude behavior. Luckily, Mavis appears completely unperturbed as she slowly draws the spoon between her lips. "This sauce is delicious," she says, dipping her spoon into the casserole dish again, scraping it against the sides for more. "I do need to work on remembering names better, Sage."

They are all laughing, even Mavis, though she looks slightly confused, when the car comes down the road, slowing in front of the house.

Nan is proud of her shoe garden, pleased to have it admired in front of her friends, but when the driver sticks his head out the window, she immediately suspects he has not come with compliments.

"Hey look, it's a witches' party," he shouts, making an unidentified, but almost certainly obscene, gesture, before speeding away with his hooting passengers.

"What did he say?" Ruthie asks.

"Just kids being silly," Nan says. "You know how they are."

Mavis stops spooning sauce to study Nan, who pretends not to notice.

"I also write poetry," Howard says, refilling his wineglass. "But that won't pay the bills."

Mavis turns away from scrutinizing Nan to address Howard. "Life," she says, "is not a bank account."

Bay, who looks oddly like she's just swallowed a bug, stares at Mavis, the disturbed expression replaced by something like wonder.

So it begins, Nan thinks with a thorn in her heart. After all these years, Mavis still has the power to charm, which is what Nan hoped for, isn't it? Even Howard looks as though he is reassessing. Nan isn't so foolish as to imagine there is any sexual element to Howard's new interest in Mavis, but how shocking is it to discover it doesn't matter? Once, Nan believed that when Mavis lost her sexual power she would be left completely depleted, but this is not the case.

After dinner, Mavis, Howard, and Bay sit on the front steps, chatting. Nan's bones are too stiff for such a posture, especially with all the cleaning she did to prepare for her guests; she remains at the table with Ruthie.

"When I go to Africa," Mavis is saying to her young audience.

"Oh heavens," Ruthie whispers, "she's not still talking about Africa!"

Nan and Ruthie muffle giggles behind their hands. Howard and Bay sit at Mavis's feet, their backs toward Nan; she imagines adoring expressions.

"I plan to live in Africa." Mavis's raspy voice rises out of the dark.

Ruthie turns to Nan, eyebrows raised. "Doesn't she realize she's old?"

Nan shrugs. Mavis can't be serious. Had she really wanted to go to Africa, she would have done so, instead of talking about it for sixty-some years! The realization makes Nan sad. If there was anyone who seemed destined to follow her dreams, it was Mavis. How does it happen? Nan wonders. How do the girls with dreams as big as the world end up old women with regrets?

Bay appears to be focusing most of her attention on Howard. It is difficult to hear what he is saying, his voice is gently modulated, but it sounds as though he might be reciting a poem. Nan wishes she could hear better, but Howard has one of those voices that always makes the listener lean close. It would be annoying, if he didn't have such a pleasant face for leaning closer to, in spite of the troublesome bruise.

When he finishes, there is a long silence until Bay and Mavis speak at once. Bay stops short, of course. Mavis has a powerful voice.

"That needs work, darling."

Howard lowers his head. Bay's sweet voice gushes, "It's a really nice poem."

"It's not good enough, not nearly good enough, but who knows how good you could be if you dedicate your life to it?"

Howard speaks, again too low to hear.

Ruthie sighs. "Here she goes again. How does she make people listen to her?"

Well, there it is, the unbearable truth. When it mattered most, when Nan knew better, she buckled under the great weight of Mavis's certainty. It's a wonder thoughts of Eve stayed at a distance this long. She should be at this reunion, sitting at the table with them, talking about her family, her own children and grandchildren. After all, Eve was the one out of the four of them who the children really loved.

Mavis was so bossy, the kids at camp were afraid of her. Ruthie liked the children, and they seemed to like her, but she was forgetful, tended to be late to activities, and had trouble with the physical exertion. Nan tried to be interested in the young campers, but the truth is she'd taken the job to be with her friends and get away from her mother. Also, Nan can admit this now: she much preferred reading books in the shade of her porch, a big glass of lemonade nearby, to the buggy forest, or the stinky glue of pinecone crafts, which gave her a headache. Eve taught the girls how to weave dandelion chains and do water ballet, cheering the little ones whose toes barely cleared the surface. It was Eve who organized the campfires and told the best stories. "They have to be just a little scary," she scolded Mavis one night after she'd offered up a terrible tale about a murderer in the woods. Later, when the girls had nightmares, it was Eve's name they called.

Of course, Eve was made immediately older by her mother's death. She had to learn at a very young age how to take care of her little brothers and run a household. Now Nan wonders if Eve's wild side was part of her character or a rebellion of sorts.

She was the one, after all, who stole the bottles of wine from the camp kitchen after the end of summer dance, saying she didn't care that James never arrived, getting quite drunk until the rain that held off for hours exploded onto their cabin, and Ruthie said it was a shame, because whatever had kept James away, he wouldn't be able to come now. That's when Eve, lying on her bunk with that orange dress fanned around her pale face, surprised them by saying he never existed. "I made him up," she said, smiling through her tears. "I guess I fooled you all pretty good."

Nan shakes her head, glancing at Ruthie, who sits with her hands folded neatly in her lap, staring off into space, while Bay and Howard sit at Mavis's feet, looking up at her admiringly. "In Africa," Mavis starts, and Nan sighs, remembering Eve as a girl in ankle socks, her dark braid coming undone in loose curls around her face, showing Nan how to eat the honeysuckle growing up the side of the house. When Nan asked how she'd learned to do it, Eve said her mother taught her, which Nan found remarkable. She couldn't imagine having a mother who would encourage such a thing. It was Eve who showed them the back way to school, past the neighborhood gardens, picking beans and pulling carrots, brushing them with her fingers and eating through the dirt.

She was the smallest, but that didn't stop her from scrambling up and down the Haverstone's apple tree, her legs red as though the tree had clawed her, showing the bottom of her white underpants as she ran toward them, half her skirt tucked under her elbow, making a bowl for the stolen apples.

"I'm not sure you should be playing with Eve so much," Nan's mother said. "I'm afraid that girl's going wild. Why don't you play with that nice Mavis more?"

Nan's mother thought Mavis was a perfect little girl. Once, when Nan was caught in some transgression, she can't remember what it was, her mother embarrassed her by saying, in front of the others, "Why can't you be more like your friend Mavis here?" which might have ended the friendship right there, had Mavis not been standing behind Mrs. Singer, mimicking her sharp gestures and pursed lips.

They grew up together, but they also grew up apart. *Isn't it true*, Nan thinks, *that all intimacy is defined by the space between distant points?* Wasn't that the terrible lesson of her life? Who can ever really know anyone?

Nan can't bear it. She rises quickly and bumps the table, causing a clatter of plates and silverware; the candles waver, but she ignores them, stacking the dishes, not caring about making a ruckus.

"The lasagna was divine," Ruthie says.

Nan nods, perhaps too enthusiastically, trying to shake the past from her mind.

Ruthie collects the silverware tenderly, as though the forks, knives, and spoons are made of glass, as though any rough movement will cause a disaster.

"Ruthie," Nan says, "you have to tell me what happened to you."

Ruthie stops in midreach, her thin hand hovering over the table. "I didn't think you'd notice."

"Not notice?" Nan looks up, startled by Ruthie's eyes. Were they always so blue? "How could I not notice? You must have lost fifty pounds at least."

"Oh, you mean—" Ruthie spreads her arms out wide beside her hips.

"You were never that big."

"I got to be. I was huge. One of those women people fear, a monster."

"Oh, Ruthie, no."

Ruthie shakes her head. "You don't know what it's like. I can say this now because I'm...I'm—"

"Thin," Nan says. "You're quite thin."

68

"Well, normal size at least. I'm a bit of an expert on the way fat affects how people are treated, and I guarantee you, it wasn't pleasant."

"I wish I'd known."

"What was I supposed to do, call and say, 'I've gotten horribly fat, would you like to visit?' I wish I'd known about Bay. It can't have been easy to raise her alone, Nan. My son was enough to keep both my husband and me pulling each other's hair out. I always wanted a daughter, but it was not to be." She leans close and lowers her voice. "I lost all my girl babies before they were born. I always felt like it was, you know, some kind of curse."

Nan feels the pain in her chest like the crushing of a flower. Sometimes she thinks her whole life is best described as a ruined garden. Well, not everything. Not Bay, of course.

"I can't tell you that I didn't think of you and her"—Ruthie juts her chin toward Mavis, still sitting on the steps, enchanting Bay and Howard—"and wished we'd stayed in touch. I never had any other friends like you girls. If we'd stayed in touch—"

"If we'd stayed in touch, everything would be different."

It is true that they are old and given to sentiment, but Nan and Ruthie look at each other across the table. The candlelight softens the wrinkled dimensions of their faces, and for just a moment, Nan actually sees Ruthie the way she was as a young woman: earnest, trusting, innocent. Nan never took Ruthie seriously. Mavis didn't either. They thought she was silly.

Nan pretends absorption in the stacking of plates. Had she really been the sort of person who let such cruel judgment cloud her affection? How could she not have remembered this about herself? How could she have let so much time pass? How different her life would be if they had remained friends! How tragic, really, to be lonely all these years.

Snap out of it, Nan tells herself. There's business to be taken care of. They are here now, and everything is going rather well. The recipe Bay found for the lasagna turned out to be quite good; what a wonderful invention no-boil noodles are! There's only one sad-looking, sauce-depleted piece left. There was that business with the boy yelling out the car window of course, but things went no further. It was unfortunate, but it certainly didn't prevent them from sharing a lovely evening. The phone hasn't rung for days, ever since Nan had the number changed. She isn't so foolish as to think Sheriff Henry won't appear eventually. In fact, he almost certainly will. By then, Nan hopes, she'll have made arrangements. Obviously, it isn't a perfect solution, but she is far too old for perfection.

"Why settle when you're young?" Mavis's voice coils out of the dark. "You can do anything, be anything, live any way at all. Why choose to be ordinary? Why choose to be boring? Of course you can choose that sort of life, almost everyone does, but why?"

With a grunt, Nan picks up the stack of dishes. Ruthie follows, carrying the nearly empty lasagna pan and silverware through the foyer, past the dining room, pushing the swinging door open into the kitchen, which is its own little climate zone, overly warm and humid, with the mingled scents of chocolate tomato sauce and the persistent moonflowers whispering through the screen door and open window.

"I forgot how bossy Mavis can be," Ruthie says. "Where's the dishwasher?"

Nan points at herself.

Ruthie runs hot water and squeezes out a generous portion of dish soap. "Nan, I have to say, listening to Bay scold Mavis for getting that boy's name wrong was the high beam of my day, after seeing you again, of course."

Nan widens her eyes, pulls her chin in slightly, and lowers her voice, trying to affect Mavis's rasp. "In Africa, there will be no young people with impossible names, like Howard!"

Ruthie has a surprising laugh, girlishly clean and light. She lifts a soapy hand, waving tiny bubbles in the air, signaling Nan to stop, which only inspires her all the more.

"In Africa, there will be no tiresome people. I shall sleep with lions and dine with kings."

Ruthie splashes one hand into the bubbles and presses the other tightly over her mouth. Nan suspects immediately what has happened. She composes herself as she turns, but how funny is this, Mavis standing there, holding the door open with one foot, her red lips smeared, her drawn eyebrows sharp against her pasty skin, blinking like someone surprised by the light.

Nan steals herself for the imperious remark sure to come, but Mavis only cocks her head ever so slightly, shakes it a bit, and says, "I wonder if either of you have seen my cigarettes?"

Nan points at the pack on the kitchen counter. "Mavis, I hope I didn't make you feel bad. The wine has made me silly and..."

"Feel bad?" Mavis says sharply as she drops one hand, clawlike, across the cigarettes. "Why would I feel bad about being made to look ridiculous?"

"Are you upset?" Ruthie asks.

"I'm too old to be upset, don't you know? Too old for Africa, but you do know that, don't you? Just too damn old for almost anything."

It is quite shocking to hear Mavis's voice tremble. Ruthie rushes to give her a hug. After a moment, Nan joins them, noting that Ruthie smells like lemons but Mavis smells like dust. Ruthie, though she has lost all that weight, is soft and easy to hold, while Mavis is hard as stone, which has the effect of quickly dispersing them.

"We need to discuss why we're here," Mavis says.

"Well, I figured it out." Ruthie squirts more dish soap into the water; Nan makes a mental note that she'll need to restock soon. "I wrote the date down correctly. I know because I have my book with me. Every time Nan and I talked, I checked. I always had it right. I had the date right, it's the day I got mixed up. Do you see? I had the right date all along; I just thought it fell on a different day! I do this sort of thing frequently. My husband says I'm an idiot half the time and the other half…well, any who, do you see what I mean? Am I making sense?"

"What are you talking about?" Mavis asks. "This is the right day. I wouldn't make a mistake like that."

Nan looks at the plate she is drying, a white plate with a border of pink and yellow flowers. Strange, the things one remembers: the sunny morning when she bought it at a tag sale forty-some years ago, when she thought mixed china would be her pattern of choice for all those dinner parties that never happened. She tries to concentrate, but she is tired, and nothing Ruthie says makes much sense.

"I'm just saying it was meant to be, that's all," Ruthie says.

With a grunt, Mavis pulls out a chair and sits, taps out a cigarette and places it, unlit, between her lips, where it droops from her bright red mouth. Beneath the glare of kitchen light, the lipstick's glamorous effect has been replaced by something else; her complexion, white, her hooded, lashless eyes, the drawn eyebrows beneath the shock of lavender hair—why, Mavis looks a bit clownish! She turns slowly, her head held at an odd angle as if burdened by some invisible weight, as though she read Nan's mind while Nan, for her part, is suddenly filled with dread. After all, in spite of Mavis's new appearance, her attitude remains unchanged, as if she has never been guilty of anything.

"Where's Bay?" Nan asks.

Mavis talks around the unlit cigarette dangling from her mouth. "She's with the boy."

"You left her alone with him?"

"She's perfectly safe."

"How do you know that? How do you know she's safe? Have you seen the way she looks at him?"

Mavis takes a cold drag on her cigarette. "And?"

"And what?"

"Have you noticed what part of the formula is missing?"

"Mavis, I don't—"

"The boy is not interested."

Of course Bay is too young for romance and doesn't need some boy to save her life. Yet, how could Howard not feel honored to be a recipient of her affection? "How is that possible?"

"Gay."

"Howard? Are you sure?"

"He told me so himself. That's why he came home this weekend. To tell his folks."

"They don't know?" Nan asks, wondering at Mavis's power to charm deep secrets from dark hiding places.

"They know now. They didn't take it well, especially the father. Trust me, Nan; he has absolutely no interest in Bailey."

Nan can't help but feel a little sad. It's ridiculous, of course. Doesn't she know she can't protect Bay from life's disappointments? Isn't that why she's invited her old friends here? On the scale of disappointments, an unrequited crush, given no chance for hint of blossom, is very minor as opposed to, oh, having a mother sent to prison, for instance.

"Can we get back to something that matters?" Mavis rasps.

"Right," says Nan, already annoyed with Mavis's bossy ways. "I think I might be going away for a while, and I need someone to take care of Bay. You can see for yourself what a remarkable child she is, no trouble at all." Nan works against the grimace engendered by the salty lie. "Well, hardly any."

"Remember when Grace Winter went away," Ruthie says. "Oh, remember that weekend?"

Nan finds herself quite relieved to be taken off this difficult subject by one of Ruthie's strange associations. "I haven't thought about that night in years," Ruthie says. "We were such bad girls."

"Bad girls?"

"I'm not talking about what happened with Eve," Ruthie says, which in itself is shockingly close to doing so. "I haven't forgotten our promise."

Nan tries to hold her breath against the scent of memory, but there they are, the three of them in whispered conference, standing in the snow, promising to die with the secret of Eve's last hours, bound by the very oath that would tear them asunder.

"I'm talking about sneaking into Miss Winter's house." Ruthie's voice, cheery even in dispute, breaks through the past, and Nan squints at the summer kitchen with its divine perfume: floral, savory—a fertile scent, Nan thinks, shaking her head at the irony.

"We didn't sneak in."

"Nan had a key."

"Well, of course we weren't robbers. I'm just saying Miss Winter wouldn't have wanted us going through her personal things. I know how I would feel if someone went through all my stuff like that. Besides, isn't that the night we..." Ruthie stops midsentence, staring into space for so long Nan begins to wonder if she will have to slap her old friend to bring her back to her senses, but before there is time to act, Ruthie walks across the room, trailing tiny bubbles, to sit on the chair across from Mavis. "Oh, remember?"

Nan doesn't know why they have to talk about this now. Unlike Ruthie, apparently, Nan's spent most of her life avoiding the memory of the string of events that led from Eve's death to Miss Winter's house burning down: the flames swallowing the pine-swathed arbor, the snow melting at Nan's feet, that strange noise that sounded so much like moaning. Nan pictures, as if it were a memory, though it is not, the cat's corpse; poor Fairy, dead. She remembers Miss Winter, wrapped in an old quilt, slowly turning away from the burning to look across the not very large distance at Nan—both of them standing alone, neither making a move toward the other.

"With all this talk of being bad girls," Mavis says, her hand shaking slightly as she fumbles with the cigarette, "I take it, Ruthie, you no longer believe?"

"Believe? Of course I believe! Oh, wait, are you saying you..."

do you mean…you…well, don't be silly. Are we talking about magic? Who would believe in such nonsense? Not me, that's for sure."

Nan is stunned. How could she not have thought of this possibility?

"Ruthie?"

"Yes, Nan?"

"I don't understand what… It's wonderful to see you after all these years."

"I feel the same way. I thought we would never see each other again. When I think of how often I wished I could call you girls, well, that's water under the table now, isn't it? What's done is done. Who would have guessed? When we were young?"

"Guessed what?"

"Well, you know"—Ruthie frowns—"how long the past is. The way it just goes on and on."

Ruthie always did have a way of veering off subject, and Nan refuses to be dragged into one of her wanderings now. "This isn't about us. We need to talk about Bay."

"Well, that's my pointer," Ruthie says. "We need to let go of the past so it doesn't weigh down the child."

Nan and Mavis exchange a look.

"Even as we speak, there is a circle, yes there is, a prayer circle I meant to say, in my community for Bay, and us as well. I asked them to remember all of us. Don't look so worried. I didn't tell them why. I just said we could use their help, isn't that right?"

Nan mumbles a thank you as she pulls the chair away from the computer table and sits, suddenly possessed of a need for more wine.

"Now, look," Ruthie says. "We've come to this naturally. We are in perfect position for a circle ourselves."

Mavis coughs, or gasps. She makes some indefinite noise between the two. Nan rises to fill a glass with water, but Mavis waves her away, and the strange noise dissipates into a throat clearing, during which she scowls at Ruthie. When silence finally settles on the kitchen, it seems unusually thick.

"Ruthie, honey?"

Ruthie, who is looking at Mavis as though she emits a sour odor, turns to Nan with a beatific smile. "Yes?"

"I think, what I need to know, what I wonder after all these years, it's just lovely, I mean, just lovely to see you again."

"I feel the same."

"Yes. But what I wonder, now that the conversation has turned this way. I understand that you, yourself, don't believe in…well, you know, but how do you feel about, well…believers?"

Ruthie sits up, her posture, from the top of her copper-colored hair to the soles of her white-shoed feet flat on the floor, erect. She pulls her lips in tight, a morning glory shut against the dark. "Sinners? Is that the word you're looking for?"

Mavis breaks into another coughing fit. This time Ruthie fills a glass with water. Nan studies the way Mavis arches her neck, hunching into herself, making a rather convenient ruckus, which stops abruptly when she takes the glass Ruthie offers, eyeing Nan over the rim.

"Ruthie, what I'm trying to understand is what you would do if you found out someone was an actual witch?"

Ruthie, her lips pressed thin, her eyebrows drawn close to her narrow nose, shakes her head. "No, no, no," she says as if accused. "What are you saying? Is this some kind of trick? Did my husband put you up to this?"

"I'm talking about the way we were. I don't even know your husband."

"Well, you're beginning to sound an awful lot like him. I think we can all agree that life is not a fairy tale."

"Well no, of course not," Nan says. "But we did read her book, didn't we? We did try a few things. Remember?"

Ruthie's hands are folded neatly in her lap, her lips pursed.

She shakes her head. "We were playing. We didn't understand. We were practically children ourselves. We weren't"—she leans over to whisper the word—"witches."

"All right then," says Nan. "What about Miss Winter?"

"What about her?"

"Let's say she lived here. Next door, for instance."

"But, Nan, you don't have any neighbors."

"Pretend I did. It doesn't have to make sense, Ruthie. I'm just trying to understand your position. Say, through some impossible way, Miss Winter was my neighbor today—"

"She would be well over a hundred years old by now!"

With an exhalation, Nan slumps in her chair.

Mavis raises her gaze from the glass. "What Nan is asking," she says, drawing out the words, "is what you would do if you met a witch today?"

"A real witch?"

Mavis nods.

Ruthie looks from Mavis to Nan, settling at last to stare at some distant point between them. "Obviously, I would pray for that person to be released from evil."

"But, Ruthie," Nan says, "what if the person, you know, is young?"

"Young?" Ruthie says as though it is a dirty word. "Well, that would be easy enough then, wouldn't it? The young can be retrained. Also, I'd consult an exorcist."

Mavis, her spotted hand shaking, fumbles with the matchbook tucked into the cellophane of the cigarette package, dropping it at her feet. Ruthie leans over, but Mavis makes an odd noise—a bark? a growl?—picks it up herself, strikes the flap, and lights the long-abused cigarette.

"Ruthie, what did you think when I told you about what happened to Bay at the river?"

"Well, I, Nan, you can't be—"

"We understood you were speaking figuratively," Mavis says.

"Well, of course. Nan, you can't be thinking…oh my. Nan, Nan, Nan. People get stuck in ghostwort all the time without drowning. You can't possibly believe that sweet child out there is a witch?"

Ghostwort? Nan has never heard of such a thing. Ruthie has been mixing up words all day, and somehow she turned duck-weed into ghostwort. Nan smells the sharp odor of salt permeating the scent of lemon, smoke, and the flower-scented dish soap before she even opens her mouth, but what is she supposed to do? It's obvious she can't tell the truth.

"Don't be silly. Of course I don't think Bay is a witch."

"Well, I hope not. Teenagers are difficult, Nan. It's just their nature. Why, my own Billy got so upset he shot his father once."

"He shot his father?"

"Just a graze. He suffers from poor impulse control, as well as poor aim." Ruthie sighs. "A trait that runs in the family."

Nan starts to speak, but is cut short by a sharp throat clearing from Mavis. It is just as well. How can things be so completely messed up before they've even begun?

"Time for bed," Mavis says, looking meaningfully at Nan. "We can take care of this mess in the morning."

"Bed?" Ruthie squints at the stove-top clock. "Oh my heavens, well would you look at that? I had no idea it was so late."

"I told the boy to stay the night." Mavis turns to Nan, blowing smoke in Ruthie's face. "He's a bit drunk."

Nan wouldn't want anything bad to happen to Howard, who seemed to enjoy the evening thoroughly and did appear especially fond of the wine, but where will he sleep?

"I told him we'd set a pillow and blanket on the couch. You have a couch, don't you?"

Nan nods even as she muses over Mavis's use of "we." Mavis isn't going to set up a bed for Howard any more than she helped with dishes or dinner. She certainly won't wake up in the morning to tidy the kitchen. That's just the way

Mavis is and has always been. Nan is too tired to think about this now. Her plans are in complete disarray. How can she possibly make sure Bay will have the life she deserves, with Ruthie lurking about, threatening an exorcism, and Mavis too lazy to help?

When Mavis struggles to stand, Ruthie and Nan move to assist her, but she ignores them, walking over to the kitchen counter, where she takes one final, languishing puff on her cigarette before tamping it out into the saucer. "I don't know about you two," she says, "but I'm ready for bed."

"Aren't we going to pray?"

"You go ahead, why don't you?"

"Nan?"

"I have to get Howard's bed set up. Mavis is right, Ruthie, this can wait until morning."

Nan walks down the hall, past the dining room to the narrow window beside the front door, where she parts the lace curtain, looking for Bay and Howard.

It's not prayer that bothers Nan, but the fact that Ruthie's sense of what is good and evil puts Bay on the side of corruption. *What have I done?* Nan thinks.

"What are you looking for, Ruthie's torchbearers?"

Nan takes half a step sideways to accommodate Mavis at the window. "I don't know what I was thinking. How silly of me to believe she stayed the same all these years."

"Oh?" Mavis says. "Do you think she's changed?"

Of the three of them, it had been Ruthie who had to have it explained. No, Eve had not just gained a little weight. No, she wasn't crying tears of joy.

"What are you staring at?"

"It is like old times, after all," Nan says. "Isn't it?"

Mavis laughs, a broad cackle that reminds Nan of Grace Winter laughing in the garden all those years ago when Nan asked what herbs repel a man.

They stand at the window, like ghosts themselves, Nan thinks, *sentenced to watch life on the other side of darkness.* For a moment, she smells the scent of honeysuckle, a pleasant odor in spite of its implications, quickly followed by the taste of ash. What is she doing? What has she done? She steals a look at Mavis, hoping to discover an unmined tenderness in her countenance, but Mavis stares straight ahead, a strange expression on her face as if, she too, has the flavor of death in her mouth.

MOONFLOWER *Moonflower, used for centuries as an intoxicant, provides protection against evil spirits, but is highly dangerous and can kill.*

⤳

O n certain August nights there is a promise of rain that carries with it the scent of summer: the ripe odor of dirt, the lingering effusion of dew on grass, the rich fragrance of chocolate mint, the stony scent of water, and the sweet aroma of moonflower intoxicating anyone who breathes.

This is such a night, and Bay, who sipped only a little wine, feels deliciously drunk (or what she imagines of drunkenness) lying in the backyard, her arms opened wide, embracing the dark, while Howard lies beside her, reciting one of his poems.

"What tree within its limbs knows sin?
What flower within its stamen?

I am not a wild thing,
A rooted weed or demon.

What night would cast its stars to sea?
What morning rejects its sun?

This is a natural course
Though I often wonder

What it means to live
Without being denied my water?"

What is he talking about? Bay has no idea, but what does it matter? She is hugging the night, though truthfully, she would rather be hugging Howard. Who cares about Wade Enders pulling her from the duckweed's grasp? Who cares about the beating of her heart as she stood there, adjusting her twisted swimsuit while Mrs. Desarti made a big production out of Bay almost drowning? Who cares about the slimy bits she found hanging in her hair later, remembering then the way she smiled at Wade, not knowing how she looked? Who cares that he turned out to be as mean as the others? Who cares (she is almost positive) that he, just before, hollered out the car window? Who cares about stupid Wade Enders when there's a boy lying on the grass beside her, reciting poetry?

"I guess that one's a piece of shit too," Howard says.

"No, oh no, it's good. It really is. Mavis doesn't know what she's talking about."

Howard looks at Bay with the kind of expression she imagines an older brother might give his sister, which is not the expression she was hoping for.

"You know, you're lucky to have all these old ladies around."

"I am?"

"They know stuff. At least Mavis does. You should take advantage. Learn something while you can."

Bay feels vaguely insulted. Is he implying that Mavis is the only one who knows anything?

"My Nana teaches me a lot. Once we made dandelion wine, though that didn't turn out too good. We make lavender soap every summer. Well, I help with the beginning, and she does the rest. I know she's kind of different, I mean that's obvious, but she's also kind of wise, actually." Bay is surprised to hear herself say this. She would never say it to anyone at school, where such a confession would almost certainly be cruelly used against her.

Howard rolls on his side, playing with the blades of grass. (Bay can't help but think that her hair would make a much better place for his fingers.) "What happened to your parents?"

The circumstances are so well known that no one asks Bay anymore. "Nana found me on her porch." She hardly ever has to think how strange her birth story is, weird enough even before she learned about the caul. Strange, strange, "strange." She hadn't meant to say it out loud. She shoots a look at Howard. "What are your parents like?" she asks, hoping to deflect more questions.

Howard squints at Bay as though she is disappearing, then rolls onto his back. Bay stretches her bare foot, accidentally scraping his pant leg, sending a delightful tingle through her body.

"Do you ever feel like the sky might crush you?" he asks.

Sometimes, Bay feels like her ribs squeeze into her, that she is not being held together by that structure of bone, but imprisoned by it. Trina Heckworth, walking down the school hallway, even when ignoring Bay, gives her that feeling, because when Trina isn't absorbed in conversation with her own group of friends or smiling up at Dale, she locks her bright eyes on Bay, leans her head back, and pretends to howl, like a wolf. Bay acts like she doesn't even notice, though of course she does. Bay sometimes feels like she is being crushed, not from the sky, but from within, as though she can't survive herself. But Bay doesn't want Howard to know what a freak she is. He hasn't seemed to realize it yet, and she doesn't want to give him any hints to look for it in her. "No," she says, "I never felt like that."

"Right. You're all set, aren't you? Living here in your enchanted kingdom, huh?"

Bay doesn't know why Howard sounds mean all of a sudden. It makes her heart skip a beat. Is he one of them? Is he a tormentor too? "There's a boy living in our garden."

"What? Where?" He sits up (which Bay is sorry to have induced, because it was nice to have his face so near) frowning at the shoe planters as though he expects to see a fairy-sized child among the wild strawberries or hanging from the foxglove.

"Back there. In the forest."

"Does Nan know about him?"

"He's a runaway," she says. Then it occurs to her to try something she never thought she'd attempt. "He's pretty cute."

"Oh yeah?"

Bay nods, pleased that Howard's face, which she only recently assumed could bear no unpleasant expression, does. "He's good-looking, for a boy." She emphasizes the word "boy," meaning to say that he is not in the same league as Howard, who is, after all, in college.

"I can't believe she told you," Howard says.

From her position lying on the ground, Bay thinks Howard looks particularly handsome, the bruise on his cheek swallowed by shadows.

"It's not like I'm ashamed, 'cause I'm not. It's just I told her in confidence."

Bay mentally goes over their conversation, trying to understand what he is talking about. Howard is acting unreasonable, and Bay believes that unreasonable behavior is one of the signs of jealousy. She's sorry she mentioned Karl now. What was she thinking? Who did she think she was? Just to make everything worse (and okay, a little better, because she does feel some relief from the interruption) Nan is standing in the yard, calling. "I'm out here," Bay shouts, and, "Coming, Nana." She presses against the ground to stand, glancing at Howard, who sits with his shoulders hunched as though the night has turned suddenly cold. "I'll be right back," she says, though she's not sure she will be. He's acting so strange.

Nan takes a good look at Bay when she comes walking out of the darkness, blades of grass tangled in her red hair, an odd expression on her face. "Are you all right?"

"Sure, Nana. Great."

"What were you doing?"

"Talking."

Nan sniffs. She smells the vague hint of rain and the flowers' perfume, particularly heavy with their last gasp of life, and that sour smell from way in the back where something has died, but there is no trace of salt.

"I think I made him jealous," Bay says.

"Jealous of who?"

"I told him about a boy I think is cute."

Nan notes that Bay wears an expression much like the one Nicholas assumes after he has had his saucer of milk. Nan squints into the moonlit night until she locates Howard, sitting all the way at the back of the yard, gesticulating as though talking to someone.

"It's late, Bay, we have a big day ahead of us, and Howard is drunk. I think he might be quite drunk, actually. He can't drive home. He'll have to stay the night."

"Really?" In spite of his very recent behavior, Bay feels a tingle of excitement at the thought of having Howard as an overnight guest. "I'll tell him," she says.

"No. You go to bed." Nan is still not sure how much time she wants Bay spending with the boy. After all, he is an odd boy and while Nan normally considers oddity an attribute, she won't risk Bay's safety.

Bay watches her Nana walk carefully across the yard toward Howard, who is either talking to himself, the lilacs, or Karl. Bay is kind of relieved she doesn't have to find out which. Howard was right, in a way, when he said that living here must be like living in an enchanted kingdom. *When I was a little kid, I really believed it was*, she thinks as she walks up the back steps and opens the screen door. She used to pretend the house and yard were a land called "Forever." How could she have forgotten that for so long?

In the kitchen, which is shockingly lemon-fresh clean, Ruthie sits at the table, haloed by the bluish glow of stove-top light, eating chocolate cake.

"I didn't know we had dessert."

"I brought it from home. Would you like some?"

"No, thanks," Bay says, surprised at herself. After all, chocolate cake is her favorite. Did Ruthie actually pack an entire cake? She shovels a large piece into her mouth, smiling around the tines of the fork at Bay, who, with a quick wave, heads up the stairs to her bedroom where she stands at her window, watching the fireflies below. *What's happening? Why are they here? Fireflies aren't usually out at this time of night or this late in the season, or before it's going to rain, and it's going to rain tonight.*

"Forever," Bay says, brushing her fingers against the screen, forgetting for a moment that it is there, as though she could reach through the open window to touch the night, catch a firefly, touch forever, the way she believed she did when she was young and her happiness was certain, her life always wonderful, and her home forever safe from harm.

FOXGLOVE *Foxglove, also known as Fairy Caps, Bloody Fingers, Dead Man's Bells, and Witch's Thimbles, contains cardiac glycosides that slow the heart. If the foxglove poison goes undetected, the brain will be starved of oxygen and the heart will go into arrest. However, foxglove tea, added to water in vases, helps preserve the life of cut flowers. A common heart medication, Digitalis, is derived from foxglove.*

⤜⤛

N an considers not disturbing Howard, but she hasn't gotten to be her age without developing a fairly large imagination for all the possible ways the most innocent solution can go wrong. Howard is her responsibility, after all. Though she can think of another troubling reason for him to appear to be talking to himself, Nan suspects he is only drunk, which sets her mind at ease somewhat; but what if the night ceases to entertain, and he decides to walk home? That could be dangerous.

This is the culmination of my life, Nan thinks, *to be prepared for the worst possible outcome of any situation.* Hasn't she tried hard to keep everyone safe? Hasn't everyone who traveled in and out of her life done so unscathed ever since she failed so completely with Eve? *Well no, actually*, Nan thinks, *isn't that the point?* How could she forget for even a moment? It's almost enough to make her go back to the house. How nice it would be to crawl into bed and pull the covers up to her neck until everyone is gone. But can Nan really leave Howard in her garden so near the dangerous foxgloves? She shakes her head at the thought of another dead boy.

Calm down, Nan tells herself as she walks carefully in her clogs across the uneven ground, peering into the dark; Nan has surprisingly good night vision for someone her age. Howard is alone, not commiserating with the dead.

"It's time to come in," she says, hoping this simple statement will be enough to induce him to stand. Nan is tired. It's been a long day, and tomorrow will be even longer.

Howard shakes his head.

"It's quite late. I think you should get some sleep."

"Sleep?" he says. "I'll sleep here. No more rooms. I need space. Look at those stars, will you? No more walls. I'm finished with walls."

Resisting the unkind temptation to roll her eyes, Nan thinks how drunk people are the most stubborn weeds of all. What is she supposed to do, drag him across the lawn? She carefully lowers herself, making so much noise groaning and mumbling at the effort that Howard comes to his knees to help ease her to sit, though he does waver slightly to do so. Close like this, Nan realizes the smudge on his cheek she had thought was dirt is actually a bruise. When he catches Nan staring, he turns away.

How fitting that the lilacs, long devoid of their May flowers, smell so strongly of them tonight. This is wrong, but then again, her garden hasn't been right forever; it's not a topic she can examine at the moment. Instead she concentrates on the foxglove. Trying to forget its disturbing implications, she remembers instead the lines from Christina Rossetti's poem: *And the stately foxglove / Hangs silent its exquisite bells.*

It is with great reluctance that Nan pulls herself away from this pleasant rumination to fix her eyes on the bruised Howard, who sits staring glumly into the space he says he desires.

"All my life. Walls," Howard says. "Walls in rooms and walls in minds. Walls in bodies. Walls."

Nan nods. Just because he is drunk doesn't mean the boy makes no sense.

"I am so sick of walls. I just realized."

"Yes, well," Nan says. "Being a poet, you will notice such things."

"Not everyone thinks I'm a poet. My parents think I should be a doctor. My father—never mind. It doesn't matter."

Did Howard's father give him that bruise? *Of course*, Nan

thinks with despair. Why else would he be hiding out here with a bunch of old women and a girl he doesn't know?

"I'm going to tell you something I've hardly told anyone," Howard says.

Nan prepares to act surprised at the secret Mavis has already revealed. She closes her eyes, trying to send him courage. After all, Nan is well aware of how dangerous secrets can be, how they have a way of taking over an entire life.

"You know what I think about mortality?"

"What about mortality?" Nan asks, confused by the unexpected turn.

"Okay, I know those movies about vampires have been really popular and shit. Excuse me."

"That's quite all right, dear."

"But mortality is—I think it's awesome!"

"Oh, you do, do you?"

"Doesn't it make everything matter?" Howard asks.

Nan leans back, blinking against the dark.

"I probably shouldn't try to explain right now. I think I might be a little drunk. Am I shouting?"

"Yes, dear, you are."

Howard leans so close Nan can taste the wine on his breath, which she considers a pleasant sensation.

"I dream words, you know," he whispers. "Pages and pages of poetry."

Nan doesn't know what to say. How strange is it to discover this boy who dreams poetry sitting in her yard, to have Mavis and Ruthie in her house after all this time, when her life has been so dull! Nan's bottom feels damp, and, in spite of the heat, her bones are cold, but how nice it is to have the taste of wine on her tongue rather than the bitter flavor of ash.

"I wish I knew what to do," Howard says. "Some people are just so certain, you know? Sometimes I think I'd like to be a doctor, and sometimes I think no, I want to write."

"Well, why do you have to choose? Why can't you be a doctor and a poet?"

"Mavis? You know Mavis? She says I have to choose one career, or I'll be mediocre at both."

"Listen to me, Howard. Mavis doesn't know everything. None of us do. We muddle through the best we can, but in the end, all the people with ideas of how you should live your life are going to be gone, and you'll be staring into the mirror, looking at an old man's face, wondering how he got there. The question you have to ask yourself is: Did that old guy have a happy life?"

Howard nods as Nan speaks; he continues to nod even when she is through. He nods far longer than necessary, then stops abruptly. "But how do I know? What will make me happy? In the end?"

"It's starting to rain. Come inside. I'll make a bed for you on the couch."

As Howard helps Nan stand, she realizes, with a sudden ache, how long it's been since she's been touched by a man, especially a young one with a strong grip. "You know, Howard, you're lucky to be living in this time when people are so accepting of differences."

"I can't believe she told everyone. And they aren't all so accepting."

The rain falls swiftly now, though the drops are soft. Howard tries to speed Nan along, but she is taking her time of it. Her clothes dampen against her skin; her hair flattens against her head, a few wisps wet against her face.

Why, this night! This night! Nan thinks. She stops so suddenly Howard almost stumbles over her, though he rights himself.

Nan looks up at the night sky, closing her eyes against the rain. Howard hangs on her elbow like a burr she picked up in the garden, until she shakes him off.

"You're getting wet," he says. "We should go in."

What is the power of rain to make Nan feel young again? She doesn't know. Is there something in the water, in the wine, in the dark, or is it all in her head? She doesn't care what the explanation is. "Make memories."

"What?"

"How do you know what will make you happy? In the end? Ask yourself what kind of memory you're making."

He is squinting through the rain at her, his hair plastered against his face. "What are you talking about?"

"Remember when you were young, and that old lady hired you to chauffeur her friends from the airport, and you drank too much wine, and stayed out late, and then you danced in the rain?"

"But we're not…"

Nan waves her arms, barely moving her feet at all. There is the sound of falling rain, and then there is the sound of laughter. She opens her eyes. Howard is dancing, exuberant as the young will be, flailing his arms and legs, fairly wild. It isn't long at all before the back door slams open and Bay runs down the stairs, spinning in her flowered nightgown, her red hair quickly dampened dark, her skin glistening. The door opens again, and Mavis stands there, saying, "What are you doing? What are you doing?" until she joins them, spinning slow circles and waving her fleshy arms. Ruthie comes to the porch in her robe, buttoned all the way to the lace collar, her face pinched as she scolds them. She begs them to come in, but they continue their dance, until she is at the foot of the stairs, saying, "Are you all crazy?" though she does not go back to the porch or into the house. She doesn't dance, but she does stop scolding, and before they all go inside, soaked to the skin, trailing puddles into the kitchen, Ruthie smiles.

Nan tells everyone to leave their wet clothes in the downstairs bathroom; they can be dealt with in the morning. She lends nightgowns to Mavis and Howard. They laugh when he comes out of the bathroom wearing his. She offers hot chocolate to everyone, but thank goodness there are no takers, and they all go, yawning, to their separate beds.

It's one of those steady rains that last for hours. The windows of the old house are open, because it's also one of those reasonable rains that does not slant sideways into the room or onto the wooden sills. The sheers billow throughout the night, diaphanous as angels.

The sleepers turn to the accompaniment of squeaky springs; there is soft snoring, the occasional sleep-spoken word; it rains, making fairy ponds in the hosta leaves, dropping blossoms from the foxglove; the little bells fall without a sound. The rain pelts the grass until the grass resists no more and gives up its green perfume to the night; the scent wafts through the house, causing the dreamers to wake and, invigorated by the delicious aroma, make plans for escape of one kind or another before once more sinking into the dark.

LILY OF THE VALLEY *This highly poisonous plant protects the garden from evil spirits. The distilled water of the flowers is very effective as an application against freckles. Whoever plants lily of the valley invites death into the house.*

❧

Though the birds sing dawn's arrival, Nan is not quite ready to leave the comfort of her feather bed, a luxury she indulged in when she was going through menopause and the nights were long, her mattress hard. Now, all these years later, her body entered into a new rhythm of restlessness, Nan remembers how she slept when she was young, as though it were something easy, no kind of achievement at all. How long has she been staring at the ceiling, pondering how to proceed with the day? It seems her mind keeps spinning like an autumn leaf about to fall.

Nan shakes her head at the dismal metaphor, thus discovering how sore her neck is; actually, she realizes, her whole body hurts worse than usual. Why? Oh yes, dancing in the rain! Foolish. Risky, even. But Nan can't say she regrets it. What had she said last night about making memories? Before she can recall, she sneezes. Nicholas uncurls from the foot of the bed. Nan sneezes again, and Nicholas, never a good nurse, jumps to the floor.

Nan turns to her nightstand for the box of tissues there, fumbling through all the clutter, the candles, the stones, the feather (remnant of Nicholas's sad offering), books, an empty glass, the mug with a film of moldy tea at the bottom, and the digital clock, which signals the late hour. As she sneezes a third time, her hand at last finds the tissues. She blows her nose loudly, finally remembering her advice to Howard. How to know what will make you happy in the end? Ask yourself what memory you are making in the present.

As such things go, Nan suspects an oversimplification. But maybe it's just what's needed to enjoy this odd reunion. Clearly, Ruthie is out of the question as any kind of guardian for Bay, and Mavis seems an unlikely candidate. Perhaps the best thing to do with this mess is to make a good memory of it. It seems a rather meager ambition, but Nan is old enough to know how much of life is lost. This does not, of course, solve the problem of what to do about Bay when Sheriff Henry arrives. In spite of the early morning heat, Nan shivers at the thought. Suddenly, and for no reason she can measure, Mrs. Desarti's face comes to mind. Thalia's mother has always been kind. Perhaps she would make a good guardian. Nan decides this might be an idea worth investigating further, though really, it is almost unbearable to consider. In the meantime, Nan thinks, "Let me have this week-end." She had not meant to speak, but having done so, she does it again. She says it like a prayer but means it as a bargain with a ghost. In case one is listening.

She eases herself out of bed, surprised that her clogs aren't there where she always leaves them, before she remembers they are in the bathroom with the other wet things. She grabs a pair of old boots from her closet. They were left in one of the donation boxes, but they are red, so she kept them for herself. She tries to stand on her left foot to put the boot on her right and almost falls in the process. What is she thinking to attempt such a trick? Sighing, she hobbles back to bed, boots in hand. It's one of those secrets no one ever tells you: when you get old, all the padding wears away from your feet, and you are left to walk on bones.

Nan glances at her reflection in the mirror and lets out a little yelp. Her hair has gone absolutely wild in the night, a result of her little rain dance. There's nothing to be done for it except a good brushing, and she doesn't want to squander her time on personal hygiene right now. She shuffles down the hall, thankful to see the other bedroom doors remain closed, a sign that everyone else is still asleep.

Nan is neither surprised nor alarmed when she finds the sheets and blanket neatly folded on the couch in the parlor, Howard nowhere in sight. The headache he most likely suffers from this morning can be alleviated by time or the herbal remedy Nan has had memorized for decades, but his disdain for walls can only be treated by wandering. Nan sighs on Howard's behalf. The poet's journey, while often quite interesting, is never an easy one.

Actually, Nan feels the vague beat of a headache herself. She has had so many lately, she is not sure whether to attribute this one to a disturbing pattern or to last night's party. Either way, she decides to step outside before she makes the coffee. She cherishes the idea of having a little quiet time to herself on the porch.

Later, Nan will struggle to explain how she didn't notice immediately everything was wrong. She settles for the fact that she was focused on the sky, which, that morning, is the shade of the rare blue poppy.

Oh, Nan thinks when she opens the front door, *it's as though I'm in the center of a flower!*

She inhales the wonderful scent of rain, dirt, and grass, enjoying the warmth of the sun on her upturned face before she lowers her chin, opens her eyes, and notices shoes on the porch. This, in itself, is not unusual, but these shoes look entirely random, as if someone simply threw them, which hasn't happened for a while.

Well, if that's the worst of it, it's not so bad, but what's this? Nan picks up a black-eyed Susan, its stem torn, the usually cheerful flower hanging. Then she sees the ripped purple phlox, the scattered sedum, the beheaded hollyhock. She recognizes the boot from the garden, the toddler shoe with the pink ribbons, which she had lovingly restored for the baby's breath, the blue dance slipper, its small heel dangling. What happened here? What is this? What has become of the garden? Shoes everywhere, everywhere torn flowers! Can she save any of them? Are they all lost? She kneels down before remembering how much it hurts to do so, shoving dirt into the nearest shoe and stabbing a stem into it.

She is working like this when Ruthie comes to close the front door, and without a word, sets to help, carefully sinking to the ground in her pink nightgown, her copper hair in tubed curls like the mud dauber wasp nest Nan found early that summer on the side of the house. She stops working long enough to give a nod of appreciation, and Ruthie nods in return; they work in silence until Mavis comes to the door and says, "You two do realize how you look?"

Nan observes that Mavis is in no condition to be casting aspersions on anyone's appearance, with her violet hair wild around her face like one of those troll dolls so popular in the sixties. Ruthie sits on her black-socked heels, pressing dirt around a small daisy in an old loafer, ignoring Mavis, which Nan decides might be the best course. After all, they are saving lives here. She concentrates on stuffing dirt into a little pink shoe. By the time she looks up again, Mavis has joined them, sitting on the ground beside the sedum, the sun shining through the white nightgown, revealing that she has experienced the course of age, her breasts so depleted they look nonexistent, her stomach, a paunch.

When the car pulls up, Nan thinks she can't stop what she's doing, even for a shoe donation, even to sneer at some teenager who's come to call her names, but when she sees, out of the corner of her eye, the unexpected vehicle, her fingers hover above the dirt long enough for her to wonder why anyone would take the single local taxi all the way out here. *It must be a mistake*, she decides as she presses dirt around the astilbe, which just might not make it, poor thing.

At the sound of the car door opening, Nan peers through the bright sunlight at the emerging woman and gasps. Of all the impossible things, how can this be happening? She shakes her head as the name falls out of her mouth. "Eve?"

"Don't be silly." Kneeling in the midst of several planted shoes, Ruthie wipes her hands on her nightgown, a pink, lacy thing that exposes a surprising amount of bosom. She turns with a pleasant expression toward the stranger.

Eve's hair was curly; this woman's hair is straight, but cut short, just as Eve's was, revealing Eve's long neck and square jawline. Of course it is not Eve. Nan has seen Eve, and she has always been blurry, like an image under water, while this woman is sharply focused and alive. She watches the taxi as it pulls away, possibly reconsidering.

Trying to offer a reassuring countenance, Nan stands slowly, pushing against the memories that arrive with Eve's look-alike, the young woman, for some reason unable to maintain her composure, her small mouth opening and closing as if chewing air.

It's the boots, Nan thinks, though later she wonders what made her believe the three of them, gardening in their night-gowns, would have looked normal had she only been wearing clogs instead?

"Can I help you?" Nan is surprised to hear the tremble in her voice. Maybe it *is* Eve. *Maybe the force of all of them together again has caused her to appear*, Nan thinks, though she immediately rejects the notion as ridiculous. The fact that she believes in ghosts doesn't mean she believes in nonsense.

The young woman raises her chin, which breaks the illusion. Eve was never the chin-raising sort. "Yes, my name is Stella Day? My grandmother suggested…she said Nan?" Her eyes scan past Nan and Mavis to linger on Ruthie, before finally returning to settle, with a disappointed cast, on Nan.

"She said you were friends with my great-aunt Eve? She thought you would be able to tell me about her. Eve, I mean. I'm writing a book. Trying to, at least. I mean, don't get me wrong, I've had a few things published. I'm not a complete beginner, though most of it has been frankly derivative. Doesn't every female writer go through an Anaïs Nin period? Anyway, it's kind of a family history/memoir thing, I think."

She shuts her lips into a chiseled, false smile, and Nan is struck by the incongruity of this breathlessly chattering person, so different from the girl she resembles.

"I wouldn't just drop in like this. Normally. But I was in the area. With my boyfriend. My ex-boyfriend. I mean he's my ex-boyfriend now. Anyway, I thought, you know, why not? Why not just take a risk for once in my life? Why not just stop by and see if we could have a conversation? I wouldn't normally do something like this, but I recently lost my job, and so, anyway, here I am."

"How interesting," Mavis says, rising to stand with such effort that for a second she appears near to toppling. "How very interesting to be named after a cookie."

"Dora," Ruthie hisses. "Stella Dora are the cookies. Her name is Stella—"

"Day. Stella Day. If this isn't a good time—"

"What?" Mavis barks. "You going to wave down a taxi?"

"I have a phone, of course."

Of course. Everyone does these days, though cell phones don't work out here, much to Bay's dismay, but that's not really the point, is it? Goodness, it is very difficult to organize her thoughts with Eve's doppelgänger standing on the front walk. *Now? After all these years someone has finally come with questions?* So confused is Nan, it takes several breaths before she is able to determine that the sensation of something uncoiling deep in her pelvis is the feeling of dread. After all, she smells the salt of this Stella's lies. Does she really expect Nan to believe that her arrival, this weekend of all the weekends, is mere coincidence?

So deep in thought is she, Nan doesn't even realize she is staring until the young woman shifts uncomfortably and once more does that thing with her eyes, casting about for better options.

"Is there a shoe store around here? Was there a tornado?"

"Just a little wind and rain," Nan says, waving at the over-turned shoes and flowers, sniffing against her own deception. "You brought luggage?"

"I was with my boyfriend? We were going somewhere? That's why I have my bag. I don't plan to stay. Or anything."

"What's the matter?" Mavis says. "Afraid we're contagious?"

"I don't want to impose."

But of course you do, Nan thinks. "You say your grandmother told you to talk to me?"

"That's right."

"She would be Eve's…"

"Eve's brother, Daniel? He was my grandfather. Eve was my great-aunt. I never met her. She died before I was born. Well, you know that. All my life people told me how much I look like her. People said some strange things to me over the years. Anyway, Daniel Leary was my grandfather."

"Daniel?" Nan shakes her head, trying to fathom the little boy with big ears, always hanging about and bothering them, an old man now.

"Danny?" Ruthie says, her voice trembling. "How is Danny?"

"He died before I was born. I never knew him. We Learys tend to die young."

"That's good," Ruthie says, which is plainly strange, but she has been strange since her arrival and likely doesn't mean to sound menacing.

"This isn't a good time," Nan says. "As you can see, I have visitors and—"

But Ruthie, in her black socks and dirty nightgown, com-pletely oblivious to the effect of her appearance, walks across the grass with open arms. "Don't be silly, Nan. It's perfect time! Stella? It's Stella, isn't it? I'm Ruthie. Now, isn't it just, what is the word? Seren…serin…ser-something-or-other that you should arrive when we've gotten together for the first time in years?" Ruthie wraps her arm around Stella's narrow shoulders.

"Is this your luggage? I once had nice luggage, but you know how that goes. My son took it with him to Mexico, and that was that. I never saw my suitcase again."

"Ruthie!"

Her arm still around the girl, Ruthie stops at the door and turns, her smile unbroken by Mavis's sharp voice.

"Serendipity."

"Yes!" Ruthie shouts, which startles everyone. "Oops, sorry. I haven't done that in years. My husband hates it when I talk loud." She turns to open the door. Stella quickly steps out of Ruthie's grasp into the dark maw of the foyer.

"Ruthie!"

"What?"

"Remember?" Mavis hisses through clenched teeth. "Remember our promise?"

"Well, of course I remember," Ruthie whispers hoarsely. "What do you take me for? A terrorist?" She leans into the door, almost closing it entirely. "I'm not going to talk about that, but there's no reason we can't talk about her. She was our friend, wasn't she?"

Mavis stares, as though considering the point, which Nan finds shocking.

"Of course," Nan says, and when Ruthie turns to look at her, she says it again. "Of course Eve was our friend."

Ruthie nods abruptly before she steps inside. Nan, who only wants some relief from the scent of salt permeating the air, brings the flower she has been holding to her nose. For a moment it works, the salt replaced with the sweet smell, until she comes to her senses and realizes she is clutching a lily of the valley.

"What's wrong with you?" Mavis asks.

Nan spins an awkward circle in the oversized red boots. The garden is a disaster, shoes splattered in dirt and filled with damaged flowers, but as near as she can tell, no one has planted the dangerous lily.

Where did it come from anyway? She tosses the withered thing away and sinks carefully to the ground. Not for the first time in recent weeks, Nan recalls the old-fashioned hourglass Miss Winter kept in her house, but this time Nan pictures it with all the sand run out.

Life is what you remember, Nan thinks as she shoves dirt into the old sneaker. *Who can remember everything? Well, no one, and that's a blessing. Life is and always has been a composition, much like this garden; it will not be contained and cannot be determined.*

She first noticed it years ago, when the shoe plants thrived long past the time for doing so. What about roots? she wondered. What about seasons? What about nutrients and rain and rot and decay? And yet, somewhere in all this mess the sneaker remains, as well as the old lady's slipper, until this recent vandalism, the container for Grace Winter's pennyroyal. It is impossible, of course, against the laws of nature. Everything here is. The elm tree, somehow surviving the disease that left main streets all over the Midwest blighted, thrives, as do the weeping apple trees she planted when she first bought the place. Things die, of course, but Nan has long observed that the passage between life and death is different here than anywhere else. This lily of the valley, for instance, its pretty May flower ringing on this August morn. Nan has no control over any of it. Life and death happen in a cycle she can't anticipate, all out of order and uncertain, and it's simply futile trying to figure it out.

Nan winces at the drumming of her headache as she plucks a sad sweet pea from the ground, so fragile, she's afraid there's no way for it to be saved, though she intends to try. She scoops dirt into a woman's boot with a ridiculously narrow heel, pouring handfuls of soil littered with stones and broken flowers into the cavity until she is overcome by the intense feeling of being watched. It makes her bones cold, until she realizes it is only Mavis, her wild hair eclipsing the sun.

"What are you staring at?" Nan asks.

"I didn't come here to exorcize your demons."

Nan pats the dirt around the tender stem. "Whatever do you mean?"

"You don't really expect me to believe that Eve's relative showed up here today, of all days, by coincidence?"

"Well, I certainly didn't invite her."

Nan's headache burrows into her forehead. She's been getting them more and more lately. She worries it is something insidious, the sort of thing that kills old women, though she doesn't dare feel sorry for herself, thinking of all the years she's lived while Eve died at eighteen.

Not realizing she'd been holding her breath until she let it go, Nan inhaled as she stepped out of the cloying heat of Eve's house into the gray light of that December morning, filling her lungs with cold air—the scent of snow freezing out the stench of blood. She stared at the streetlights, thinking how they looked like miniature moons gilding the flakes that floated to the cracked sidewalk, and dusted the old houses with a sugary glow, turning the dismal neighborhood into someplace almost beautiful, before she came to her senses.

Run, Nan thought. *You will regret standing here the rest of your life*, and she was running down the creaky steps, careful on the ice. "Everything is going to be all right," she said over and over again, so innocent she still believed good thoughts made things so.

She ran all the way to Miss Winter's house, its gingerbread trim caked with snow, the windows filled with caramel light.

Nan pressed on Miss Winter's bell until she opened the door, her pleasant expression quickly replaced by one of horror, as though Nan explained everything, though she had been made mute by things too dreadful to say out loud.

They ran. Nan stumbled, but Miss Winter kept running, wearing no hat, gloves, or coat. When Nan caught up, she led the way to Eve's house, which they entered without knocking, squinting in the pea-green light. Had the hallway to Eve's room always been so narrow? Had the door to her bedroom always been so heavy? Had Ruthie and Mavis always looked like ghosts?

Snowflakes melted from Miss Winter's hair and clothes onto Eve's breathless body, a benediction of ice.

"What have you girls done?" she asked.

"Nothing," says Nan, then, realizing that the purple-haired Mavis is looking at her strangely, adds, "is going to make our past go away, you know."

"I'm not spending the last days of my life in prison," Mavis says, "to make you feel better."

"Prison? Who said anything about you going to prison? Oh! For Eve? Is that what you're talking about? I hardly think that's on the table."

"You don't know, do you, Nan?"

"It's not like—"

"We committed a crime."

"Well, yes, but—"

"Is this why you invited us? For revenge?"

"Revenge?"

"I know you blame me," Mavis says.

How could she possibly know that? Nan hasn't talked to Mavis or corresponded with her in decades. Mavis has no way of knowing what Nan's been feeling or thinking. "I haven't, I—"

"Don't lie."

Nan squints up at Mavis, who, through some trick of the light, looks like one of those fake statues, a person painted as stone, until she turns her head, and her lavender hair emits a shower of tiny rainbows. Is Mavis's hair still wet from last night's downpour? How is that possible?

"What are you up to?" Mavis asks.

"Up to? Up to?" Nan ponders the question, even looking at the sky for a moment as though the answer might be floating overhead. "I'm not up to anything, Mavis. Anything sneaky, that is. I told you about Bay. You remember that, don't you? I asked you to come so you could help with her."

"Bay seems quite capable of taking care of herself."

"I don't want her to feel abandoned. The way Eve did."

"Eve? We're talking about Eve now?"

Nan worries Mavis's mind has lost its edge. It is not the first time during this visit that she seems confused.

"Nan," Mavis says. "Eve is dead."

Nan presses a calendula into a dirty white shoe she doesn't have time to clean. Can the plants survive lying on the ground with their roots exposed? Why is Mavis standing there as if there is nothing to do, no one to save? Then again, isn't that what Mavis does in times of trouble—stand around giving orders?

"Don't you remember, Nan? Don't you remember Eve dying?"

"Of course I remember." Nan can barely control the spit in her words. As though she would ever forget! As if it were just another mundane moment in all the forgotten hours of her life. She peers up at Mavis, who, haloed by the sun, looks blurry, like someone stuck between life and death. The thought makes Nan incredibly sad in the midst of her irritation. They waited too long for this reunion. It can never make up for all they lost. All this life lived that Eve never had. Gasping at the realization, Nan sits back on heels. "She did this."

"Who? Who did what?"

"Eve. I don't know why I didn't realize sooner. Of course she would be upset. All of us together again, after all these years."

"You think Eve vandalized your garden?"

Nan nods slowly. "Who else?" she asks.

"How about the hoodlum who called you a witch last night? How about his friends? How about Bay? She seems like an angry child."

"Bay? You can't be serious. Why would—"

"Do you actually believe the most rational explanation for this destruction is Eve?"

Nan wipes her face with the sleeve of her nightgown. It certainly has gotten hot quite suddenly. "Bay would never do something like this. Eve—"

"Is dead."

"Why do you keep saying that?" Nan shoves a plant, so damaged as to be unrecognizable, into the baby shoe, roughly pressing the dirt around it with shaking fingers. "Clearly, I'm talking about her ghost."

"Her ghost? You don't actually believe Eve's floating around here with gossamer wings, do you?"

"Don't be silly." Nan rolls her eyes at Mavis. "You're confusing ghosts with angels."

Nan remembers the time Eve dressed as a fairy for Halloween. Funny, Eve was always dressing up as someone with wings: fairies, angels, butterflies. Though it makes sense, doesn't it, that Eve was drawn toward creatures of flight? Oh, poor Eve!

While Mavis stands in her dirt-streaked nightgown, staring into space, Nan plants two more shoes, appreciating the silence until she is overcome by her duties as hostess. She can't allow her guests to become catatonic, no matter how much she regrets their presence.

"Mavis?"

She turns her neck so slowly Nan almost expects to hear it creak. "You've seen her?"

"Who?"

"Eve?"

"Yes, of course. Well, sometimes. Occasionally. Mostly it's a scent or an unpleasant taste, but yes, I have seen her."

Mavis looks as though Nan were a ghost herself, a shocking presence among the flowers.

"What does she want? What does she say about death? Does she say anything about me?"

Isn't it just like Mavis to make herself the topic of concern? "She doesn't talk. Sometimes she sings. You know, 'Happy Birthday,' things like that. She never tells me what she wants. You remember how she was." Nan pats dirt around a cosmos, trying to recall when the taste of ash arrived. She hopes it leaves soon. She doesn't want the weekend ruined by the bitter flavor. "I don't understand why you're surprised."

Mavis waves her hand, the way she does, as though what anyone says is just an annoyance. "Why would she appear to you? What's so special about you?"

Nan picks up a long, winding red stem that might be a wild strawberry. It should be planted in a tall boot, something where it can cascade and show off its tendril of pink flowers, but there is no time for that. What's so special about Nan? It's just the sort of thing Mavis would say, insult disguised as query.

"It's the house. It's some kind of portal, I guess. Like in that movie. You should have seen it. What a mess—the broken windows, the rotting porch wood—it stood abandoned for twenty years, which is why I could afford it. From my inheritance, you know. Who would have guessed that little bit of money could buy all this?" Nan waves her dirt-streaked hand like a conjuring magician. "Of course the yard was overgrown and wild. But once I saw the place, I knew it was home. The locals tried to talk me out of it. They said it was a bad-luck place. A doctor built it for his wife, and she died on moving day, right on the front staircase, rubbing her hand over the calla lilies carved in the banister. They said it was haunted like that's a bad thing. Truth be told, I considered it a positive point, but it turned out to be difficult. She shows up whenever she wants to. She doesn't wear gowns or rattle chains or such nonsense, of course. She won't talk to me. I've always thought she's just waiting."

"Waiting for what?"

"For me. For when I die. For revenge. Oh, don't look like that, Mavis. I remember how sweet Eve was, but we were all changed by her death, weren't we? It makes sense she would be too. It's all right. I figure it's what I deserve." Nan picks up another lily of the valley, its leaves torn. Where are these coming from? She tosses it aside, reaching for the foxglove instead. It, too, is a dangerous flower, but only if a person is foolish about it. No one should ever imbibe the water any flower has been sitting in (or accept a drink of any kind from a stranger), for instance. Nan shakes her head, slightly disgusted with herself for blaming the boy for her own criminal behavior.

"Why would you deserve to be haunted?" Mavis asks, easing herself down to kneel on the damp ground. She grabs an old saddle shoe and a fern frond, which likely won't take root, but Nan is not really sure of anything in her garden, and besides, she doesn't want to risk discouraging Mavis with details. "I'm surprised you believe in 'deserve.' I got over that a long time ago."

Of course Mavis has never been hampered by expectations or accounting. She always has been capable of setting her own rules, an annoying trait Nan now wishes she possessed and passed on to her daughter. If Bay didn't worry so much about being normal, Nan wouldn't be so worried about her now. Is Mavis capable of understanding any of this?

Nan explains how Bay was left all those years ago in the caul-draped box. "I told her almost everything right from the start," Nan says, "but I said it was lace. I wanted her to have a nice picture in her head about her arrival. And I think I was right to do so. After all, she only recently learned about the caul, and even at her age, reacted poorly. I didn't even get to the part about her special talent for ghosts. I didn't get to tell her that she'll be able to see them and talk to them as though they are still alive, before she ran out of the room. I thought… well, I don't know what I was thinking. I thought she would see the three of us together and realize it's not a terrible thing to be a witch. I thought that would make things easier for her after I was gone. I had the silly idea, I realize now how silly it was, that you and Ruthie could take care of her. You know, if something ever happened to me."

"A witch?"

Nan is having difficulty adjusting to this aged Mavis who has trouble staying on topic. Who would have guessed Mavis would get funny in the head?

"Yes," Nan says, careful to speak clearly. "If she saw the three of us and how normal we are…" But Nan doesn't know how to continue, looking at Mavis with her lavender hair and pasty face, thinking of Ruthie with her prayer circles and exorcists.

"Oh, Nan," Mavis sighs.

"What?"

In this bright light, Mavis, frowning broadly beneath her frantic hair, looks like an unhappy chrysanthemum. In spite of everything, Nan giggles.

"I'm glad you find something amusing," Mavis says. "Apparently, my face." She wipes her hands on the nightgown, sets aside the saddle shoe she's been working on, and with a good deal of effort, stands. "Come. You need to get out of the heat."

Nan looks at the flowers lying in the sun; there is still so much to be done. But when Mavis extends her hand, Nan takes it, rising to her knees, slowly standing. Mavis puts her arm around Nan, in that stiff way she has. It's not a comforting hold, Mavis being more mast than sail.

"But the flowers—"

"What about Bay? We can't leave her alone in there with Ruthie and Stellora, can we? Who knows what they've been telling her."

Why has she been worrying about the garden when Bay is alone in the house with Stella's questions about Eve and Ruthie's way of speaking without censure? It is disturbing for Nan to realize she's lost her focus so entirely. "Wait," she says, stopping on the porch. "We need a plan."

"A plan?"

It's distressing, Nan thinks. Mavis, who used to be so wickedly smart, standing there frowning as if Nan makes no sense at all.

"You know, how should we act around Stella?"

"How should we act?"

Nan decides right then that the best way to proceed with the weekend is to rely on her skill for subterfuge. It's clear she can't count on Mavis, and Ruthie has never been a serious contender for cunning. "We need to act like we have nothing to hide. We need to act normal."

Mavis turns to look at the front door as though she doesn't know how they have arrived there. "Okay," she says, "we'll act normal. Whatever that is."

In spite of the solemnity of the situation, Nan is giggling when she enters the house, blinking away sunspots in the dim foyer.

"Good morning." Bay's voice floats from the top of the stairs. She seems to have taken special care in dressing, wearing her yellow sundress, languidly descending the steps like a 1940s film ingénue, stealing a look in the direction of the parlor.

Bay kisses Nan's cheek and turns to Mavis. "I can't believe everyone is up! I slept terribly late!"

Nan exchanges a look with Mavis. Obviously the girl is over-doing it, but why?

"Isn't it a beautiful morning?" Bay says, glancing at the parlor.

"Don't do anything drastic," Mavis says to Nan. "I'll be right back. I have to take care of a little business." She walks up the stairs, clutching the banister like a seasick cruise passenger.

At the end of the hallway, the kitchen door swings open. Ruthie, wearing an apron over her nightgown, takes short, quick, black-socked steps toward Nan and Bay, pausing at the open front door to shake her head and wave her spatula, turning to point it at Nan. "What are you doing? Breakfast is ready. Come. Eat!" Without waiting for a response, Ruthie pivots, pushing the door as she does, though it only closes halfway as she glides across the wooden floor to the kitchen.

Before Nan can stop her, Bay strolls over to look outside. It's one of those habits she inherited from Nan; they both like to begin the day by greeting the garden. Nan steels herself for the hysterics sure to erupt. Bay always has hated the tricks people play, and as she's gotten older, her despair over such behavior has gotten worse. Also, Bay loves the shoe garden, though she won't admit it. Nan suspects Bay loves the garden more than she loves breakfast, which is saying a lot.

"What a beautiful day," Bay says, turning to step back into the foyer. "Do I smell pancakes?"

Nan watches Bay, with her new languid walk, stroll toward the kitchen. How could she not have noticed the destruction? Maybe she was stunned into a stupor; she's in shock, poor thing, but when Nan rests her hand on the door to close it entirely, she finds that she is the one stunned. She shakes her head in case she's having one of her memories again, in case she isn't really seeing what she thinks she sees.

The walk is clear of dirt, flowers planted in shoes that only moments before were scattered in the yard, the hollyhocks returned to their boots, the cosmos happy in their sneakers, the daisies in their slippers; every flower in a shoe, every shoe standing. Nothing is in the right place, but the entire front yard is restored to some semblance of its own, quirky normalcy.

"Pancakes!" Bay hollers from the kitchen.

Nan loves pancakes! She swallows, licks her lips, and swallows again. The taste of ash is gone, replaced by a slightly sweet, floral flavor, as though instead of planting flowers this morning, she's been eating them.

Nan closes the door and turns to smile at Mavis as she comes coughing down the stairs, clutching a pack of cigarettes. She looks startled but returns the smile, a fleeting expression that subtracts a great deal of age from her face. Nan understands. The thing about witches, after all, is that they must learn to wear masks. It's something almost all of them do as protection against judgment. Even in the midst of this summer morning, Nan shudders at the history of witches: tortured, burned, hanged, or strangled. Horrible things were done to them as ward against their rumored strength. It is so easy to forget that they were real women. Nan decides not to frighten Mavis (who apparently still does have her power after all) with words of gratitude, but what harm can there be in a smile, even if Mavis now scowls in response? They walk to the kitchen together, inhaling the wonderful aroma of coffee and pancakes.

WILD CARROT *Wild carrot, or Queen Anne's lace, is an aromatic herb that soothes the digestive tract and stimulates the uterus. It bears a striking resemblance to the poisonous hemlock.*

⟋⟍

Ruthie, humming at a surprising pitch, stands at the stove, flipping pancakes. "Good morning, Sunshine!" she says. "Bay, this is Stella."

Stella? Bay doesn't remember anything about someone named Stella. The newcomer sits at the table with her chin in her hand. Her smile reveals dimples and small white teeth. Bay wonders what her Nana could possibly have to do with someone so young? She suddenly realizes that the stranger, her head tilted, is studying Bay as though thinking the same thing.

"She makes the best pancakes," Stella says. "I mean, seriously, what's your trick?"

Bay pulls out a chair, and Ruthie sets a plate of pancakes before her.

"No trick," she says.

"No trick?" Stella shakes her head as she eyes Bay's plate. "I find that hard to believe."

"Well, you don't really expect me to give away all my secrets, do you?"

"I was hoping you might," Stella says, watching Bay fork a triple-decker slice of pancake into her mouth. "You know, I think I will have one more!"

"Oh my gawd," Bay says, maple syrup dripping from the corner of her mouth.

Stella nods. "I know, I know. They're not even pancakes."

"They're...they're heaven—"

Together they exclaim, "Heavencakes!" which makes them laugh.

Mavis, wearing a dirty nightgown, her violet hair spiked like an attack on her head, pushes through the swinging door, followed by a smiling Nan, also still wearing her pajamas accentuated by red boots. She glances sideways at Bay and Stella smiling at each other across the table. "What's going on here?"

"Pancakes. They taste like heaven," Bay says.

Nan drags the computer chair across the floor to the crowded kitchen table. Stella offers Mavis her chair, but she replies with one of her looks, as though the suggestion she might need to sit is insulting. Ruthie flips a perfectly round pancake from the spatula to Stella's plate.

"How many for you, Nan?"

"How many what?" Nan asks, which has the effect of freeze tag on everyone. Ruthie stops between table and stove, her spatula held upright, a cook's exclamation point. Mavis stands with one hand on the coffee pot, the other holding a mug; even Stella stops chewing to frown at Nan, who, Bay realizes, looks especially odd this morning, her hair dotted with petals and stems.

"Nana?"

"Yes, dear?"

"Do you feel all right?"

Nan presses her fingers against her temple. "I'm having one of my headaches."

"How many would you like?" Ruthie asks. "How many pancakes, that is?"

"Oh, I don't know," Nan says, "perhaps six."

"Six?"

"Nana loves pancakes."

"Do you need an aspirin? I think I have some with me," Stella offers.

"I'll just have my headache tea."

Nan moves to stand, but Ruthie tells her to stay put. "I'm right here. I can get the kettle on." She veers around Mavis, leaning so far into the refrigerator she is all backside. "What are you looking for?"

"Apparently the only thing not here," Mavis says. "What is all this? Why are there all these flowers?"

"Flowers? In the refrigerator?" Nan asks. "Why ever would you be looking for flowers in the refrigerator?"

Mavis backs out, standing to her full height of shocked purple hair, a small pink petal dangling above her ear. "I don't suppose there's any cream."

"Right there." Ruthie uses the spatula to point at the blue pitcher on the counter.

How fun, Bay thinks, *to have a whole kitchen full of people for breakfast. Is this what it feels like to be part of a large family?* Ruthie hums something unidentifiable and off-key as she flips pancakes. The stove is remarkably clean, Bay notices. When she makes pancakes, the batter gets everywhere.

Mavis stands by the screen door, staring into the backyard as she drinks her coffee, which gives Bay a chance to observe that even someone as intimidating as Mavis looks frail in a night-gown, positioned in such a way that the light appears to pass right through her.

"Nan," Mavis says. "Do you know that Howard is in your backyard?"

Howard! Bay can't believe she forgot about him—well, not forgot, because she had been disappointed not to see him when she came downstairs, thinking nothing could distract her from him, until breakfast did.

"Six pancakes!" Ruthie announces, setting a large stack in front of Nan.

"Howard? I thought he left."

"He appears to be doing something untoward to the flowers."

Nan's forkful of pancakes stops halfway to her mouth.

"You eat, Nana," Bay says.

"Yes. Eat. You need your strength." Mavis sets her mug firmly on the counter. The teakettle whistles, and Ruthie yelps, which causes a distraction. The next thing Bay knows, the screen door is banging shut, and Mavis is gone.

"I'm surprised at Howard," Ruthie says. "He's starting to remind me of my son. Now, where's this headache tea of yours?"

"I'll get it." Bay says, glancing out the window beyond the glass jars filled with cut flowers and various stones littering the sill, to see Howard, who is sitting in the backyard, look up at Mavis's approach. Even at this distance it's clear he's surprised, and perhaps a bit horrified. *Well, Mavis is looking pretty scary,* Bay thinks, though Howard looks kind of odd himself, still wearing her Nana's nightgown and holding a bouquet of Queen Anne's lace surrounded by... Bay leans across the sink to peer at the backyard littered with overturned shoes and tossed flowers.

"I wonder what caused him to act so criminally," Ruthie says. "Maybe he's had a seizure of some kind."

"A seizure?" Stella asks.

"You know. A fit," Nan says. "Ruthie, these are the best pancakes!"

Not wanting to alarm Nan, though her gut quivers with that feeling of wasps building their nest again, Bay opens the herb cupboard (really an old broom closet fitted with shelves) and easily finds the headache tea; it's been used so much lately. She turns, jar in hand, surprised to find Ruthie and Stella watching with peculiar expressions, as though it were a closet of bones.

Stella turns slowly to address Nan. "Is Howard your husband?"

"No, he's just a boy she hired," Ruthie says, "to transport us about. Nan never married."

"He's very nice," Bay adds, pouring hot water over the filter of herbs.

"She thinks she's in love with him."

"Nana!"

"Oops, it's just these pancakes."

"Isn't it unusual for someone of your generation never to have married? I don't mean to pry, if you don't want to talk about it, though that is part of what my book is going to address, I think. You know, how you were when you were young, and how you are now. Well, not you, specifically, of course."

"Here's your tea," Bay says, frowning at Stella.

No one ever asks Nan about a husband. Bay hasn't thought about it since she was a little kid and used to fantasize a wedding for Nan and a father for herself, until she decided she liked her family just fine with only the two of them.

Nan doesn't seem to mind the question, however. In fact it is unclear if she heard it; she appears entirely absorbed in eating pancakes and doesn't seem to notice that Stella sits across from her with an expression that reminds Bay of Nicholas stalking a bird.

Who is she, anyway? What is she doing here? Bay wonders, suddenly eager to leave the warm kitchen, with its heavy scent of coffee and pancakes and an uncomfortable feeling she can't quite name, the way the air feels before a storm, though it isn't going to rain. "I'm gonna see if I can help," she says, which no one seems to notice, so absorbed are they in their separate tasks: Nan eating her pancakes, Ruthie pouring batter onto the griddle in what appear to be perfect heart shapes, and Stella, her dark eyes slit, watching them both.

Bay carefully closes the screen door behind her. *It's one of those days, a Sugar Day,* her Nana calls them, when the sky is bright blue and the sun polishes everything to a glow, like the sparkle of sugar-dusted frosting. She wishes she could enjoy the sweet feeling, but how can she with the entire back garden destroyed?

She runs down the little hill, remembering how easily she used to run to her special place, while now her feet hit the ground with a shock. When she stops in front of Mavis and Howard, they are both frowning. "This isn't how it looks," Howard says from his position among the ruin.

For some reason Bay feels like crying. She can't imagine any good reason for Howard to be in the midst of this destruction, but having so often suffered cruel conclusions based on incomplete evidence, she decides to give him the benefit of a doubt.

"It isn't how it looks," she tells Mavis.

"Why don't you go back inside, Basil? I need to talk to Harvey."

"She can stay," Howard says, casting a wary look at Mavis.

"Your nightie is bunched around your hip," Mavis says.

Howard pulls at the gown, which, ruched high on his thigh, reveals the tiny hairs there, golden and pretty as saffron. In this light, the bruise on his cheek looks pronounced; Bay wonders if he is the sort of boy who always gets in trouble.

"Aren't you a little old for this sort of game, Basil?" Mavis asks. "You have Nan fooled, with your tricks, but I am well aware that you are the culprit here."

"Me?" Bay thinks it is bad enough to see the beautiful garden destroyed, the entire backyard a mess, all these flowers dying, all the pretty shoes her Nana so lovingly restored thrown about like trash. How many nights has Bay looked out her bedroom window at the fireflies blinking over these flowers? How many times has she leaned close to the screen to inhale the scent of home? It's bad enough that this terrible thing happened, without being accused of doing it.

"I didn't," Bay says. "Why would I?"

"It's obvious you're an angry child," Mavis says. "Maybe you've been given too much to deal with, Nan being the way she is."

Bay makes a sound, a strange, abrupt noise somewhere between laugh and bark. Yes, *Nan being the way she is* has been a challenge. But that's not really Mavis's business, is it? Or Howard's. Bay realizes they are watching her as though she might do something terrible, which gives her a confused thrill. *Like I'm one of the mean girls, like I have power.* It is almost funny, as is the look on Mavis's face, her frown deepening until it morphs into a coughing fit that goes on so long Bay reluctantly steps closer to pat her on the back until the cough subsides.

"Are you all right?" Howard asks.

"No. I am not. I think that's obvious. I want to talk to you," she says, pointing a bony finger at him, but the cough returns.

Mavis shakes her head at Bay when she raises her hand for further back-patting, which she appreciates. Her palm burns for some reason. *Probably just another one of the freaky things about me,* Bay thinks.

"I need to go back inside, but I don't want you to leave until we have our conversation," Mavis rasps to Howard in that way she has of making it seem like no isn't even an option. She turns to wag her finger at Bay. "Don't you break Nan's heart, young lady. Do you hear me?"

Bay is tempted to think really mean things about Mavis, with her clown hair and drawn eyebrows, but she resists. Bay isn't one of those mean girls, and she determined, some time ago, that she wouldn't let all the meanness in the world make her so.

"Of course I won't break my Nana's heart."

Mavis nods abruptly, turning to address Howard. "There's pancakes for breakfast," she says before lumbering across the yard toward the house, a green vine trailing from the heel of her dirty foot.

Bay kneels to the ground, trying to decide what to save in the damage around her. She didn't realize how brittle she felt until she softens at the sight of Howard tenderly handling a white phlox. She had been right about him, after all. This would be a happy thought if it didn't arrive with the unpleasant conclusion that some unknown person caused this damage. Remembering all the smashed pumpkins of her life, Bay wonders if this is going to become something seasonal. She reaches for a red lily, torn from its stem; already dying, it can't possibly be saved.

"I would never hurt my Nana's flowers," she says softly, holding her breath until Howard answers, which seems to take a long time.

"I know. Hand me that sneaker, will you?"

Bay's hand, gold with lily dust (a flower's kiss, her Nana used to say) hovers above the dirt-streaked shoe when she realizes. Karl! Of course! This is one of the pair she left out for him. She picks up the shoe and hands it to Howard.

"Don't you like pancakes?" she asks. "Ruthie makes the best ever."

"I do," Howard says, pouring dirt into the high-top and making a hole for the sad phlox.

"This'll take all day," Bay says. "You should go eat. Find out what Mavis wants to talk to you about."

The phlox droops across the dirty shoelace like it's depressed, Bay thinks.

"I do kind of have a headache," Howard says. "But you can't do this all by yourself."

Bay shrugs. "I'm just going to see what I can get done before it gets too hot."

"Is there maple syrup?" he asks.

"Of course."

"Real maple syrup?"

Bay nods solemnly. This is a matter her Nana takes quite seriously, buying it by the gallon from that guy with the big mustache at the farmers' market. "There is no other kind," she says.

In spite of everything, when Howard smiles, Bay does too. *It's as if our happiness is connected,* she thinks.

"Well, then." Howard rises awkwardly, still adjusting to the nightgown. "If my dad could see me now," he says, turning toward the house.

Bay watches him walk the whole way, until he has gone up

the back stairs and steps into the house, before she starts calling for Karl—not so loud that those inside can hear, only loud enough that he will come, if he dares.

POPPY *The poppy, a symbol of fertility, is known as "the flower of forgetfulness" because of its association with sleep and death. The seeds are used as a source of cooking oil, in baking cakes and breads, and as bird food. The smoke of poppy seeds has been used in divination.*

ere she is at camp. She's wet in almost all these pictures, isn't she? Eve loved to swim, you know." Ruthie leans across the dining room table to hand one photograph to Stella and the other to Howard. Nan sits stiffly in her chair, peering down her nose at the black-and-white photos spread across the table like a game of "Go Fish." She feels a little bit like a ghost herself, looking at the young woman she was, so different from the old woman she's become. There they are, the four of them in the last great summer of their lives. Well, she assumes. What does she know, after all, of the summers Ruthie and Mavis spent during the years apart? And what, really, did she ever know of Eve? Nan's fingers hover above the photographs, as if a firm grasp would be too intimate.

Why, look at Eve smiling in picture after picture, flattened in framed space, captured forever like an anesthetized butterfly. Only now does Nan consider how the constancy of Eve's smile was, in fact, a clue. Who can be so happy all the time? Who thinks she has to be? They were so young! They had not yet learned about false smiles and desperate lives.

"That's funny," Stella says. "Everyone always tells me I'm just like her, but I don't like to swim at all."

"Hilarious," Mavis says as she walks into the dining room, clutching her package of cigarettes.

"Oh, Eve loved the water," Ruthie says. "She swam every chance she got. She swam before breakfast and after lunch. She even swam in the middle of the night! Did I ever tell you girls? Once I woke up and Eve was gone. Well, naturally I assumed she had nature's call. I wasn't worried. We didn't worry so much in those days, we were…well, we were young, and it wasn't like it is now, everyone expecting something terrible to happen to pretty girls, but when she didn't come back after a while, I wondered what she was up to. I didn't even need a flashlight. The moon cast everything with a silver glow. I remember thinking how it was enchanting, walking through the forest like that.

"When she wasn't at the outhouse, well, then I would say I was concerned, but I thought of the lake right away, and James. That was before…well, sure enough, there she was. Swimming. All by herself. I didn't disturb her. I assumed if she wanted company she would have had it, though now I…"

Nan can't believe how dangerous Ruthie is. She seems so sweet and simple, and yet here they are, everyone struck still, as though turned to salt in the old story of Lot's wife, for daring to look back. Nan should say something, anything to break the spell, but she can't think of anything other than Eve swimming alone in the dark.

"I sat on that rock. You know the one, right, girls? It was a boulder, really. I sat and watched her swim. I don't know why. It seems like such a strange thing to do, now that I think about it. You know how we were back then. We were all a little strange, weren't we? Eve especially. I didn't think she'd want company, yet I felt compelled to find her. And I remember how I could feel the moon on my skin. What do they call it? The glow, just like the sun, only cooler?" .

"Moon glow," Mavis says through clenched teeth.

"Well, of course! Why couldn't I remember such a simple thing? The moon glow. The lake was black, but it had that silvery light all over it, like a web. That's the way everything was, the trees, the sky, and Eve, swimming like she thought if she swam long enough she could swim away from there, though naturally she was surrounded by shoreline on all sides."

Howard frowns at the photographs littered across the table. "You all look so young."

"Hard to fathom the ravage of time, isn't it?" Mavis rasps.

"Here's a picture from the dance," Ruthie says. "You can't tell, 'cause it's in black and white, but that dress was the most amazing shade of orange, like nothing Eve had ever worn before. Though it would look good on you too, Stella. The color was, well, what was it like? I wish I could think of—"

"Poppy," says Nan, remembering Eve wearing that orange flame, her lips painted red.

"Well, yes, of course! Poppy." Ruthie shakes her head. "Pity not to have it in color. It was quite striking, really. I wonder whatever became of that dress?"

"What's in her hair?" Stella asks.

Ruthie shakes her head as she frowns at the photograph.

"Carnations," says Nan. "They were on the tables at the dance, and she took three for her hair."

"Do you have any pictures of her with James?" Stella asks.

"There was no James," Ruthie sighs.

Nan closes her eyes.

"That night," Mavis says, "he didn't show up. He was a cad in the end."

"Oh. She must have been upset."

"She wasn't very," Ruthie says.

"Really?" Stella frowns at the photograph. "I didn't realize how beautiful she was."

"But if she were still alive, she'd be a dinosaur, just like us."

"Mavis, could you help me in the kitchen?"

Nan knows that only half an hour ago she looked as bad as Mavis does, but now that she, Ruthie, and Howard have made themselves presentable, Mavis, with her wild hair and dirty nightgown, looks like the crazy woman from the attic. Instead of getting the hint and following Nan into the kitchen, however, Mavis just stands there scowling and scratching her backside.

"Are you coming?"

"Yes, Nan, I'm coming to help you in the kitchen," Mavis says in an overly loud, dramatic voice. Mavis was always interested in the theater, and while certainly no Meryl Streep, she's a better actress than she's being now, making a point of letting everyone know it's a ruse. Nan doesn't need her help, but is summoning her, and frankly, Nan resents it. This is her house, these are her guests, and strange as the circumstances are, she means for people to be comfortable, even Stella the spy, and Howard, who told Nan earlier that he planned to stay to "keep an eye on things" because of the garden vandal, which is what Nan tells Mavis when she walks into the kitchen, clutching her cigarettes, her spiked hair giving her the look of a recent electrocution.

"What possible good can come of her presence? Don't think I believe, for one minute, that she just miraculously showed up this weekend," Mavis says. "And what does Howard think he can do about some hoodlum that we can't do ourselves?"

"Obviously, Howard is unhappy at home. I think that's clear. I don't mind offering a little shelter. As to Stella in there, how many times do I have to say it? I did not invite her. I didn't even know of her existence. But we will only arouse her suspicions if we act guilty. We need to behave as though there's nothing to hide. Think, Mavis. Be reasonable."

"Are you accusing me of being unreasonable?"

"Of course not. There is no accusation intended at all. Can't you forgive me for not being precise? I'm just saying that all of us—well you and me, that is, I don't think we should bring Ruthie in on this—we have to stay focused. Of course we don't need Howard's help, but I do believe he might need ours. Besides, it can't hurt to have him hanging about. Stella showing up like this is disturbing, but we don't have any idea how much she knows."

"Do you think Ruthie told her—"

"No, no, no. Ruthie certainly wouldn't want her church folk learning about our history. We just need to be careful, that's all I'm saying. We'll send Stella on her way with a few of our old stories about Eve, and she'll never be any the wiser. I don't trust her either, Mavis. She might look like Eve, but she's a liar."

"Well…"

"Yes, well," Nan says, "That was different, of course. Eve's lies were…"

"What do you propose we do?"

Though the day has only just begun, Nan is tired. While she has developed an unexamined affection for Howard, and it has been wonderful to see Mavis and Ruthie too (in spite of her new, frightening beliefs) Nan wishes everyone would go home now. What she needs to do is take a nap to clear her head. She'd like to enjoy what she can of the rest of this time with her old friends before they all die, which, Nan knows, some would consider a morbid notion. The young would say so, but the old live with constant reminders of life's morbidity, and after a while, one gets rather used to it.

"Let Ruthie entertain Stella and Howard. If she says something unfortunate about Eve, we can attribute it to her general confusion. Ruthie is our secret weapon," Nan says. "She's such a secret, she doesn't even know it."

Mavis stares at Nan. "When did you get like this?" she asks.

Nan blushes with the compliment, turning to look out the screen door just in time to see Bay walking up from the yard, her yellow dress streaked with dirt and grass, an unusually grim expression on her face.

"I told you she's an angry young woman," Mavis says.

"Shh." Nan turns away from the door, almost walking into Mavis in the process. "It wasn't her. She loves the garden."

"Right. It was Eve's ghost, or an elf, I suppose. Perhaps a trampling unicorn."

Bay enters the kitchen, distracted, mumbling to herself, well into the room before she even notices them and smiles. But Nan suspects it is a false smile, which sets her heart to racing. Everything Nan has done, everything good and bad, has been so that Bay will never have to be a girl with a false smile. What happened out there? Nan trembles as she eases herself into the nearest chair.

"Nana? Nana?"

"Goodness, Bay, don't shout."

"I just said, are you expecting more company?"

"No, of course not. Where would I put anyone else? Everyone is here and then some. Why?"

Bay frowns at the large bowl filled with fruit. Where did it come from? Ruthie is some kind of super homemaker, all the pancake mess cleaned, and a fruit bowl on the counter. "I just saw an old woman." Bay picks up an apple and places it on the cutting board. She pulls open the silverware drawer and selects a knife.

The woman frightened Bay actually, suddenly arrived among the shoes and flowers, standing so still that for a moment Bay wondered if she was dreaming.

"She was really old. And she was dressed like it was the middle of winter."

"What do you mean?" Nan asks.

"She had on a long black skirt and a little knit thing, like a sweater, and a big sun hat, only it was black too."

This is just too much. Anyone would agree. Why does everything have to happen at once? "Well, she's no one I invited," Nan says, pleased with how normal she sounds.

"Was she anything else?" Mavis asks, her head slowly turning, as if it is the weight of a bowling ball. "Other than old?"

Bay sighs. How did her Nana, her sweet Nana, who doesn't even realize when she's being insulted half the time (Bay remembers how once they were at the grocery store and Nan called the bag boy a nice young man after he asked if she needed a broom; they were having a sale, he said), become friends with Mavis, who sees everything as an insult?

"I asked if she was looking for you, Nana, but she just walked into the forest. Remember when you used to make those apple dolls with cloves for eyes? That's what she looked like."

"Well, she must be someone from that subdivision," Nan says, trying to assume a neutral expression, though Mavis is clearly suspicious. "Probably out hunting mushrooms."

Bay picks up an apple slice. Why would her Nana say such a thing, as though lost people were always showing up around here, hunting mushrooms?

Nan breathes deeply, locating the apple's sharp scent through the memory of smoke. She can do this. She can pretend everything is normal. Hasn't she done so for most of her life?

"Also, there's something else." Bay would prefer to wait until Mavis is no longer lurking about, but what if she puts ideas into Nan's head about Bay tearing up the garden?

Something else, Nan wonders, *what else could there be?*

"There's a boy," Bay says. "He's been hanging around here. I'm sorry, Nana, but I think he messed up the shoe garden in the backyard. Someone did, and I think it was him."

"A boy?"

"Don't worry. Most of it is fixed, but I came inside because he was acting like a jerk."

"You see him?"

"We're not... I mean, yeah, I see him, but you know, not like that. At first I thought he was nice, but now I'm not so sure. Do you think we should call the sheriff?"

"Oh, no, we don't want to do that," Nan says.

"I thought he was just, you know, weird, but now I think he might be mentally ill or something."

"Why would you say such a thing?"

"Well, he expects me to believe he's a ghost."

Mavis eases herself into the chair across from Nan.

"I said to him, 'What do you think I am, stupid?' And he said…"

Nan can hear Ruthie, Howard, and Stella laughing in the dining room. They seem to be having a lovely time remembering Eve, though Nan can't think of anything funny about her.

"What?" Mavis barks. "What did this boy say?"

Nan closes her eyes, bracing for the worst.

"It doesn't mean anything. He called me a witch. I've been called worse things, that's for sure."

Oh! Nan tries to stop smiling when she notices Mavis studying her. *But really? Is that all?*

"His feet were cold. That's what he said. I left some shoes out for him weeks ago. He said he never found them, which is a lie. I mean, they were right there. Anyway, last night with the rain and all, he said he was trying to put on shoes, and nothing fit. It was like putting on water, and all of a sudden he remembered."

"Remembered what?"

"That he was dead. But of course that's just an excuse."

"Well, how did he die?" Nan asks, hoping her voice sounds innocent.

"He didn't, Nana. He just made that up. He said something about a car accident, but of course he doesn't have a scratch on him. He just doesn't want to get in trouble."

"Oh, I don't know about that," Nan says, pretending only casual interest. "He wouldn't be the first ghost in our garden."

"He wouldn't?" Bay asks.

"We'll have him on his way in no time."

How is it possible, Bay thinks, *that my Nana, who is, okay, weird, but much more normal than others realize, how is it possible that she not only believes in ghosts but thinks they live in her garden?* Bay feels herself blush, embarrassed on Nan's behalf.

"How do you propose to get rid of him?" Mavis asks.

Nan waves her hand, pretending nonchalance so thoroughly she almost believes herself. "We'll have a little ceremony. We'll tell him to go to the light. We'll tell them all to go. I have long suspected there are quite a few hanging around here. I should have done it years ago. It's best for everyone."

"But, Nana," Bay says, "he isn't a ghost." She turns to address Mavis. "I don't believe in ghosts. He's just a boy. His name is Karl."

Mavis cocks an eyebrow, but Nan slumps in her chair; she cannot stop herself from doing so. It is as if she is struck to hear the name again after all these years. "You need to stay away from him."

Bay shrugs that one-shoulder shrug of hers, which always drives her Nana crazy. "Use both shoulders," she'll say. "Who shrugs like that?" Bay is almost positive she didn't do it on purpose to get on her Nana's nerves, which judging by the deepening scowl, it has.

"Just keep away from him."

Mavis and Bay are both staring now, Bay looking hurt, Mavis with that knowing expression she gets. Nan sits up and assumes a smile. Goodness knows how far a false smile will take you! "As I said, we'll have a ceremony." She is pleased by the brightness in her voice. "Won't this be fun?"

He isn't a ghost, Bay thinks. She considers arguing her point, but her Nana is obviously upset, and Bay doesn't want to ruin the special weekend. After all, she knows how she would feel if she and Thalia were separated for decades. Well, on second thought, she has no idea, though she thinks she's starting to understand. Thalia has been so distant lately. Suddenly, Bay is filled with fear. Are she and Thalia already beginning the sort of separation that kept Nan and her friends apart for all these years? Thalia, Bay realizes, is the only person she can talk to about this. Thalia, who believes in ghosts, would find the notion of one in Bay's garden thrilling. "Can I invite Thalia?" she asks. "To the ceremony?"

"Well, I don't know…"

"Please. You have your friends."

Nan pretends not to notice Mavis, standing behind Bay, vehemently shaking her head and cutting the air with her hand. "Oh, all right, as long as it's okay with her mother."

"Thanks, Nana," Bay says.

Nan feels pleased, listening to Bay run happily up the stairs, the scent of apples trailing in her wake, but the pleasant feeling quickly dissipates. It's disturbing, quite disturbing, actually, to think that Grace Winter (for who else would the old woman be) and Karl, who most certainly is dead, have been in contact with Bay; more than disturbing, dreadful.

"Why don't you just invite the entire local community?" Mavis drawls. "We can have a bonfire. That's always been popular for witches."

"You're not funny, Mavis. What am I supposed to do?" Nan lowers her voice. "Tell the child she can't have friends?"

"Don't be silly. Why can't she have friends?"

If it weren't for the fact that, after this weekend, Nan won't see Mavis again, she would be quite annoyed with her. But how can Nan indulge in such pettiness when they will be dead soon? *Part of growing old*, Nan thinks, *is that every thought of the future becomes a funeral.* In fact, when she really thinks about it, Nan suspects she will be long dead before any trial. In spite of the dismal context, this is reassuring.

"You two should come see this picture!" Ruthie calls from the dining room.

"We need to talk," Mavis hisses. "Somewhere private."

Nan doesn't see why. What is there to say? Further conversation is not on her agenda.

"I do believe I'll take a nap," Mavis says loudly. "Didn't you say you were going to take a nap for that headache of yours?"

Nan nods.

Mavis points at her own mouth. "Speak up, so they can hear you."

"Are you hungry?" Nan shouts.

Mavis rolls her eyes as Ruthie, Stella, and Howard exclaim from the dining room that they couldn't eat another thing. "Say you're going to take a nap," Mavis whispers.

"Well, I think I'm going to go take a little nap," Nan shouts. "Oh, yes. I will go to take a nap now." Nan, unlike Mavis, always was a poor actress.

They go up the back stairs together, passing Bay's room, with her door closed, and the story room, where Ruthie slept, the door left slightly ajar. Glancing into it, Nan is surprised by the mess. Frothy piles of summer-colored clothes litter the floor and cover the bed. The dresser and bedside table are crowded with flower-filled vases. Is there more than one garden vandal lurking about? The last thing Nan sees, and she's sure she must be imagining it, a trick of the light, a confusion of shadows as she reluctantly turns to face forward (at her age one has to be careful) is a chocolate cake, poised atop a large stack of books, fairy tales, if Nan remembers right, the old copies of Grimm and Andersen though of course it can't be a cake; it must be a hat.

Nan follows Mavis down the hall, past the pink room, which is the one Mavis is using, to Nan's room, where she immediately closes the window and draws the drapes. The old house stays cool on hot days if she remembers to block the heat this way. She should have done so in the parlor and dining room as well, but she's too tired to attend to it now. She eyes her unmade bed. There is something so depressing about an unmade bed.

"What are you doing?"

Nan is tempted to respond with Mavis-like sarcasm but settles on transparency instead. She straightens the quilt and fluffs the pillows, then sits, thinking that's where she'll remain for the conversation. But once there, she can find no good reason for not lying down.

"Are you taking a nap?"

"I just need to close my eyes, Mavis. We can still talk."

After a moment, Mavis tells Nan to scoot over, which she does, though it is no longer the easy maneuver of her youth.

"We have to send that boy to the light, or wherever he must go," Nan says. "Mavis, I don't want Bay to speak to him under any circumstance."

Mavis sighs. Nan opens one eye to look. Why hasn't she noticed before? Mavis looks quite unwell. "Are you—"

"There's something you need to know," Mavis says. "You aren't falling asleep, are you?"

"No," Nan lies. "I'm glad you're here, Mavis. It can be difficult enough to send one ghost toward the light, much more the three we know of, and all the others besides."

"What three? What others?"

"Well, there's the boy, Karl." (Nan hopes that Mavis, so close on the narrow bed, doesn't notice the shudder his name induces.) "And Miss Winter."

"Grace Winter?"

"I've actually suspected for a long time, but I never had proof. Strange things happened. Candles blown out on windless nights, fires roaring in the hearth going suddenly dead, doors held shut as though locked, that sort of thing."

"But, Nan—"

"And then there's Eve, of course. I don't want her talking to Bay."

"That seems unlikely, since you said she can't talk."

"No, no, you're not paying attention," Nan says. "She can talk. Why wouldn't she be able to talk? She just won't talk to me."

"I have to tell you something."

Nan feels the slightest tremor, reminiscent of that long-ago sensation of sleepovers and sharing sweet secrets. "I have something to tell too," she whispers. "You first."

"I don't believe in ghosts."

She tries not to judge, but how could Mavis let herself go

like this? Nan cannot believe the mess she's gotten herself into, only to discover that she must deal with it all alone. Eve, with her tragic death story, would shock Bay, and Karl could destroy her world, though Nan is almost positive he remains ignorant of the facts of the matter, which is to her advantage, of course. Apparently even Grace Winter has shown up for the party, and why wouldn't she betray Nan, who betrayed her so horribly? How will Nan deal with all that needs to be done? Obviously, Bay will have to accept her own ghost-filled life, but Nan can't bear the thought, she won't bear it, of Bay being damaged by Nan's half-dead past.

She pats the bed until she finds Mavis's hand. How strange it is that Mavis (Mavis!) would have this old woman's hand.

"I thought these were supposed to be my golden years," Nan says. "I didn't expect them to be so tarnished."

Mavis's hand lifts beneath Nan's. Well, Mavis never could stand intimacy. But she is not trying to end the touch, only reverse it. Mavis pats Nan's hand and says, "I thought I would have beautiful white hair but no wrinkles."

"I thought I would be wise."

"Oh, but you are," Mavis says, "all old women are terribly wise."

"And cute," Nan says, because she especially hates that word.

"I thought there would always be someone to go to dinner with."

Nan sneaks a look at Mavis, who has taken on a disturbing, corpselike appearance. Is Mavis lonely? Whoever would have imagined it?

"We didn't know," Nan says. "How could we guess what our lives would be like?"

"I really thought I would move to Africa."

"Oh well, maybe you will. You're not dead yet."

They lie side by side on the small bed, not holding hands exactly, but touching fingers.

"I thought it wouldn't hurt," Mavis says.

Nan thinks of the pain in her feet, the ache in her legs, the headaches, how her skin sometimes feels pricked with needles.

"I thought there would always be someone who loved me."

"Oh, there is," Nan says. Just like that, she realizes it's true. In spite of everything, and all the years, Nan still loves Mavis.

"That's a nice thing for you to say," Mavis murmurs.

How tired Nan is of the past. After all, what are the hurt feelings of an old woman? Just another thing that passes, and there is so much that passes as time goes on, that life, which once felt like an eternally replenished cup, is emptied until only the essential remains. The heart, Nan has discovered when relieved of the burdens of hate and anger, can be quite buoyant.

Mavis, always an untroubled sleeper, is already snoring softly. How are two old ladies going to fight dark forces, send ghosts to the light (or wherever; she doesn't actually care where they go, so long as they leave, though truth be told, she has no real idea of how to make this happen), keep Ruthie distracted, two teenage girls entertained, and get dinner on the table besides? It is too much to do and too much to think about. *How can Mavis fall asleep at a time like this?* Nan wonders, and so thinking, her mind drifts toward all Mavis is capable of, the memories torn like the flowers in Nan's garden, the peppery scent teasing, until she finds herself longing for the full aroma, the perfume of their innocence that last summer.

◦◦◦

They gasped when Eve came out of the cabin, dressed in orange, her lips a deep red. Brazen. "What? Do I look bad?" she asked, her smile collapsing.

"Oh my Lord, no." Ruthie broke the silence to go to her, passing Nan with a swish of petticoat, and perfume of Ivory soap. "You look beautiful."

"You do. You look so beautiful," Nan said as she, too, rushed to embrace Eve. They were always hurrying to hold her close, as though she needed to be reassured of gravity.

"You look fine," Mavis said, standing there in her white dress, with her slash of signature red lipstick, which no longer seemed extraordinary. "What's everyone waiting for?" She turned toward the path in the woods, and they followed, because of course they always followed Mavis. They followed her into the forest, torches lighting their way, the air scented with skunk cabbage, the dusty aroma of burnt moth wings and ferns, the scent of the end of summer, monkshood, virgin's bower, hellebore, the wild wood, the mineral scent of water, the smoky scent of fire.

PEONY *A symbol of love and affection, the peony's roots are protection against evil spirits. The seeds prevent nightmares. Peony grants its recipient the power to keep secrets.*

⁓

Ruthie has kicked Bay out of the kitchen, and she isn't sure what to do about it. She wishes her Nana could explain, but she has been napping all afternoon! Ruthie says this is understandable. "It takes a lot of energy to get ready for a whole houseful of guests. Let her sleep. I'm enjoying myself. Ever since my son left, I haven't done much cooking."

Bay has observed, mostly among her schoolmates' parents, that there is a mysterious system of offer and decline. People offer to do and give, and it is up to the intended recipient to refuse. There seems to be a certain number of times (two? three?) before the once-insistent giver happily rescinds. Bay noted, years ago, the stunned expressions of mothers when Nan bypassed the polite decline for immediate acceptance and said, "Why yes, it would be lovely if you could transport the girls both ways." (Her Nana hates to drive.) When Ruthie tells Bay to stay out of the kitchen, she is happy to fall on her Nana's example rather than argue the point. While it's true Bay might want to be a chef when she grows up, she doesn't want to start now. There is too much going on; she's afraid of missing some new excitement. "Just let me know if you need help," she says.

"I don't want you sneaking in here." Ruthie sounds stern but looks so sweet, smiling and wearing an apron patterned with peonies as big as cabbages, that Bay doesn't mind being scolded. "Use the front entrance the rest of the day," Ruthie says.

Which is what Bay does, wandering in and out of the house

and restlessly around the yard. Eventually, she feels sleepy. Maybe it's the heat, or the boredom. Maybe she should have insisted on helping Ruthie in the kitchen after all, though it doesn't seem like a good idea to try now. Nan would probably say Bay is tired because of all the growing she's doing. "It takes a lot of energy to grow bones," Nan likes to say.

Delicious smells waft from the kitchen into the upstairs hallway when Bay walks to her bedroom, only to discover Stella sprawled across the bed. "What is she doing here, anyway?" Bay mumbles as she backs out of the room. "Where's Thalia going to sleep?"

Bay tries to decide if the bed shortage is good reason to wake Nan, then scolds herself for not acting her age (always running to her Nana like a baby!) when she remembers the tent. Thalia is nervous about sleeping outside, but nothing bad happens around here, except a few car accidents caused by taking the curve too fast. Bay goes downstairs and starts toward the kitchen with its access to the basement (where the tent is kept) but stops short. She stands in the hallway, inhaling the wonderful aromas: onion, butter, and curry—she thinks she has these right—and chocolate. It's definitely chocolate, one of the best scents of all, even better than the lavender her Nana loves. In fact, there is also a scent, faint but distinct, of lavender, though that doesn't make sense. Maybe the aromas from the kitchen and garden mingle in some previously undiscovered way, at just this juncture in the hall.

Bay might have stood there a good deal longer, enjoying the kitchen smells, had Mavis not come down the stairs, wearing a bright gold dress with long sleeves belling out at the wrists, carrying the heavy odor of too much perfume. *Flowers' Doom*, Bay thinks.

"What are you doing, Sage? You look… What—is that—smell?"

"Ruthie's cooking."

"It reminds me of something," Mavis says, her bracelets clanking when she gestures. "What? I can't remember, but it's a good memory, I'm sure. Where's Nan?"

"Taking a nap."

"Still?"

"Maybe her bones are growing," Bay says, immediately feeling ridiculous when Mavis's eyebrows, darkly drawn on her pale forehead, rise like the antennae of a giant insect.

At the sound of someone moving in the upstairs hallway, Bay feels unreasonably excited, as though her Nana has just returned from a dangerous trip, but it is Stella, not Nan, stretching as she comes down the stairs.

"Oh, I didn't know you were here," Stella says, her cheeks pink, her short brown hair tousled. "I don't know what happened to me. I don't usually sleep like this in the middle of the day. I felt like Dorothy, you know, in *The Wizard of Oz*? Remember that scene where she's walking through the poppy field? I felt like that, but now I'm wide awake. Maybe this would be a good time to talk, Mavis. About, you know, Eve."

Mavis responds with a grunt.

Stella's little mouth in the midst of a frown repositions into pursed lips. "Oooooh, what is that smell?"

"Ruthie's cooking," Bay says. "No one's allowed in the kitchen."

Stella closes her eyes and inhales deeply, reminding Bay of the yoga teacher who came to her school last year, the way she breathed so loud that it was inevitable she be mocked for it. Later, she made things worse by talking about the "spirit" of yoga, which Karen Hander's mother says is a cult.

Mavis edges closer, inspecting Stella the way someone might study a sculpture in a museum. Stella's expression, for a moment rhapsodic, turns sour. She opens her eyes and, apparently startled by Mavis's proximity, steps back.

"You do bear a remarkable resemblance," Mavis says.

"Thanks? People say we could be sisters."

"I hardly think so." Mavis claps her hands, one loud clap. "Come along."

Stella and Bay exchange a look that suggests neither of them care to take orders from Mavis, but because there is little avenue for escape, they follow her out the door to the backyard, which Bay notices has been restored to some semblance of order, though it still has a messy quality about it, a few errant shoes in the middle of the grass, as if caught in the midst of fleeing. *Well, no wonder Nan needs a nap*, Bay thinks, feeling guilty for having abandoned the job.

"This is where we'll have the ceremony." Mavis gestures broadly at the yard. "Just in case."

"A ceremony," Stella says. "What kind of ceremony? I didn't know anything about a ceremony."

"In case what?" Bay asks.

"A sudden downpour. Or any reason why we might want to get inside quickly. For the autumn equinox."

"The equinox isn't for another month."

Mavis turns to assess Stella with narrowed eyes. "For a young person, you are really stuck in your ways, you know."

"But it doesn't make sense."

Mavis laughs, nodding as she reaches up the long bell of her sleeve to remove a cigarette and matchbook. She places the cigarette between her bright red lips, turning away to strike the match.

"I wanna talk to you," Stella whispers. "Somewhere private."

Bay nods, pretending nonchalance, as though she is one of those girls frequently pulled aside for whispered conferences, used to being considered someone whose opinion matters. Mavis, who seems to have forgotten all about them, stands with her face tilted up to the blue sky, where a rising snake of gray smoke lingers overhead. Stella turns toward the house, but Bay pretends not to notice and walks farther into the yard, beyond the lilacs, through the pampas grass, and into the small clearing, Bay's special place she's shared with no one, not even Thalia. Bay doesn't know what came over her to share it now. Stella seems entirely unappreciative as she follows Bay into the clearing, brushing her legs, complaining about a sticky web. When she looks up, she wrinkles her nose and asks, "What is that smell? That's not a skunk, is it?"

Stella scans the clearing, and Bay looks too, imagining what it must be like to see it for the first time. A small blue butterfly hovers over the wild honeysuckle, and the sunlight laces through the weeping apple trees' gnarled branches that arch above the patch of tamped down grass, sheltered on all sides. "You wanna talk here? Doesn't the smell bother you?"

Loneliness, Bay thinks. That's why she never shared her secret place with Thalia. What if she reacted like this? What if she didn't understand that this small patch of grass matters to Bay? She doesn't think she could stand how lonely that would make her feel. She shrugs. *What smell?*

"This could be nice, I guess," Stella says as she sits on the grass. "You know, if you had a little table and some chairs back here."

Bay has been noticing the smell much of the summer, though it seems worse today. Is the forest dying? Her Nana says, years ago, this used to be a real forest with deer, coyotes, raccoons, skunks, mice, and birds, the population greatly diminished when they built the subdivision, a project that took many years, and even now isn't finished but abandoned, a few houses occupied, but with yards unseeded.

"I'm not the outdoors type, myself. You seem like you enjoy it, though. You seem like you have a nice life. It seems really…normal."

Bay smiles, what she hopes is a normal smile, not overly eager, merely courteous. She thinks of her Nana wearing that stupid walnut wreath in the front yard, where anyone can see her, or her muddy clogs to town, once to school to watch Bay in a swim meet, not meaning to doom her as strange, though that's what happened. And really, in spite of this, Bay wouldn't trade her Nana for anything. Thalia once even said she wished her mom were like Bay's, which would probably mean more if Bay hadn't said she wished her Nana was like Mrs. Desarti, who wears lipstick and high heels, and whose idea of making dinner is opening the Chinese take-out cartons. In reality, Bay is almost certain, neither would trade mothers. What is that thing Nan sometimes says? "Love has thorns?" Yes, that's it. For the first time, Bay thinks she understands.

"Obviously," Stella says. "I mean who wouldn't?"

Bay, used to tuning out Thalia's constant stream of chatter, suddenly realizes Stella is talking and has been for a while. Reluctant to assent to something unknown, Bay assumes an expression of interest, her eyebrows raised, her gaze steady.

"People change, I get that. We aren't, none of us, any one thing, right?"

When Stella frowns, a small heart-shaped furrow appears in her forehead, which Bay studies closely. She wonders if any hearts appear in her own face when she frowns; she wishes one would, it's very pretty. She'll look in the mirror later.

"Then there's time, of course," Stella says. "I mean, I'm not who I was at eighteen. I'm sure you're not who you were as a kid. I get it. I can see how sweet she is, but that doesn't change what she did."

Clearly, Bay has lost track of the conversation. She has no idea who or what Stella is talking about.

Stella cranes her neck to look over her shoulder, as though there might be spies hiding in the apple trees. "I know she doesn't seem like it, but that might be a trick, acting sweet, though maybe she really is now. She used to be dangerous. I mean, I think she outgrew all that, but I wouldn't feel right if I didn't warn you. One thing I know for sure is you are innocent."

"Who are you talking about? Who's dangerous?" Stella better not be talking about Nan. Stella better not be one of those witch haters. Not that Nan is a witch, because she isn't, but some people who think she is are really mean about it.

Stella exhales the name as though it is too bitter to have in her mouth. "Ruthie."

Ruthie? Ruthie, of the heavenly pancakes, mixed-up words, and sweet smile? Ruthie who brought a chocolate cake with her on the plane? Ruthie, who at this moment, is making dinner for everyone? Dangerous?

"You have to take this seriously."

"But, Ruthie is—"

"I'm not saying she's dangerous now. Obviously. I wouldn't be here if I thought so. When she invited me for this weekend—"

"Wait. What? Who invited you?"

Stella bites her lip. "I wasn't supposed to say. She doesn't want Mavis or Nan to know. See, that's what I mean. I like Ruthie. I like her a lot, actually."

"Why would she invite you if she has something to hide?"

"I know, right? I mean, how does that make sense? I feel like there's something really obvious I'm not seeing. They're so secretive. That's why I thought we should talk. I thought you could help. As my grandma says, 'little pitchers with big ears,' and all that."

Bay doesn't know what Stella is talking about. What do pitchers have to do with ears, anyway? She has an idea, however, that she's being insulted. She's pretty sure she's the "little" in that saying, which makes her feel stupid. Stella isn't trying to be her friend, after all.

"Have you noticed how they won't really talk about Eve?"

Bay opens her mouth to object, but closes it without making a sound. It has been Bay's experience that when confronted with accusations, the best defense is often silence.

"I mean, we looked at some old photographs, but it's not like anyone told me anything I couldn't tell from just looking at them myself. 'Here's a picture of Eve in her bathing suit. She liked to swim,' you know? I mean, come on!"

"Well, if you don't know anything about Eve, why are you writing a book about her?" Bay asks.

Stella exhales loudly. "Okay, here's the thing. I wasn't writing about Eve. Not at first. I was just going to write about my grandma, you know? She's getting old, and well, you know. I thought it might be research for a novel, or something. Then, when I lost my job—"

"You lost your job?"

Stella purses her lips and nods. "But that's not the point. It might even be a good thing, all right? I mean, I kept saying I wanted to be a writer, but when was I even writing? Not much, let me tell you. Grading freshman comp is actually soul sucking, just so you know."

"Why'd you lose your job?"

Stella shakes her head. "That's not the point. Where was I? Okay, I thought I'd write this family memoir thing, or maybe a novel, and there were always stories, you know, family stories about my grandpa and his brothers and sister, and their dad, and Eve's mom, who also died young—very *Grapes of Wrath*, if you know what I mean."

Bay shrugs. She's not sure she's following, though she does enjoy the feeling of being confided in.

"So you see," Stella says.

"Not really."

"Okay, there were all these rumors, right? Grandma told me there were rumors about an old witch, of all things. Can you imagine? I mean, really. I couldn't believe Grandma was talking like that. There was an old witch, she said, a rumor about Eve and her friends, how they joined a coven. I know. I can tell by your expression you think this is really nuts, and I do too. But I thought, well, you know, Grandma's getting old, though she's not as old as they are, but I thought, dementia, right? And then she said she had something to tell me. She said Grandpa saw it with his own eyes."

"Saw what?"

"You can keep a secret, can't you?"

Though Bay isn't even sure she likes Stella, she does enjoy the thrill of secrets. She nods.

Stella takes half a deep breath, briefly covering her nose and mouth with her hand as she inhales. "Grandpa saw Ruthie shoot someone."

"Ruthie would never—"

"I know. Believe me, Bay, I know. I've met her, all right? Just 'cause it turns out she's all Mary Poppins now doesn't change what she did."

"But you don't know—"

"Grandma wouldn't lie. And my grandpa didn't lie to her. He saw the whole thing. He told Grandma he never forgot the look in Ruthie's eyes. He said they were killer eyes."

"But who—"

"I'm not ready to say who yet, okay? You don't really need to know that right now, anyway. I don't actually know why she did it. That's what I'm trying to figure out. That's why I'm here. I was using Eve as a cover. 'Cause she died young. I thought they would talk to me about her. But of course I started with the source, right? I called Ruthie, you know, pretending I was trying to find out about Eve, and she was so sweet, Ruthie I mean, and invited me to come this weekend, but she said we had to act like it was just a coincidence. See how sneaky she is? She also said that maybe they were ready to finally talk about 'what happened to Eve.' That's how she said it: 'what happened to Eve.' And just like that I knew I had a bigger story than I thought. I know there's a connection. I just don't know what it is yet."

"She's not your usual bird," Nan will say, for instance, when Mrs. Hevore drops off a donation of unmatched shoes, no pairs in the entire box, which always makes Bay wonder if Mrs. Hevore has a secret shoe garden of her own, though the few times Bay has seen her at the supermarket, her cart filled with red meat and yogurt, or at the summer theater production of *A*

Midsummer Night's Dream, sitting stiffly in a folding chair, wearing her social worker clothes, she has appeared far too tame for secrets. "Oh, she's not your usual bird," Nan says, as though that explains everything. *Clearly,* Bay thinks, *Ruthie is "not your usual bird" either, but that doesn't mean she's a murderer.*

"You're wrong. Ruthie is—"

"I went back there, where they grew up. Do you know about Eve's grave?"

Bay shakes her head.

"Grandma said I would smell it before I'd see it. Because of the roses. Grandma says no one knows how they got there. She said Great-Grandpa Leary tried to dig it out once, but all he got was scratched up, and besides, who goes digging up someone's grave, anyway? It's kind of stunning, really, beautiful in a forbidding way, you know, because of the thorns. The headstone is almost covered, the roses wrapped around it. People were so much more dramatic back then. Anyway, carved into her headstone are these lines: 'Did not the whole earth sicken when she died?' It's from a poem by Ben Jonson. Grandma says the roses were a sign."

"A sign of what?"

Stella shakes her head. "Well, you know. A sign of a witch, or maybe a ghost. Some say it's a sign she's a saint, like a miracle, but no offense, I don't believe that. And you know, of course, I don't believe in, like cartoon witches, but everyone these days knows about Wicca." Stella stops abruptly, eyeing Bay from beneath lowered lids. "I'm just trying to figure out the truth. I mean, if I'm wrong, then fine, I'm wrong. All I'm saying is they're acting secretive. All of them are, even Ruthie, who invited me and now talks nonsense half the time. I really don't know what's going on. I still don't know what she meant about 'what happened to Eve.' I'm not trying to hurt anyone, but I think I have a right to know. Don't forget, this is my family."

When the pampas grass rustles behind her, Bay wonders if a

deer will walk in on them. Once, when she was a child playing here, a deer did wander into the clearing. Her Nana was upset when Bay told her about it afterward. "Deer are dangerous," she said. "Their hooves are like razor blades. Don't ever get so close to one again." Bay never said how close she'd gotten, lying down next to it, falling asleep until a sharp sound like a bough breaking or a gunshot woke her, and she found herself alone, though the ground beside her was still warm.

This time, however, it is not a deer, but Howard, apologizing when he sees them.

"Oh, I get it," Stella says as she stands and brushes blades of grass off her legs. "Secret assignations? I guess I'm in the way here."

Bay feels herself blush as Howard protests more vehemently than seems necessary.

"I was just leaving anyway," Stella says. "Don't worry. I won't blow your cover. I can keep your secret too."

Howard and Bay both start to speak, but Stella waves her hand, dismissing them as if they are the last people on earth to explain themselves. She gives Bay a long look and says, "I hope we have an understanding," before exiting through the tall grass.

"Well, that was awkward," Howard says.

Right, Bay thinks. *Because why would you have anything to do with me?*

"This is a nice spot. I was here earlier, but that smell got to me. Doesn't it bother you?"

"I don't notice anything." At this point Bay is lying, for no reason she can think of, other than she doesn't feel like agreeing with Howard.

He studies her, his eyes narrowed, forehead furrowed. "What's wrong? Why are you angry?"

"I'm not angry," Bay says, though she is beginning to suspect she is. "Why is everyone saying that? Mavis—"

"Yeah," Howard says. "I know how angry I was that she told everyone I'm gay—"

"Wait. What?"

"Not that I'm ashamed. I mean, that's why I'm here. Well, not here, but home this week."

"You're gay?"

"You knew, right? Mavis told everyone."

Bay shakes her head.

"Are you… I mean…" Howard shifts from one foot to the other, and Bay realizes he is mistaking her silence for judgment.

"Oh, no. I don't care," she says. "I don't care about stuff like that at all. It doesn't matter."

This isn't completely true, because it does matter, but not like that. Of course it matters. Howard's sexuality is an important part of his life. Bay doesn't mean to suggest it is trivial. That's not what she meant. It's just, she liked Howard. She likes him. She thought…well, what was she thinking? Even if he weren't gay, he's in college and way too old for her. Still, Bay feels sad to lose the fantasy she's been imagining. It's not horrible, it's just not the story she thought she was in, that's all.

"I have to get out of here," Howard says. "The smell is really bad."

"It's not that bad," Bay says, though truth be told, it is. They walk through the bank of grass into the yard, the odor dissipated by the mysterious scent of dead lilacs. Stella is nowhere in sight, but Mavis still paces the yard, taking what appear to be measured steps in starts and stops, punctuated by exhalations of smoke, her dress aglow against the blue sky. She signals Bay to join her, but Bay pretends not to understand and waves without enthusiasm until Thalia rounds the corner of the house, stopping briefly to speak to Mavis.

As Thalia walks toward her, Bay is filled with an odd feeling: both happy and sad, as if they have been separated for decades. And while it is true they haven't spent as much time together in the past month as they usually do, it's not as bad as years; it's only been a few weeks.

"Is she one of your Nana's friends?" Thalia asks.

"What did she say?"

"She said something like, 'Oh, that's right, you can represent normal.' What's that supposed to mean?"

"Just ignore her."

"But what does she mean?"

"Just ignore her. No one knows what she's talking about half the time."

Bay watches Mavis stop short, halfway up the back stairs, descend, and walk to the front of the house, her lips moving as she gestures with her cigarette, smoke trailing behind her like ghosts.

"Are we having meat tonight? 'Cause you know, I just turned vegetarian."

"Thalia, I have to tell you something."

"It's okay. I'll move stuff around on my plate and bury it in the potatoes—"

"No, I don't know what we're having. Ruthie's making dinner. It's a surprise."

"Thanks for inviting me. I'm so excited. What kind of ceremony is it? Hey, who's that? He's cute."

"Thalia, wait."

When Howard, who is standing beneath the lilac trees turns at their approach, Thalia giggles. Bay understands; seeing him is like finding the guy from *Twilight* in her yard.

"This is my friend Thalia. Thalia, this is Howard."

"Hi," Thalia says too loudly with a giggle.

"Come on," Bay says, "we should see if Ruthie needs help setting the table or something."

Thalia beams at Howard. "See you at dinner?"

"Oh, I didn't know you were having a party. Maybe I should leave."

"Don't be stupid." Bay cringes at how mean she sounds. "Of course you're invited."

"I'd like to. I'd like to stay."

"Good," Thalia says. "We would like it too!"

Bay grabs Thalia's elbow, steering her away from making a fool of herself and up the hill toward the house.

The light has taken on that polished look, the way it gets on summer evenings, that small space of time that always makes Bay a little sad. Stepping around several runaway shoes, she inhales the delicious air, scented with savory herb, onion, and chocolate. These are the smells Bay can identify. She doesn't know what else composes the delicious aroma, though it's a pleasant problem to work out. *Onions, chocolate, lavender, and curry,* she thinks, *but what else? Roses?*

The back door screeches open, and Ruthie steps out, changed from her peony apron into a brightly colored striped skirt, its fullness achieved with layers of petticoats and a white sleeveless blouse that reveals the loose flesh of her freckled arms.

"Oh! I was just coming to get you young people. It's almost time. Where's Howard?"

"He's back there, he's—"

"I'll get him," Thalia says.

"No. You need to get dressed. This is the Flower Feast, you know."

There's no way Ruthie ever killed anyone. Bay can't believe Stella would say such a thing. Then again, look what people say about Nan. Look at what the kids at school say.

"I didn't bring anything special to wear," Thalia says. "I didn't know I was supposed to."

"Not to worry, dear. I put some things on your bed, Bay. Nothing either of you girls would be interested in normally, I am sure, but there should be something fun for tonight."

"You didn't have to do that."

"Of course I didn't. Go on now. I'll get Howard."

"Did Nana wake up yet?"

Ruthie's smile collapses, and the screen door she's been

holding open with her foot falls shut with a screech. "Actually, I'll see about Nan. You girls tell Howard there's a suit laid out for him in the parlor. Don't dwiddle. You don't want to be late."

Her Nana never sleeps all day. What can it possibly mean? What if...but Bay won't let her mind go there. Thalia chats happily about the mysterious Flower Feast and the opportunity to dress up, which segues into a rumination on whether she'll be seated next to Howard, and why didn't Bay tell her about him, where did he come from, anyway, and is that why she's been acting strange lately?

"It's not like that," Bay says. "What do you mean I've been acting strange?" *Don't be dead,* she thinks, sending the thought all the way to Nan. "Don't be dead."

"Who's dead?"

"No one's dead," Bay says, perhaps too vehemently. She doesn't want to talk about the fear she has of her Nana dying, as though naming it will make it so. Nan is not dead. She's taking a very long nap—an all-day nap. A nap longer than any nap she's ever taken.

"Are you sure?" Thalia squeezes Bay's arm so hard it hurts. "Do you think Howard's a ghost? Did you feel cold around him? I did. I just realized. I think I did. Don't you think it's possible? I mean, if your Nana is a witch? It would make sense, wouldn't it? That there would be ghosts around here? Is that why they're having a ceremony? To send him to the light?"

"Howard's not dead, and my Nana's not a witch, and I'm not the one who's been acting strange."

"Are you okay? You seem—"

"I'm fine."

"I'm just saying it makes a lot of sense, you know? Maybe she has a special ability. My mother says when my grandmother died she used to visit all the time to rearrange the spices. She says some people have the sight, and—"

"Thalia, stop."

"I'm sorry, Bay. Don't cry. Why are you crying?"

"Hey, what's wrong?" Howard has joined them, so quiet they didn't hear his approach.

"Ruthie says she has a suit laid out for you in the parlor," Bay says through her tears. "I am such a freak."

"You're not," Howard says, and Bay realizes she's done it again, spoken out loud what she meant not to. "I mean, maybe you're a little different, but all the best people are." Howard wraps one arm around her shoulder, and Thalia, standing on the other side of Bay, does too.

"Yoo-hoodle! Bay! Yoo-hoodle!"

Ruthie stands at the back door, waving her hand high. She wouldn't deliver terrible news with a yoo-hoodle greeting, would she?

"You don't want to be late for the Flower Feast! You need to get dressed. Bring your friend. Howard, you come too."

Maybe it's a trick. Maybe Ruthie wants to get me close before she delivers bad news, Bay thinks as Ruthie pivots back into the house.

"She's probably emotional because of her hormones," Thalia whispers to Howard.

Thalia, who has several older aunts in various stages of menopause, has recently begun attributing everything to hormonal flux. Bay would laugh were she not so distracted by the beating of her heart. They are at the foot of the stairs when Ruthie pops out of the door like one of those Glockenspiel dancers at German Fest.

"You almost came into the kitchen. I've told you and told you not to come into the kitchen, and you almost did." Thalia says something about hormones. "Don't be ridiculous," Ruthie scolds. "I got over all that decades ago." She frowns down at Bay. "You promised. You promised several times. Now I understand why Nan is worried about you."

"Nana's worried about me? That's what I wanted to ask, about Nana."

"What about her?"

"Did you remember to wake her?"

"Of course I remembered! What do you take me for? You sound like my husband."

Bay isn't sure how to proceed. She apologizes profusely to Ruthie, whose drawn lips loosen with each sorry, until at last she is smiling, telling them to hurry and get ready. "Nan is taking her bath, but you three are so young and fresh, you'll be fine as rain with soap and a bowl of water, which I left in your room, Bay. Howard, you can use the sink in the downstairs powder room."

They walk to the front of the house in silence, Thalia taking sideways looks at Howard, which Bay notices with sinking recognition. It would be embarrassing, because really, she knows she looked at him the same way, except that now, Bay realizes, Howard probably has no idea about any of it. He probably gets looked at like this all the time. He probably thinks the whole world is composed of beaming females.

When they step into the foyer, all three of them are struck still with the pleasure of entering a home filled with the pleasant air of a holiday feast.

"What is that?" Howard says.

"I hope it's not meat."

Bay can hear water running through the pipes, the reassuring sound of her Nana taking a bath. The scent that fills the house is divine. Bay hopes for a peek at the setting for the feast, but the dining room doors are closed. She and Nan rarely use them, ever since the time the old pocket doors got stuck one Christmas. (Which actually was one of the best Christmases ever, and the start of Bay's favorite tradition!)

As Bay and Thalia ascend the stairs, the scent of vanilla bubble bath mingles with the delicious kitchen aromas. When they arrive at the landing, Stella comes down the hall, wearing a dress the color of blue morning glory, with a full skirt, much like Ruthie's, though Stella's dress is strapless. She spins for them, modeling how nicely it fits and how pretty the color is on her.

"I was wearing heels, but Ruthie made me take them off," Stella says, displaying her bare feet, the toenails painted red. "Apparently no one wears shoes to a Flower Feast. Who knew?"

How can she act so sweet? How can she say such things and then act like she's accused Ruthie of nothing more than stealing cupcakes?

"Bay, are you all right?"

"I'm fine. I'm good."

"'Cause you look a little odd."

"I'm fine."

"You look like you're almost crying."

"It's her hormones," Thalia says.

"Bay, did Howard bother you in some way…or did Ruthie—"

"No, Howard's not like that. And Ruthie isn't either."

"She's overwhelmed," Thalia says.

"I'm fine. We have to go get dressed."

"You'll let me know, right, Bay? If there's any problems I can help you with? And you, too," she says to Thalia, though it's clearly an afterthought.

The girls promise as they back down the hall, Stella frowning her heart-making frown, until they enter Bay's bedroom, closing the door behind them.

"Would you stop telling everyone my hormones are bothering me?"

"Look at these. Oh, Bay, look at these."

A dozen dresses are laid on Bay's bed, each at least as pretty as Stella's, the colors of summer blossoms: sundrop yellow, snapdragon white, hydrangea blue, a hollyhock pink. Bay runs her finger lightly over them, as if they are too fragile for touch.

"Where did she find these? I can't believe they were all stuffed in her suitcase along with a chocolate cake," Bay says. *Is that something a murderer would do?*

Thalia squeals as she sorts through the dresses, apparently equally delighted with each, until she holds up a white one trimmed with glass beads and silver thread. "This is the best, don't you think?"

Bay thinks it might be, but she tells Thalia she should wear it. "Are you sure?"

Bay nods, though she wishes she'd seen it first, until she finds a pale green dress embroidered with tiny butterflies and pearl buttons up the back that she thinks might, in fact, be the prettiest dress she's ever seen.

ROSEMARY *Symbolic of remembrance, fidelity, and friendship, rosemary is frequently used as a funeral wreath, wedding herb, and as a guard against pregnancy. Rosemary is a remedy for diseases of the brain. Bathing in rosemary makes the old young again.*

⁓

N an can't believe she slept all day. She'd be worried if she didn't feel so good. She feels wonderful. Why, when Ruthie told her it was time to get ready for dinner, Nan didn't believe it. Dinner? How was that possible? She had the strangest dream, though right now she can only remember the odd feeling and no details, which is fine, actually, because the odd feeling makes her feel, well, odd, and there's no reason to linger with that sensation when she can enjoy feeling good instead. This bubble bath, for instance, feels very good indeed. She hasn't taken a bubble bath in years. Why is that? There seems no reason for denying herself such a simple pleasure for so long, though she's sure she did have a good reason once.

The bubbles feel like kisses, though of course that's just silly. The bubbles are soft and warm against her skin; they pop, nothing like lips at all, though a definite pleasant sensation. Nan closes her eyes and leans back against the tub, remembering how she was once possessed of a body that was kissed; she once knew what lips felt like and made no uncertain comparison of lips to bubbles. Nonetheless, it is very pleasant indeed to be caressed by bubbles, so pleasant in fact that she responds to the knock on the door with something close to a growl.

"Nan, are you in there?"

"I'll be right out, Mavis." Nan tries to sound cheerful. After all, she has a houseful of guests; she slept right through the day and did nothing to help with dinner. The least she can do is be accommodating and not hog the bathroom.

Mavis, however, cannot wait. She sidles in, closing the door behind her, waving her hand as Nan tries to cover herself. "Don't make a big production. There's nothing there I don't already know about. We need to talk." She sits on the toilet, crossing her legs beneath the caftan she wears, leaning forward to fix Nan with an inquisitive look.

"Are you enjoying your visit?"

"Don't be coy, Nan. We haven't time for it. We have to decide what we're going to do."

"Do?"

"You haven't forgotten, have you?"

Nan shakes her head, which she immediately regrets, because the lovely vanilla aroma is ruined by the scent of salt. She sighs. "Don't look at me like that, Mavis, my memory isn't what it used to be. Just catch me up so we can get on with it."

Mavis does, first reminding Nan about Karl (the "interloper" Mavis calls him) tearing apart the garden, which, Nan thinks, is as understandable as it is devastating. Young ghosts are said to be quite dramatic and erratic in their behavior. Who can blame him? A dead adult is sure to be greeted on the other side by a welcoming crowd of loved ones, whereas a young ghost might not recognize anybody. Young ghosts can be so confused that they experience the act of being sent to the light as violent. Even if they understand they are dead, they recognize all they lost in the process, and are determined not to lose again. Rather than welcoming the light, they consider entering it to be another death of sorts, an unknown destination that entails leaving the existence they do not necessarily like or understand, but at least have come to know. Young ghosts can be very difficult, stubborn and clingy in general, though Nan knows that Karl has a particular bone to pick with her. In spite of the heat of the bathroom, she shudders.

"Are you cold?" Mavis asks.

"You let in a draft."

Mavis frowns at Nan, who takes the opportunity to comment on the matter of Eve and Grace Winter hanging about. Mavis looks like she doesn't know what Nan's talking about. Well, there's no time to linger over how Mavis has lost her mental acuity. They've all lost something, after all.

Mavis waves her hand, her Bakelite bracelets clanking against each other; she has a way of sounding like she's always breaking something. She says Karl isn't a ghost, but a hoodlum. Stella, she says, is the dangerous one, in spite of her innocent appearance. "Be reasonable," Mavis says (she dares to say this while perched on the toilet after having invaded Nan's bath). "Think of how damaging she could be to us."

Nan is annoyed by Mavis's continued demonizing of Stella. *What does the girl know? What does she suspect? On the other hand, what does it matter? Do they really have to die with this secret?* What Nan wants from this whole mess is that she be the one to reveal her criminal past to Bay before someone else does.

"What?" Mavis squawks, interrupting Nan's reverie. "Don't just stare, say something!"

"As I've already said, we have to act normal. We have to pretend we've got nothing to hide. But also, we must have this ceremony," Nan says, not admitting she has no idea how to proceed in this direction. Though Mavis tries to talk her out of it, Nan won't make that mistake again. After all, she won't be bullied by Mavis as she has been in the past, which she finally says, not thinking before she does. Mavis leaves the bathroom in a huff.

It's all rather complicated, Nan thinks later, dressing alone in her bedroom. She might be discouraged were it not for the enticing aromas and the pleasant sound of voices in the rooms below, the chatter of a house on holiday.

Ruthie is apparently under the impression that they all know what a Flower Feast is, though none of them do. They are to dress for dinner, but not wear shoes, which Nan finds distressing. She has gotten over vanity for the most part, but her feet are particularly unpleasant, odd little misshapen things with bunions and crooked nails that she would rather not reveal. What has made Ruthie so bossy? Nan shakes her head as she looks through her closet, lingering over the old velvet dress several times before deciding no harm can come of trying it on. Velvet in summer doesn't usually work, but it is her favorite frock.

Nan is relieved to discover that the dress holds a lovely scent of lavender, not the dusty odor she thought it might. Oh, how she loves velvet! She steels herself against getting her hopes up. *It probably won't fit*, she thinks as she drapes it over her head. For a moment in the dark, she thrills at the feel, the scent, the swish sound of the lining. Nan thinks she can almost forgive Ruthie the silly rule about bare feet, if that is the exchange she must make for wearing this dress again. It's the dress she plans to be buried in, so isn't it a pleasant surprise to be wearing it tonight? *Why*, Nan thinks, *my white hair looks quite nice with the midnight blue, and my cheeks, not pink of course, but there is something there, something vaguely lifelike.*

Nan turns in a slow circle, enjoying the feel of the skirt brushing her legs, her bare feet strange on the hardwood floor but also nice, which Nan would clarify had not that single turn left her a little dizzy. She sits on the edge of the bed, waiting for the spinning to stop.

Ruthie is another issue they have to work around. Earlier, Mavis pointed out all that Ruthie's done, from helping in the garden to making breakfast, as well as preparing tonight's entire feast. From the sound of it, poor Ruthie hasn't taken a break since her arrival; she must be exhausted. Even so, Nan has to consider the possibility of a fatigued Ruthie lingering around for the ceremony which she would not approve of. This is an uncomfortable issue for Nan, who has worked hard to maintain her lifestyle without endangering herself, her home, or Bay (though Nan suspects Bay has been persecuted on her behalf), but what can be done about it? When Mavis mentioned locking Ruthie in the basement, Nan wasn't sure it was a serious suggestion, but pointed out that such a drastic measure would probably cause more trouble than it would be worth. Besides, Ruthie is a guest.

The room returned to focus; Nan stands to brush what there is of her hair. She has kept it long all these years, even when it began falling out during menopause. It's quite thin now, a matter she usually covers by bullying it into an untidy bun, which she likes to think creates the illusion of volume. She turns her head, trying to determine if the pink of scalp shows through. It does a little, but when will she ever do this again? When will she ever wear this dress, if not in her casket? When will she ever wear her hair down, if not in her grave?

Nan shakes her head as she sets the brush firmly on her dresser. Just like that, she remembers. The night garden dotted with points of light. Candles brightening at her approach until she was surrounded by an aura, like a moon glow brightening a dark corner of the yard, a neglected plot, hidden behind the trees, where a blue poppy bloomed, and then she disappeared? No, that's not right; it was more like a melting, but without a burn. She just faded into everything. It sounds frightening, but it wasn't. It was a lovely dream.

Nan faces herself in the mirror. Her hazel eyes blink back at her. "What are you still doing here?" she says softly to her reflection, and watches herself not answer before she turns away to join the party.

VERBENA *Very effective for ailments of the womb, verbena also arrests the diffusion of poison, mollifies enemies, and helps reconcile differences. If a dining room is sprinkled with verbena-steeped water, the guests will be merry.*

F eeling too excited to sit still in their party dresses, Bay and Thalia flit about like butterflies. Banned from the kitchen and barred from the dining room, they whisper, giggle, talk too loud, and are struck silent when Howard appears in a tux, which he models for them with a flourish. Coming upon them like this, Stella runs to the kitchen and hollers, "Howard is wearing shoes!" which causes Ruthie to push through the swinging kitchen door to order him to take off his sneakers. "It's the Flower Feast after all," she says, as though Howard has lost all reason. She hurries past them to the dining room, opening the pocket door just a crack, a space impossibly small, which she nonetheless slips through.

This starts the four of them laughing, though Bay cannot set her mind on what is so funny. She wonders if, after all these years, she finally understands her Nana's experience of unreasonable laughter, a sobering thought as Bay does not like to think of inheriting such odd behavior. Thalia laughs so hard she collapses on the stairs, the white dress merengueing around her. Stella, her hand on the staircase newel, creates a perfect arch up her arm and over her shoulder, to the curve of neck, where laughter flutters in her throat as though she just swallowed a hummingbird. Howard tries to stand on one foot to take off his shoe, but failing this (he totters but does not fall) sits on the floor to untie the laces and remove the socks, revealing hairy toes and crooked nails accompanied by an unfortunate odor, which no one comments on, but does have a subduing effect on the assembled.

When Mavis appears at the top of the stairs, first Howard, then Stella gape, which causes Bay to turn; she doesn't know what she was expecting, though certainly not this. Thalia whispers, "Oh my gawd," but no one else speaks as Mavis comes down the stairs, her gaze impervious. She slows considerably near the bottom, giving Thalia (with a prompt from Bay) time to unfroth herself and step aside.

Mavis is wearing a one-shoulder gown in leopard print, paired with an orange feather boa twisted about her neck, draped like its namesake across her chest and down her back. Her bare feet make intermittent appearances, revealing toe rings and crimson toenails (the color at the edge of a scab) which is also the unfortunate color of her lips. At the bottom of the stairs she turns to Howard and says, "I'm sure your shoes and socks will not be lonely without you," which causes Thalia to giggle. Howard backs out of the room to discard the offending items.

With a rattle, the dining room door slides open just enough to reveal lace and candlelight. Ruthie sidles out like one who's had much experience with narrow passage, though she immediately spins on her heels, apparently having forgotten something. Bay tilts her head to spy on Ruthie dipping her fingers into a bowl and flicking the air a few times before once more squeezing through the slim opening, pulling the door firmly shut behind her. The whole thing makes Bay uncomfortable, but then Howard returns, creating his own splendid entrance, though he is not in any way changed, but one of those fortunate people whose very beauty, even bruised, will cause a stillness from which they are broken by the sound of an upstairs door closing. Bay is surprised by the quickening of her heart. Of course her Nana is not dead, what a thing to have thought, but why is Bay's heart beating like this? She doesn't know if she's excited or afraid.

Nan walks down the hall with her familiar lope, the blue velvet dress revealing her vein-lined calves and small bare feet. *She looks good,* Bay thinks. Nan looks pretty with her hair down, like an angel, and why, oh why does Bay feel like crying?

Nan descends the stairs in her own quiet way, greeted at the landing with compliments exchanged all around. They tell each other how pretty they look, how beautiful, how handsome. There is twirling of skirts, adjusting of tie, fingering of boa, and brushing of velvet, accompanied by much smiling, interrupted finally by Ruthie, whose return went unnoticed, clearing her throat until they pay attention, at which point she invites them into the dining room.

When Nan sees the closed pocket doors she shoots Bay a look. Bay tries to signal everything will be all right; Ruthie has gone in and out of the room several times without incident. The doors slide open with only the vaguest complaint, revealing the dining room in splendor of lace, candlelight, and flowers. *Who knew,* Nan thinks, *that I had so many candles?* They shimmer soft golden light just like that poem, what is it again, the one by Yeats?

"Go ahead," Ruthie says. "Sit."

Howard hurries to pull out chairs for Nan and Mavis. Stella, Thalia, and Bay seat themselves. Bay remembers the lace table-cloth but never noticed the gold thread before. Nan is thinking the same thing as her fingers gently brush the material. Stella holds a white lily, looking at it as though it were strange. There is a lily at Bay's place setting as well. Mavis sticks hers in her hair, though Bay can't figure out how she makes it stay. Thalia has placed hers in her water glass, where it floats with the lemon. Howard tucks his into his pocket as a boutonniere.

Ruthie taps the side of her glass with her knife, ringing it as though silencing a noisy room. They wait for her to stop, which eventually she does. Bay notices that Ruthie is the only one without a flower, and hopes this is not a bad omen. She sits at the head of the table, the windows open behind her, the sheers hanging in the still air, her hands folded, which is all the prompt the rest of them need. Stella follows Ruthie's example, while the rest do vague imitations, hands in lap, or hand resting on hand, a gesture of respect if not solidarity. Ruthie does not bow her head and close her eyes, though Howard does.

"On this, the occasion of our first annual Flower Feast, we thank the darkness of the earth, the light of the sun, the nourishment of the rain, and the cold months that will soon be here. In this way we honor the living and the dead among us. No flower blooms forever. We are the living and the dead. Tonight we celebrate that cycle."

Ruthie fixes each of them with her small blue eyes, a matter lost on the still-bowed Howard. "Who mourns the cut flower?"

They hesitate, not clear about what is expected, until Ruthie stands so suddenly her chair scrapes across the wood floor. "I can't believe I forgot music."

Nan bites her lower lip, not sure if the evening is off to a wonderful start, or if it is too strange for success. She offers to help Ruthie, who only waves her hand, saying she has it all under control, leaving the dining room to a silence they mostly maintain. Thalia drinks from her water glass, working around the flower. Nan adjusts her silverware, though it is placed correctly. Stella starts to say something but is cut off by soft piano music, the source of which Nan cannot place. She's meant for years to put in a sound system but has never gotten around to it. She peers at walls and ceiling, looking for the speakers, but finds none. *What a strange thing to forget,* she thinks, *and really, what is Ruthie talking about: "We are the living and the dead?"*

Ruthie returns, carrying a large tray she sets on the sideboard. The room is immediately filled with summer, the warmth of sun, the sweet scent of grass, blossomed flowers, *the scent of laziness,* Nan thinks, though of course that doesn't really make sense. She remembers the feeling of being in a young body without bones compressed in tortured shrinking. *The scent of honeysuckle!*

Ruthie spoons tiny white blossoms from a crystal bowl onto the small pink plates Nan uses for Christmas pudding. A few blossoms flutter to the floor, making a flower snow, forging a strange confluence for Nan, who remembers, in a single breath, the honeysuckle that grew wild near Eve's back door, and the snow drifting beneath the streetlights that terrible morning.

Mavis eyes the blossomed plates with raised eyebrows and a smirk, though thankfully, she doesn't say a word. Stella looks at her plate for a long time, presenting the top of her dark-haired head with its jagged white part, until she sits back with a composed expression. Thalia watches Bay, whose confusion incites a giggle. Howard, served last, holds a blossom between thumb and forefinger, turning it this way and that.

"These are honeysuckle," Ruthie says. "Howard's correct. They are meant to be eaten with your fingers."

"Are you certain they're edible?" Stella asks.

"Of course they're edible. Do you think I would feed you dangerous flowers?"

When no one disputes the notion, and in fact Bay is first struck by the possibility of it, Nan says, "Some flowers are poisonous, you know. The prettiest things can be quite lethal."

Bay glances nervously from her Nana to Stella to Ruthie.

"Howard," Ruthie says, "show everyone how foolish they're being."

Bay has not, until this moment, believed it at all possible that Ruthie, of all people, is a murderer, but here she is, urging Howard to eat the suspect flower. Before Bay can stop him, he places the blossom in his mouth, chews, and swallows.

Stella, apparently understanding Bay's anguished gaze, almost imperceptibly shakes her head. "Actually," she says, "I do remember reading about honeysuckle. They're perfectly safe if grown without pesticides."

"As these are," Ruthie says.

Howard picks up another and tosses it into his mouth.

"They aren't meant to be shoved in your mouth like popcorn, but savored," Nan says. She uses her thumbnail to cut into the blossom and pull the stamen down to lick the flower's narrow throat, terribly disappointed that the first two are duds she tosses onto the table. Finally, the third blossom releases the sweet, honeyed flavor of her youth, too quickly gone.

"Doesn't this remind you of anything?" Ruthie asks.

Mavis, working a stamen from between her teeth, glowers at Stella, who makes soft moaning sounds of pleasure.

Bay searches her mind for a memory that tastes like honeysuckle, then realizes Ruthie is probably not addressing her. Thalia frowns as she chews, apparently still not having come to that conclusion and, good student that she is, trying very hard to find the answer.

"Eve," Mavis says, pushing away the small plate still littered with blossoms.

"They grew around her house. They're also known as woodbine, said to keep out evil," Nan says, picking up a blossom and tearing it apart.

"Remember?" Ruthie says. "How it smelled like honeysuckle after she died?"

Nan has no memory of that at all.

"'There in due time the woodbine blows,'" says Stella, plucking petals in a dreamy fashion. "'The violet comes, but we are gone.' Tennyson."

Ruthie excuses herself to clear the plates, "Sit, sit," she says, though no one has offered to help. "I can do this myself."

"I guess I don't have to worry about meat, huh?" Thalia whispers to Bay.

"You told me Eve liked to swim," Stella says. "I don't know anything about honeysuckle."

"It grew by her back door." Nan shivers at the unwelcome memory, but no one seems to notice. "Her mother, before she died, used to have honeysuckle all through the house."

"Oh? Grandma never said anything about that."

"Why would she?" Nan asks. "How would she know such a thing?"

"That's right, you don't know. My grandma's maiden name was Stenkle. Theresa Stenkle."

"Tiny Stenkle?"

"Uh-huh." Stella picks up a blossom, tosses it into the air, and swats at it as it flutters down, though she misses. "She told me they used to call her Tiny when she was young."

Nan and Mavis exchange a look. Why hadn't they thought of this? Eve's brother, Daniel, married a local girl.

Ruthie returns, carrying a large tray, the glass bowl filled with spiny green globules. "Our next course is artichokes," she says, "because of the heart."

"Well, something around here has to have a heart," Stella says.

"What's that supposed to mean?"

"It was a joke, Mavis." Stella abandons her game of swatting at honeysuckle to assess the artichoke before her.

"Just discard the leaves onto your plate," Ruthie says as she passes out ramekins of melted butter.

Nan frowns at her beautiful lace tablecloth with its never-before-appreciated gold thread, disturbed to think of it stained by oily drips.

"How do we eat these?" Bay asks.

Ruthie instructs the young people, while Stella, Mavis, and Nan begin pulling off tender leaves, dunking them in butter, drawing them between their teeth.

"Ruthie, I haven't had an artichoke this good since I was in California," Stella exclaims, winking at Bay, who pretends not to notice. "Visiting my grandmother. I couldn't have been ten years old, and I thought she was trying to poison me."

"Oh, well." Ruthie pulls a tender leaf from her artichoke. "A little poison drama is just one of those things in a family."

"It is?" Thalia asks, her eyes wide.

"I saw too many movies," Stella says. "My grandmother never would have done something like that."

"Well, it's always the least likely, isn't it?" Ruthie smiles softly.

Stella's hand hovers over the artichoke, then flutters back to her lap.

"My husband wasn't the type either. Do you think that on my wedding day I thought I was marrying a man who would one day poison me?" Ruthie asks.

Everyone is taken aback. Also, the party as a whole has apparently lost its appetite for artichokes; they sit, half-eaten, on plates littered with teeth-scraped leaves. Nan shakes her head; she is not thinking clearly. "Did you say your husband actually poisoned you?" she asks, trying to keep her tone neutral.

"Well, obviously he didn't fully succeed," Ruthie says, which makes everyone laugh. Mavis's laugh turns into a cough, finally soothed with water.

The artichoke eating resumes, all the way to the strange hearts that Thalia, Bay, and Howard greet with trepidation but devour with relish once the whole process is explained to them.

"That was filling," Thalia says.

"I hope not." Ruthie clears the plates onto the tray, carrying it into the kitchen and back again, refusing any help, returning on her fourth trip with the soup tureen. She announces the course: fennel consommé with lovage.

"Ruthie?" Stella licks her lips. "What exactly happened between you and your husband?"

"Is this a meat stock?" Thalia asks.

Ruthie shakes her head at Thalia at the same time as she says, "Let's not talk about him."

"It's my understanding that it's important to talk about difficult times," Nan says. "It helps with the healing."

"Really?" Ruthie looks up from her soup. "Then we should tell Stella everything?"

Nan doesn't understand. How did this happen? How have they traveled so quickly to this precipice?

Across the table, Mavis's eyes are two dark slits, venomous as a snake's.

"I don't think this is the time," Nan stammers.

"Oh, why not?" Mavis scolds. "Have at me, why don't you? You've blamed me—"

"I have not blamed—"

"Of course you have." Mavis raises her arms in a gesture of supplication, her bracelets clanking. She looks up at the ceiling. "I have lived my whole life with your judgment."

"You've lived with my judgment?" Nan, aware of the wide eyes watching, tosses her spoon onto her plate, making an impressive clatter. Only Ruthie continues spooning her soup as though this was the most ordinary of dinner conversations.

Nan can't focus on what she has to say. The words are mixed up. She continues saying "you," until Mavis rolls her eyes and says in that bored voice of hers, "One more ewe, and we'll have a herd," which is just what it takes to release the block in Nan's mind.

"It isn't my judgment. It was your lack of judgment. Can you at least admit that?"

"Finish your soup before it gets cold," Ruthie says over the top of her spoon.

"Maybe someone could fill the rest of us in?" Stella asks.

"What are they talking about?" Thalia whispers.

Bay shrugs her shoulder. Nan turns so quickly one of her flower-bouquet earrings falls into Ruthie's bowl. "You need to stop shrugging like that."

"Well," says Ruthie, frowning down at her bejeweled soup, reaching to pluck out the earring. "It's clearly time for the next course."

Nan and Mavis sit glaring across the table at each other, until, incredibly, Mavis collapses, like a Thanksgiving balloon sprung a leak, diminished so incrementally it is difficult to measure as it happens, though the effect is obvious.

"I thought you invited me here because—"

"You know why I invited you."

"Yes. But I thought it meant you had gotten over it. And then we had such a nice time, upstairs in bed."

"Gotten over it?"

Bay turns to assess her Nana closely. Upstairs in bed? Why does it seem like everything Bay thought was real is now only one of many possibilities? She frowns at her water glass as if it, too, were suddenly uncertain, half-expecting her hand to reach right through it, pleasantly reassured by the cool, damp feel against her palm.

"Dates with lavender and goat cheese." Ruthie returns to the table like a waitress, extending the serving plate with one hand. "Take two."

When Ruthie sits, Howard, who is displaying a curious and appreciative appetite that seems to have kept him too preoccupied for conversation, compliments her originality.

"This has always been a favorite of mine, though I haven't had them since the incident with my husband."

Bay looks at the dates on her plate, plump with cheese to the point of splitting, rolled in the tiny, rice-shaped lavender. She knows they are supposed to be pretty, but they look disturbingly insectlike.

"Are you saying this is how your husband poisoned you?" Stella asks.

"Well, who knows? He did make these for me a lot."

"Do you mean this could kill me?" Thalia asks, a half-eaten date in her hand, lavender and cheese stuck to the corner of her lips.

"It's not the stuffed dates that kill you, it's the poison," Ruthie reassures Thalia.

"What?" Nan, Mavis, and Stella speak in unison.

"Thalia was concerned about the dates. I was just explaining that they aren't poisonous. Someone would have to put poison inside them, of course."

"I notice you aren't eating yours," Stella says.

Ruthie sighs, picks up a date, brings it toward her mouth, then drops it as though stung.

Nan gasps. "We have copacetic." She pushes away from the table. "And I do believe there's a spell, and—"

"Oh, don't be ridiculous," Ruthie says, reaching once more for the stuffed date. With only the barest tremor, she pushes it into her mouth.

"But, Ruthie?"

"Yeph, Howar?"

"Why would you serve something that has such painful memories for you?"

Ruthie swallows, laughing as though this question is the funniest thing, but she laughs alone. Finally, wiping the corner of her eyes with her napkin, she says, "It's the Flower Feast"—and seeing that no one understands her point—"the feast of forgiveness."

"It is?" Mavis and Nan ask.

Ruthie bites into another date; the white cheese leaks out of the back and sides, making a bit of a mess, which she licks, revealing the surprisingly nimble point of her pink tongue.

"I think it would be hard to forgive someone who tried to poison me," Thalia says.

"Forgiveness isn't about the other person. It's about freeing yourself," Stella says. "Besides, it's probably easier to forgive someone for something you yourself have done."

"What are you talking about?" Ruthie asks.

"Listen to our little Oprah here," Mavis says. "'Forgive and you will be free.'" She rolls her eyes.

Nan knows that Mavis is mocking Stella, but can't help liking the idea of being set free. Why does the (even mocking) idea of forgiveness make Nan feel lighter, as if, in fact, she has been caged by her skeleton all these years instead of supported by it? "It's not you," Nan says, suddenly realizing the truth. "It's me I can't forgive."

Bay has been listening to this conversation with increasing confusion. What are they talking about? Her mind sorts through the various disconnected bits and lands on the only piece she recognizes. Ruthie's husband tried to poison her. Poor Ruthie. Bay is against revenge, in theory, but she knows what it's like to be tormented. No one should kill anyone under any circumstances, of course, but she can't blame Ruthie for wanting to hurt the husband who tried to kill her. "Did you forgive your husband?" Bay asks.

"Oh, no," Ruthie says, shaking her head. "It's much too soon for that. Whatever gave you that idea?"

"But you said—"

"Isn't this fun? I'll just be a few minutes with the next course."

Bay feels like they've been eating for a long time but have not yet tasted anything that would account for the diverse smells that filled the house. Also, she is still hungry.

"Your Nana's friends are really different," Thalia whispers.

Turning a honeysuckle blossom between thumb and forefinger, Bay nods. Her Nana said something about the copacetic, but then she also said something about a spell, didn't she? Bay thinks she must have heard wrong, but what if she didn't? What if her Nana is a witch after all? Bay pretends to be playing with the honeysuckle, but really she is eyeing her Nana.

Ruthie returns, carrying a tray laden with small bowls. "Elderflower sorbet," she says brightly, "to cleanse your palate. If there is any bitter taste left in your mouth, this should take care of it."

Bay loves the little spoon, small enough for fairies, though she doesn't believe in them any more than she believes in ghosts. The sorbet is quite refreshing, cool, not terribly sweet, but she's too distracted to enjoy it. She wishes everyone would leave so she could be alone with her Nana again and things could get back to normal. What did she mean about a spell?

Nan spoons the sorbet but can't taste it, the flavor lost to all this unfinished business. Her spoon clanks against the little dish as though furiously seeking solace, until she stares into the empty bowl. Elderflower sorbet? When will she ever have a chance to taste it again? Why does Mavis have to ruin everything?

"That was a totally great meal," Thalia says.

"But we haven't had the main course!" Ruthie pushes away from the table, pressing so hard that the candles tremble.

Bay is surprised when her offer of help is accepted. She follows Ruthie into the kitchen where the aromas of chocolate and curry mingle with a yeasty scent and the flowers' perfume that drifts from the vases and glass jars on the kitchen counter and table, crowded next to the computer monitor. Nicholas, curled in the chair, opens his eyes to watch.

Ruthie hums as she works at the stove while Bay unloads the tray, causing blossoms to drift to the floor. Bright yellow daylilies bow from arched green stems in a glass jar, a few blossoms littered among the honeysuckle and red tear-shaped rose petals. Lavender, in a bouquet tied with string, hangs from the cupboard handle. Every time Bay passes, she enjoys the familiar aroma.

The back door is open, giving a full view of the yard in the long light of summer when everything looks polished, all the green grass and shoe flowers shimmering. Even the grass looks incandescent.

Ruthie bends over the oven to remove a chicken, which she sets between simmering saucepans on the stove.

"You know," Bay says, "I think you could teach me some things."

Ruthie hums softly as she carves the chicken, then, suddenly, as though startled, drops the utensils, opens the oven door, and pulls out a large sheet of biscuits, which she sets on a rack to cool. Still humming, she dips the spoon into a saucepan, blows on it, and asks Bay to taste.

"Rose petal sauce; what do you think?"

"It's beyond delicious, it's better than a taste. It's like eating summer, like a spoonful of summer." Bay thinks she sounds stupid, so she clamps her mouth shut.

"Is it bad?"

"Oh, no. It's, it's…I…"

Ruthie dips the spoon into the pan, blows on it, darts the tip of her tongue into the sauce, then wraps the spoon with her entire mouth, slowly pulling the utensil out. "Well, now there's nothing wrong with that, is there?" She drops the spoon into the sink.

Bay lines the breadbasket with cloth napkins for the biscuits, which are steamy with a sweet, vaguely familiar aroma.

"The thing to remember," Ruthie says, returned to carving the chicken, "is that kitchen mistakes have kitchen remedies. Too much salt? This seems like a tragedy, until you know about lemons."

"What about lemons?"

"First," Ruthie says, "lemon, and then, just a little sugar to counter the sour flavor. Works every time."

Bay thinks she should put lemon on some of the kids at school. *If only it were that easy.* She wonders if Ruthie wishes she could squeeze lemon on some people too. After all, she has done a lot of work for this party. "I'm sorry about my Nana and Mavis fighting," Bay blurts out. "Something about Mavis gets on her nerves."

"Oh, they were always like this."

"They were?"

"Well, they didn't have a past then, of course," Ruthie says as she plates the chicken. "The past makes everything complicated. Don't worry about it, dear. They're behaving just as I expected."

"They are?"

"Oh, yes, of course. Forgiveness is often preceded by anger. I'm furious with my husband, for instance. So that's a good sign."

"Just so you know, I don't blame you for what you did."

"What did I do?" Ruthie asks, ladling pink sauce over the chicken.

"Your husband." Bay lowers her voice. "Stella told me you shot someone. I wasn't supposed to say anything."

"Well, you see," Ruthie says, not looking up from her work, "there are opportunities for forgiveness everywhere."

Bay walks to the back door, so close that the view on the other side is hatched by the screen. She doesn't know what draws her there; already the light has changed, the polish replaced by the blue hour. Karl stands closer to the house than he's been before, his hands in his pockets, his shoulders hunched as if against a chill only he feels in the warm night.

"You better get those biscuits in there, honey, while they're still hot."

After Bay and Ruthie clear the sorbet bowls into the kitchen, there is a long, awkward silence that Nan suspects she should fill. This is her house, after all. These are her guests. But she is at a loss as to what to say, her mind stuck on the past. *Why, the past has almost been a life source,* Nan thinks with a start. She doesn't like the sound of that, as if she were somehow nourished by tragedy. No, she doesn't like the thought of that at all. The dead are not meant to be a life source. She frowns at the empty wineglass before her.

Nan walks to the sideboard and peers into it, selecting two bottles of merlot. She has no idea if it is right for the main course, as she doesn't know what that is, but it's her favorite, so she reasons it's right enough. She feels better as soon as the wine is uncorked. As long as she's not expected to actually forgive Mavis or herself, it certainly isn't too soon to begin the process, and she's going to begin by not pursuing the subject further. What point is there in all this bitterness, anyway? Eve has been dead for a long time…a very, very long time.

Nan circles the table, filling the empty wineglasses. Was Ruthie just going to ignore them, or had she forgotten this detail? No matter, Nan fills the glasses near to the brim. This is not a half-full wineglass sort of occasion.

"Biscuits!" Bay enters the dining room, carrying a cloth-draped basket. "Sorry, but we're having chicken," she whispers to Thalia.

"I don't care," Thalia whispers, "this is the best party ever."

Ruthie enters the dining room, carrying an enormous tray she sets on the sideboard. "Our main event, " she says, "is chicken with rose-petal sauce and curried daylilies. Thalia, Bay told me you aren't eating dead animals. You get extra lilies, and the rose-petal sauce is divine, so I put some on the side of your plate. Bay already brought in the calendula biscuits. Now, I think we need a toast." Reaching for her water, Ruthie jerks away from the merlot, as though bitten.

Nan knows she should feel bad, but she can't. It's all she can do not to giggle. She just wants to get on with this toast so she can eat. She'll worry about everything else later. She is determined to taste this food and not let it get past her the way the sorbet did.

"To the cut flowers," Ruthie says, raising her water glass.

"To the cut flowers!" Nan responds, perhaps a little too loudly.

They raise their glasses and tap one another's, then finally, they eat. They can deal with death later. They can fight later. They can forgive later. This is time to savor. Stella murmurs with pleasure. Thalia licks her lips. There is the sound of silverware, knife, and fork against plate, the spoon Bay uses to scoop the sauce; they are nearly finished before anyone speaks.

"Ruthie," Mavis says, "judging by this meal, I expect your future includes opening a restaurant?"

"Oh goodness, no." Ruthie shakes her head and purses her lips, apparently trying very hard not to be pleased.

"You should," Bay says. "You're a totally great cook."

"I'm not."

Everyone compliments Ruthie, who shakes her head, embarrassed, though obviously enjoying the praise. Seeing this, they continue complimenting, and Ruthie continues squirming until the mood at the table is quite elevated. Mavis proposes a toast in honor of the cook, which is heartily cheered. When glasses are returned to the table, the assembled gently push away the empty plates, beaming at one another as though they have all had a great success.

Ruthie announces dessert, to which everyone exclaims, as though the idea had never occurred to them. "I hope you saved room," Ruthie says. "Some people say dessert is what I do best."

"You have the coolest family," Thalia whispers to Bay, who smiles and nods but wonders what she's talking about. After all, these people aren't her family; she's only just met them herself.

"Mavis," Nan hisses. "Pass the wine."

Mavis hesitates, then passes the bottle as Ruthie returns with a dessert-laden tray. Thalia gasps and giggles, Mavis's eyebrows swoop, Stella's mouth drops open, and Howard cheers. Bay wishes she felt happier, but ever since the subject came up, she has been distracted by the question. *Is Nan really a witch?*

"I don't know if I can eat all this," Nan says.

"Why not?"

"It's just so beautiful."

"Well, don't be silly." Ruthie smiles at her own full plate. "We have violet truffles, pound cake with blueberries and lavender syrup, and vanilla ice cream with black-pansy sauce. I couldn't decide on just one."

It is too much, on that they all agree. Yet, in spite of their full stomachs, with only the occasional pause for delicate burps behind napkins and murmured threats of never being able to, they eat, finally leaning back, moaning softly, the plates empty but for puddles of milk, a black-pansy smear, a bit of syrup, the occasional errant blueberry.

The candlelight haloes each satisfied face with gold, and for a long moment the party does nothing more than digest, until Ruthie says, "Well, that's that then. What are you waiting for?"

The young people: Bay, Thalia, Howard, and Stella, push back their chairs and rise, rubbing their stomachs, closing eyes and licking lips, dreamily shuffling out of the room, speaking softly about how delicious the food was, how full they are, stopping for a moment to consider what to do next, agreeing to go outside, leaving Ruthie, Mavis, and Nan eyeing each other.

Almost warily, Nan thinks.

"It was always you two," Ruthie says. "When we lost Eve, I lost my best friend. Or so I thought. I thought she was my best friend, though apparently she could not confide in me."

Mavis starts to speak, but Ruthie continues. "I don't know what you are up to, but I've decided to forgive both of you in advance. All these years you've had your best friend right here, on earth, and this is how you treat each other?"

Nan, who inspects the tablecloth during Ruthie's scold, looks up, expecting Mavis to respond with a sharp comment or, at the very least, a glower, but Mavis has assumed a surprisingly tender expression.

"You don't have to worry about me getting in your way with whatever you've planned for the rest of the evening."

"Ruthie, we—"

"No Nan, stop. Putting together this dinner was a lot of work, which I wanted to do, but now don't I deserve a bubble bath?"

"Of course you do," says Nan. "It was a wonderful dinner."

"I shall remember it the rest of my life," Mavis adds.

"Well, that might have meant something when we were younger," Ruthie says. "Will you girls join me in a circle?"

Nan figures it's the least they can do. She takes Ruthie's extended hand, which is shockingly cold; Mavis takes the other. Then, with only a look to make them understand, Mavis and Nan hold hands.

"This circle ends the Flower Feast," Ruthie says. "Though it does not end the cycle." As Ruthie releases her grasp, she says, "You have no idea what my life was like."

Mavis and Nan exchange a look.

"See? That's what I mean. Even after all these years, you two look to each other first."

Mavis and Nan speak at the same time. They don't mean to make Ruthie feel left out. They never meant to hurt her.

"All I'm saying is you should appreciate your good fortune. I know we parted under poor circumstances, but we were, well, not girls, I suppose, but we were quite young, and part of a terrible thing, for which we have suffered. Don't try to stop me. I'm on a roller here. I have thought about this a lot over the years. I have thought about it most especially recently. We never should have let each other go. We never should have. Nan, I thought you understood that. I thought that's why you invited us. There's hardly any time left at all now. Less for some than for others, and that means less for all of us. We're like the Beatles." Ruthie leans forward, something in the light causing her eyes to appear both closer set and brighter than usual. "Heal this thing between the two of you while you still can." Without further comment, she leaves the room, closing the rumbling pocket doors behind her.

"That," Nan says, "was not the sort of prayer circle I expected. She's right, you know."

"What are you talking about?"

"After all, look what happened to Grace Winter."

There. It's been said. Even though they promised, all those

years ago, not to speak of it; the promises of youth, Nan reasons, are not necessarily the best commitments for the old.

"What happened to Grace Winter was not our fault."

"How can you say that? What happened to her happened because of us."

Mavis sighs, quite loudly, twisting the boa around her throat. A few orange feathers float dangerously close to the flames. "Have you lived your entire life blaming us for every terrible thing that ever happened?"

"Are we really going to do this now?" Nan says. She feels a little thrill at the thought. After all these years, are she and Mavis going to have it out with each other? Finally?

"No," Mavis says, "we're not."

Nan can't believe Mavis is running away, but there she is, striding across the room, pulling on the pocket doors, though they do not open, even when she grunts and leans into them. She turns to Nan as if it is all her fault.

"They get stuck sometimes," Nan says. "We can go out the window."

"All right," Mavis says, her eyebrows low, her mouth mean. "You want to know why I could not bear to remain your friend, is that it? Do you want to make me actually say it?"

Nan is confused. Mavis sounds as though she thinks she is being held captive! "This happens all the time," Nan says. "One Christmas, Bay and I had to go out the window!" It is one of Nan's fondest Christmas memories, composed of nothing more than the silliness of climbing out the window, the shock of snow and ice, the pleasure of coming into the warm house through the unlocked front door, rushing to change into pajamas and socks, which wasn't really necessary, but felt so wonderful nei-ther of them argued against it, recounting their adventure later as though it were a grand event while drinking hot chocolate on the couch, the Christmas dishes left until the next morning, when the doors, rather magically, opened. "We've kept it as a tradition ever since," Nan says. "After Christmas dinner, we climb out the window, and when we come back in through the front door, there are two presents waiting for us in the foyer, new pajamas, which we change into. Then we drink hot cocoa, eat cardamom cookies, and watch *A Christmas Memory*, the old one with Geraldine Page."

Mavis sits down so hard that the candles tremble. "All these years, how I've missed you," she says, staring forlornly at the table still littered with the remnants of dessert, the small plates splotched with melted ice cream, pansy syrup, blueberries.

"You missed me?"

Mavis sighs deeply, still not looking at Nan. "I couldn't stand to be with you after what happened, I couldn't stand your certainty, your smug—"

"I was never—"

"You were," Mavis says. "Don't lie about it now. How could I have been so wrong? How could I have made such a tragic choice?"

"It wasn't your fault," Nan says, the words dragged out of her as though they bear thorns. "You were trying to do the right thing. We all were."

"You don't know how long I needed to hear you say that."

Nan is startled; it never occurred to her that Mavis needed anything she couldn't get on her own. "I never blamed—"

"Don't ruin it," Mavis says, "with one of your lies. Don't you know? I forgave you a long time ago."

"You forgave me?"

"Yes. I know you find that remarkable."

Nan is surprised by the expansion in her chest, right where her heart is. As though a small bird caged there for all these years is finally released. She is surprised by her tears, and surprises herself further by leaning across the corner of the table to hug Mavis, who sits stiffly but lifts a hand to pat Nan's shoulder. Nan is surprised most of all to hear herself say, "I'm sorry. I am. I forgive you too. I forgive all of us. I do." Nan detects no scent of salt, none at all, so maybe it's true.

"What about him?" Mavis asks. "Do you forgive him?"

Nan pulls away. "Well, there are limits," she says.

What is the cost of life? As she's gotten older, Nan has come to the conclusion that there is a price. Maybe it's true what they say about how the good die young, not out of some otherworldly cruel hunger, but because living involves difficult decisions, the occasional willingness to be brutal, make cold assessments, come to unkind conclusions. *Sometimes*, Nan thinks, *it all works out. Sometimes, it does not.*

There was a time when Nan thought she would always weep, until one day she didn't. She covers her eyes with her hands, as though it suddenly is unbearable to look. How can so much loss be survived?

Hearing the scrape of chair across the floor, Nan prepares to be hugged. It's what anyone would do in such a situation. She is taken somewhat out of her grief by the notion of Mavis rising to administer a hug, though it takes such a long while Nan peeks between her fingers. Mavis, clutching the feathered boa close to her chest, blows out the candles in the candelabra on the table.

"Come," she barks, "help me with the window."

They work together to push out the screen, which falls with a clatter onto the front porch. Isn't it just like Mavis to offer no solace beyond distraction? Nan steps carefully through the open window, grateful it's the sort that reaches almost to the floor, because even this small maneuver is precarious. She turns to watch Mavis exit, hiking her narrow dress high, revealing, of all things, support stockings, the kind worn for varicose veins.

When did time grow so small? The present is all they have left. Who are they kidding? Ruthie is too old to open a restaurant. Mavis is too old for Africa. They are all old now, far too old for the future; perhaps that's why they are finally able to deal with the past.

They stand on the porch, staring at the night sky seeded with stars. "Do you still plan on this ceremony?" Mavis asks.

Nan frowns as though the question is absurd, though actually she rather hoped the ceremony would be forgotten. Like many inspired ideas, it suffers under scrutiny. *What does she know about getting rid of ghosts?* All she knows is what people say: "send them to the light," and whatnot. She has grave doubts it could really be so simple. Besides, what if she got it wrong? What if instead of banishing them, she brought more into her life?

Thinking about it now threatens Nan's good mood, so she decides to think about it later. Instead, she suggests they sit for a while, and Mavis agrees without complaint.

Nan loves rocking. They had rockers on her front porch when she was growing up. She used to sit there in summer, with a big pile of books and lemonade, the good kind, not powder from a package.

"Oh, remember homemade lemonade?" Nan asks, but Mavis doesn't answer. She sits with her head back, her eyes closed, her mouth open, her purple hair oddly crooked. Nan frowns, only just realizing—a wig! Why would anyone wear a wig that color? She closes her eyes, too tired to figure Mavis out.

She used to sit on her porch, surrounded by library books and the insistent scent of rosemary, that odd herb Miss Winter planted, which produced no flower, only thin green needles yet somehow emitted the seductive aroma that filled Nan with longing as she watched the women come to Miss Winter's house. They wore big hats or hid behind sun umbrellas or turned away when they saw Nan. They mostly came in twos, though some came alone. Occasionally there was a man. Nan drank her lemonade and pondered the ignorance of those who said Miss Winter was a lonely old witch with no friends in the world. All you had to do was be her neighbor to see that Miss Winter had lots of friends.

A sound—what is it, the creaking of twigs as though someone

walks nearby—startles Nan. She opens her eyes to find herself surrounded by dark. What happened to the bright sun? Where is the lemonade? Where is Miss Winter's house, wild with overgrown vines and unkempt flowers? It's all rather frightening for a moment until Nan remembers herself, and then it's frightening in another way. *Oh, I am old.* She shakes her head and closes her eyes. *I am an old woman now.*

WILD PANSY *Known as love-in-idleness, the wild pansy was originally a white flower that, struck by Cupid's arrow, turned purple. The flower's juice can be used as a love potion and treatment for acne.*

༄

Every summer the community players put on a production of *A Midsummer Night's Dream* in the park. Though Nan doesn't like to drive, especially in the dark, she and Bay used to go, sitting on the old quilt, sharing a picnic of tomato sandwiches, pickles, and chocolate cake. Nan always offered to share her wine with Bay, who, aware of the narrowed eyes of those nearby, declined, sipping lemonade instead. After the play, when they returned home, though it was not the Fourth of July, Nan let Bay run through the yard with sparklers. Even when she was past the age for doing so, Bay liked to pretend she was lighting the stars.

Now the yard looks much the way Bay imagined as a child, before she no longer wanted to be seen in public with her Nana and lied about not enjoying the play. (They ate their picnic on the porch and watched the fireflies blink through the dark, but it wasn't the same. This year, with everything else going on, they hadn't even done that.)

Somehow, Ruthie found time to hang mason jars from tree branches and placed them strategically throughout the yard, tucked near flowered shoes, resting on flat rocks. In each jar is a white candle, its glassed flame creating an aura of light as alluring as fireflies.

Bay feels like she's just woken from an odd dream where nothing makes sense, to this golden night and Thalia making broad gestures with her small hands, saying something about ghosts.

"Do you think my Nana really is a witch?"

Thalia stops in midsentence.

"I want to know," Bay says, inhaling the scent of bee balm, cut grass, and grilled meat. Someone, probably in the subdivision, is having a barbecue tonight.

Thalia is uncharacteristically silent.

"Please, I'm serious."

Thalia nods. It takes a moment for Bay to realize that the nod is the answer.

"Why?"

"Well, you know, it's kind of obvious. Don't you ever wonder about the deer not bothering your flowers out here? Doesn't that seem strange? Nobody has a garden like this in the country, not without a lot of fencing and barbed wire. The deer eat everything except daffodils, but you have all these flowers. Doesn't that make you wonder? And what about roots? No one else can plant flowers in shoes and have them grow forever. Everyone knows flowers need to sink their roots into the earth. Don't you ever wonder about that?"

"My Nana is a really good gardener."

"But, Bay, who has friends like those? I mean were you even paying attention in there? Don't you wonder if they are all, you know, witches?"

Having asked for Thalia's opinion, Bay tries hard to be receptive to it. She bites her lower lip and nods politely, but her mind is not near as compliant as her countenance. People have always been jealous of Nan's garden. Thalia doesn't know what she's talking about. As to Ruthie and Mavis, well, that point, Bay has to admit, does sort of stick. They do seem kind of witchy, especially Ruthie. But isn't that just what people say about old women? Isn't it easy to call an old woman a witch?

"My mother says it doesn't have anything to do with Satan or stuff like that. She said a long time ago being a witch just meant someone who was good with plants. You know, herbs and stuff."

Hard as she tries, Bay can't focus. She scans the yard, as though looking for escape. Why would she want to leave here? This is the safest place she knows, so pretty tonight, the candles glowing among the branches like fallen stars, but Bay is not, as she believed for so long, standing in Forever. Things are changing.

"My mother says people started calling your Nana a witch a long time ago. Things just got worse after that boy died out here."

How is it that Thalia knows more about Bay's life than she herself does? What boy died out here? Bay scans the yard again, thinking she will understand everything if she can just figure out where to look. The flowers, in such distress only this morning, perk brightly from their shoes—though they remain in disarray, scattered throughout the yard, giving the odd appearance of a gathering where guests were suddenly possessed of a need to wander away barefoot. The house, from here, is mostly dark, but for the soft, buttery glow emanating from the kitchen. Howard sits by himself on the lawn, in a circle of candlelight, picking blades of grass. Bay has no idea where Stella went. *Probably spying on Ruthie,* she thinks.

"Bay, are you okay?"

"I need to figure this out."

"Don't be mad."

"I'm not." Bay is surprised that her tone of voice sounds as though she is, in fact, angry. "I'm not," she says again, this time softly. "I just need to think, okay?"

Bay and Thalia have been through a lot, as they say. What would their lives be like if they weren't friends? When they talk about it, as they sometimes do, they agree their lives would be horrible and lonely without each other.

"You know you're my best friend, right? Just 'cause I sometimes need to be alone, that's nothing against you. You know that, right?"

"Remember what you said on your birthday?" Thalia asks.

"About going away? I thought, when you started to act so strange, that maybe you didn't want to be friends anymore."

Bay is shocked. How could Thalia possibly believe such a thing, though suddenly it all kind of makes sense, doesn't it? How would Bay have felt if Thalia said she wasn't coming back to school? "I can't believe you thought that. I just need to figure some things out, that's all. It's nothing against you. I need a little time alone, okay? Look, there's Howard. Why don't you hang out with him? I'll be back. We're best friends, right?"

Thalia narrows her eyes at Bay, as if she can best be seen at a squint, then nods abruptly. They give each other a quick hug. Bay watches Thalia run across the lawn, the silver threads in her white dress causing her to sparkle.

How can Bay feel sad after such an amazing meal, during such a special night? She feels stuck, not sure what to do. She shakes her head and murmurs, "What's gotten into you?" She is acting just the way her Nana sometimes does, like someone who's lost her way in her own yard, which is stupid. Bay knows exactly where she wants to go. Her feet feel strange as she walks across the grass. Why doesn't she go barefoot more often?

The stench of her special place rises like a warning, but Bay can think of no better spot for solitude. Besides, she sat there just this afternoon, and it wasn't so bad, was it? There's not really anything particularly special about it. It's just a circle of grass tamped down by deer that sometimes sleep there, sheltered from the yard by the lilacs and tall grass, but it is the one place that has always belonged to Bay. She even stood here last winter listening to the snow fall through the few stubborn leaves still clinging to the weeping apple trees. She has no one to blame but herself for what she finds now: Stella, changed out of her party dress, lying on the ground like a deer, waking with a start, her eyes wide, frightened.

"Oh," Bay says, "I didn't know you were here."

"You can see me?"

"It isn't that dark."

She sits up slowly, patting her hair made curly by lying on the grass. "You can hear me?"

Bay nods, then, wondering if she's obscured by shadows, says, "Yes, I can see and hear you."

"Can you still hear me?"

Bay thinks Stella is probably a lot like the mean girls at school: someone able to smile as she ridicules, someone who knows how to make alliances but not how to be loyal, someone who drinks too much at parties. Not that Bay ever gets invited to those parties, but she hears about them, even as she keeps her face averted, not wanting to be caught watching the people at school who say she has an evil eye.

"Yes. I hear you."

"You actually hear me?"

Nana is right, Bay thinks. *Drunk people are so annoying.*

"You see and hear me?"

Bay almost feels sorry for Stella, she seems so confused. *What is she wearing, anyway? Why did she take off her beautiful dress and put on this ugly thing instead?* "How come you changed?"

"Well, now let me see if I can answer that. I haven't had to answer to anyone for so long. It isn't easy being here. I'm sure that's part of it. At first I was sad all the time. Then I was angry. And now I'm just—wait, you can hear me? I have been wanting to talk to you for so long! I used to watch you play here."

Bay rolls her eyes. She doesn't have to be polite. Stella won't remember any of this when she's sober. Bay wonders if she had too much to drink herself, though she doesn't remember taking more than a few sips of the merlot. It must be the combination of moon and candlelight, and not an alcohol-induced illusion that creates the aura around Stella, almost as though she is its source. "Listen, Stella—"

"Stella? Stella? Oh," she says, and the light around her dims.

A bat must have crossed the moon, Bay thinks.

"Oh, changed! You mean my dress."

"When did you watch me play here?"

"Oh, that." She moves her hand, a bright flash of white.

Is she flickering?

"I didn't mean it the way it sounds. I didn't mean I used to watch you. How could I? We only just met, didn't we?"

Bay nods.

"I meant to say I imagine. Yes, that's what I meant to say. I imagine you played here as a child."

Stella sounds an awful lot like Ruthie right now, Bay thinks, realizing that Ruthie, who hasn't drunk a drop of wine since her arrival, sounds like she's drunk most of the time.

"You want to know why I changed? My dress?" She plucks at the skirt but picks up nothing, her finger and thumb pinching air. "I guess I changed because I wanted...that is to say, this is more comfortable."

The dress reminds Bay of the sort of thing her Nana sleeps in. It appears to be quite loose, a dismal shade of brown splotched with red, which Bay assumes is a rose pattern on the skirt. It looks comfortable but ugly and too warm, with its long sleeves, for summer.

"Why don't you sit with me, Bay?" She pats the ground. "What did you think of the party? Did you have a wonderful time? I used to love parties!"

There is something about the way Stella is behaving right now; she seems so lonely and strange that Bay sits, letting her dress with its full skirt spread out in such a pleasant fashion, forgetting for a moment, how unhappy she is. "It was an amazing party. Ruthie did a great job."

"Oh, Ruthie. She is something, isn't she?"

The sudden infusion of honeysuckle that passes in the space between them quickly becomes cloyingly sweet; combined with the bad smell, the effect is sickening. "Ruthie's great," Bay says. "Not at all the way you think."

"But I think Ruthie is—wait—did I say something unkind about Ruthie?"

This is the weirdest conversation Bay has ever had. Can Stella be so drunk she doesn't even remember her accusation?

"I don't know why I would have said something unkind about Ruthie, unless it was, you know, under duress, but let's talk about something else. Something happy. I heard you like to swim?"

"Yeah," says Bay, though she hasn't gone back to the river since the day after her birthday. She thought her Nana would worry about that, but she believed Bay when she said she had too many things going on to go swimming. "I used to like it," Bay says. "I'm not sure anymore."

"Well, that happens. I was quite a swimmer myself for a while, which reminds me, Bay, I have something important to tell you, okay? Something you have to tell Nan, and Mavis and Ruthie too."

Bay shrugs, not willing to fully commit until she hears what it is.

"Say I'm not angry. I never was. Not at them, at least."

"Why would you—"

"You have to tell them. All of them."

"But—"

"I know not everything makes sense right now. Believe me, I remember when everything stopped making sense, though your situation is different. My goodness, yes. There are times when things just don't make sense, but that doesn't mean—"

"No." Bay shakes her head. She isn't sure what they are talking about, but she's sure about this. "You're wrong."

"Wrong? What do you mean I'm wrong? I should know, I think. I should know whether I'm angry or not."

"You're wrong. You can't call someone a murderer and make it better by not being angry about it."

"Well, my goodness, of course not, whatever would make you say such a thing?"

"Not me, you. You're the one who said it."

"Well, I, goodness. Who knows what I said at the end? I hope I didn't say anything like that, but I was entirely unprepared. I was only a few years older than you are now. I don't remember what I said. I was sad. You have no idea. It wasn't… I wasn't ready. I had, why I had dreams. I had so many dreams! Ruthie knows. We were going to leave together. Move to the city. Can you imagine what Ruthie would be like if I hadn't… I wanted to get away from there. I was going to get a job. Any old thing. I had an idea that I would save up for teacher's college. That probably sounds strange, considering. I loved children. What happened to me was… Tell them, Bay, tell them I never blamed them at all."

Bay wonders again if she might be the one who has had too much to drink, though she doesn't recall more than those few sips. Her Nana is always serving wine so it won't be tempting to overindulge at teenage parties. Poor Nan still hasn't noticed that Bay doesn't get invited to parties, which is all right for the most part. Who wants to drink so much they throw up? Bay doesn't understand the attraction.

"Can you still hear me?"

"Yes. I hear you."

"I know you're confused. I'm sorry, but I can't wait for you to understand. I've waited long enough, and who knows, maybe this is the only chance I'll get. I need to ask you to do this while you can still hear me."

"Yes. I. Hear. You. Fine."

"Well, you don't need to shout, dear. I'm not deaf just… Tell them, okay? Tell them I was grateful they were there. They were a comfort to me. I don't really like that 'Did not the whole earth sicken when she died?' I don't want to be the cause of so much sorrow."

Drunk people never make sense, Bay thinks as she pushes against the damp ground to stand. "You're not going to wander away or anything?"

"No, I can't. I depart for brief periods of time, but I always end up back here. Wait, you aren't leaving me? Don't go. We can talk about other things. Happy things. You can tell me about happiness."

Bay can't explain her desperate need for escape, how the smell she has been insisting all day is not so bad has now become unbearable. *Maybe I am angry*, she thinks as she pushes through the pampas grass, determined not to stop even at the sound of Stella's drunken pleading.

Stepping into the yard scented pleasantly of citronella, Bay glances back to see if she is being followed, but while the grass rustles as though someone passes through, no one does. Bay decides she'll sit on the porch and—what's that thing her Nana says?—she'll "gather her thoughts." Yes, she just needs to gather her thoughts.

But there really is no place left. Even the porch is occupied. Nan sits with a stream of moonlit drool dripping down her chin. Mavis sleeps in the other rocker, her head back, her mouth open beneath the lavender hair oddly askew.

Bay decides to take a little walk. So what if it's the middle of the night? It's not like she lives someplace dangerous. As soon as her bare feet touch the warm pavement, she wonders why she's never done this before. It's such a pretty road, lined with tiger lilies and wild phlox bowed beneath the moon. She answers her own question by remembering all the stories she's heard of kidnapped children then tells herself to calm down. *Nothing happens here.* Is that all there is to it, the lies her Nana told (if they were lies, that is), an attempt to keep Bay close?

Because if Nan is a witch, Bay thinks, *she's a liar as well. Did she really find me in a box? Was I really left on her doorstep? Or is there some other explanation, something sinister? What a ridiculous story, found in a shoe box on the porch!*

Bay stops on the side of the stone-pitted road to inspect her foot. Tiny spots of blood blossom on her heel. She can still see her house. She can't see her Nana or Mavis on the porch, but she thinks they are still there; they didn't look like they were waking any time soon. She sees only a glimpse of the backyard, the candle jars flickering. She imagines Stella sleeping in that mysterious moonbeam, Howard and Thalia talking within that aura of light.

Who am I? Bay turns away. *Where am I going?*

She walks on the grassy bank, pushing through the tiger lilies, parting the tall grass, safely out of the way when a car comes too fast around the curve, headlights briefly monstrous before it passes, leaving Bay once again in moonlight, and alone.

CARNATION *A girl who wears carnation blossoms in her hair will learn her fortune. If the top one dies first, the last years of her life will be difficult. If the bottom one dies first, she will have misfortune in youth. If the middle one dies first, her entire life will be marked by sorrow. The white carnation is a symbol of love; the red, a symbol of an aching heart.*

⁓

Nan wakes on the moonlit porch, thinking that Mavis's appearance is a little frightening beneath the strange wig, her face ghostly pale, eyebrows archly drawn over lashless eyes, and just like that, Nan understands. How had she not seen it sooner? It steals her breath. Mavis is dying!

How did she know, how did that young Mavis know we should celebrate our bodies while we can?

Nan closes her eyes and leans back against the rocker, remembering.

She was only supposed to be taking care of Fairy, the cat, but how could she resist the opportunity for a freedom they had all gotten used to that past summer? When she showed them Miss Winter's book with those pictures of naked women, Eve and Ruthie covered their eyes, but Mavis said they needed to stop acting like bodies were embarrassing.

Perhaps it was the dandelion wine that made them wild, because it seemed one minute they were drinking out of the bottle and the next they were standing in Miss Winter's parlor, almost naked, their skin brushed with light from the fireplace flames. When Mavis announced it was time, they dropped the towels. Eve, who had protested the plan most vehemently, was the last to do so, revealing her distended belly, lightly veined blue against pink skin, like a blossomed watercolor.

The flames crackled and wavered in the peculiar stillness that shrouded them, until Mavis spoke. "Are you pregnant?" she asked.

Eve picked up her clothes and walked out of the room. The three who remained, suddenly self-conscious, even Mavis, turned their backs to dress.

"I don't understand," Ruthie said, over and over again. "I thought she made him up. Didn't she say there was no James?"

Mavis and Nan didn't bother trying to explain the obvious. They spoke in hushed voices. Things could be done. This didn't have to happen. They spoke in code, without ever saying exactly what they meant.

"Miss Winter," Nan said. "It's what she does."

"Are you talking about witchcraft?" Ruthie whispered.

People said Grace Winter was a witch; something Nan's father called preposterous, though Nan watched her own mother hang a rosary from the kitchen window facing their neighbor's porch.

"Come," Nan said. "I'll show you."

Miss Winter's basement was not filled with tools, broken tables, terra-cotta pots, cobwebs, and clocks. *What did the witches do here?* Nan wondered when she came to feed Fairy that first night, creeping around the house like a criminal. She went upstairs before she went down. Attics were the place for secrets, love letters, wedding dresses, feathered hats, and fur coats. She didn't know anyone with anything important in the basement, but when she found the locked door, she immediately thought of the key Miss Winter removed from the ring. "Now this here one is for the front," she'd said to Nan. "And this one for the back. This one you don't got to worry about." She frowned at the skeleton key even as she worked it off, waiting until Nan's back was turned before dropping it into the desk drawer, which Nan spied quite by accident in the mirror, not really thinking much about it until her curious search led her to the locked room. It didn't take long to find the key in the desk, which is where she returned it and found it again. She unlocked the basement door, turned on the light, and with a flourish of hand, like the magician when they were little girls, presented the room with all its surgical furnishings.

"What is this?" Ruthie asked, but a moan brings Nan back to the present, where Mavis frowns at Nan as though she were a source of indigestion.

"What are you looking at?"

"Your hair," Nan says.

"What about it?"

"Crooked."

Mavis grasps the lavender wig, and with a few tugs, makes an adjustment, though it still isn't right. Nan mimes moving her own hair (which suddenly seems abundant) and, following this example, Mavis adjusts the wig to rest more realistically on her head.

"Why didn't you tell me?" Nan asks.

Mavis pats the slithery boa and picks at the drape of her leopard-print dress. She finally lifts her chin to face Nan, who observes the amazing matter of Mavis with tears in her eyes.

"Are you getting better?"

"Haven't you noticed? I keep getting better all the time."

How strange, Nan thinks, *to feel so entirely the loss of a friend she lost a long time ago. What a waste, what a terrible waste.* She starts to say this, but Mavis raises her hand, palm out. "Don't. Pity buries me alive," she says, turning away to stare into the dark.

It was Mavis, of all people, who insisted they take Eve to a "real" doctor instead of Grace Winter with her strange instruments in the frightening basement. But when they went there (and they all went with Eve, of course, "What's this, girl's day out?" the nurse said) it wasn't a doctor's office at all.

They took the train, which would have been exciting under other circumstances, watching their familiar world flip past the dirty glass, meadow to broken corn stalks, to dark trees reaching long branches, to dilapidated houses, to smoke-spewing factories, the landscape suddenly comprised of gray towers, metal, and people rushing past. The four of them, ejected in their Sunday best, wandered the terminal like summer flowers tossed in the wind, until Mavis, who acted like she knew what she was doing, led them down a frightening hallway, strangely empty, though populated with the feeling of being watched. Her confident retreat brought them to a giant room of beveled glass as beautiful as it was confusing. They found the exit; immediately hailing a taxi, which took them into a sorrowful neighborhood of dismal buildings, one with a plastic red carnation stuck oddly in the dirt by the front stairs, like a wound. Nan tried not to be superstitious about the chill that crawled up her spine when they opened the creaking door into a dark hall that smelled sour and salty.

The "office" was furnished with a desk, several uncomfortable straight-back chairs, one small table with an unlit lamp, and an ashtray filled with stubs of cigarettes shaped like tiny bones, some with red smears of lipstick. The three of them sat, waiting for Eve, who was taken behind a screen into what she later said was "just a kitchen."

"It was dirty," she said. "Maybe Nan was right."

Mavis, Ruthie, and Nan never saw him, though they heard his voice, a low, scratchy sound like sandpaper. "Take it off. Why are you crying? You want this, don't you?"

Nan, who had neglected to bring a book or knitting, searched for something to occupy her mind and remembered the afternoon she came upon Eve reaching for the honeysuckle her mother trained to trail around the door before she died. Eve was standing on bare tiptoes, reaching, when Mr. Leary stepped outside, and spoke softly to her bowed head, then brushed something from her face, though Eve's hair was short and always neat. They both jumped when Nan called out. At the time she found it strange, but didn't linger over the thought.

Mr. Leary turned away. Well, he wasn't known as a demonstrative father. Eve looked, for just a moment, like a stranger, but the moment passed so quickly Nan thought it must have been a trick of the light, the terrible expression on Eve's face replaced with that odd smile she had, her eyes perpetually sad, as if she were bifurcated.

In the dismal apartment meant to be Eve's place of salvation, Nan shifted in the chair, still not sure why the memory made her so uncomfortable. Trying to find something happy to think about, she recalled that Halloween when Mr. Black sawed the lady in half. She smiled the whole time that bloodless blade severed her, and just like that, the way inspiration or divine knowing is said to arrive, Nan understood what happened to Eve. While Ruthie sat with folded hands and erect back, oblivious, and Mavis paged through her Isak Dinesen, Nan arched forward and vomited a splash of putrid yellow mush that splattered Ruthie's white shoes.

With an exaggerated sigh, the nurse pushed back her chair to retrieve a bucket, sawdust, and a little broom, which she handed to Nan before disappearing behind the screen, returning later with a wan-looking Eve, dressed and clutching her purse.

Ruthie was the only one who talked on that long train ride home, though Nan didn't listen to the words but stared out the window at the flat landscape, the brown grass, the dead flowers, the leafless branches raised to the gray sky, vaguely nauseated by the stench that rose from her collar while Eve read a book.

"You can come live with us," Nan said. "I'm sure my parents won't mind."

Eve looked at Nan as if she had said something inscrutable. "Why would I do that?"

Nan opened her mouth but swallowed her words.

So it was decided. They wouldn't speak of it. Later, when they left the train, Eve walked ahead, not hurrying, really, just brisk, leaving them behind as though they had done something she wanted no part of.

FERNS *The root of the fern, dug under a full moon, will cause a witch to turn pale. Royal fern is soothing if laid on wounds. Moon fern is said to be so magnetic that it will pull the shoes right off your feet.*

The car has passed Bay twice, the first, going too fast on the dangerous curve, the second, much slower. Bay supposes a stranger could easily get lost out here; it's not a road that goes anywhere important, as far as she knows. East, it ends in town, where it inexplicably splits into two roads, neither of which bears its name. West, it winds past the sign for Wood Hollow, the subdivision Thalia's mom drove through once, clicking her tongue at the dirt lots and oversized, mostly empty houses. "Like a ghost town with no ghosts," she'd said, then shot Bay a look. What was that look? Now that Bay thinks of it, Mrs. Desarti is often shooting darted looks her way. Why? What does everyone else know about Bay's life that she doesn't? What did Thalia mean about a boy who died out here? Karl? Of course not, he's not really a ghost. Yet everything is confused. What is true about Nan, for instance? Is she a witch? A liar? What is the secret of Bay's life? She asks herself these questions several times, but the inquisition yields nothing.

Here it comes again, the headlights mark the car's slow progress. Bay doesn't know what makes her duck at its approach, but when the headlights blink off, she crouches lower than the tiger lily petals, her heart beating wildly. Not a lost driver, someone looking for the girl walking alone on the side of a dark road, how stupid has she been?

The car passes slowly, a red car with a missing fender, the driver a silhouette of a man hunched over the steering wheel.

Bay doesn't move a muscle. Though her feet itch, she does not move to scratch. She doesn't turn her head either. She listens to the car purr away until it squeals around the curve.

What was she thinking to come out here like this at such a late hour? How can she possibly hope to discover the truth of her life by wandering around in the dark? She scratches her ankle. What if he comes back?

She doesn't know how long she crouches there before she hears humming. Because Bay is a swimmer, or at least used to be one, she is able to hold her breath for a long time. One thing she learned the day after her birthday is that actually, she can hold her breath for a freakishly long time. Bay feels the held breath course through her like smoke. The humming grows louder. She holds so still she doesn't even blink. The person humming is now directly in front of Bay, the white sneakers close enough to touch. She closes her eyes, like a little child, and for a moment thinks it works. Maybe there is magic, after all. Maybe she can be saved by held breath and hope. The humming stops. The only sound is the peepers down the road. Perhaps Bay imagined everything else; she used to imagine things a lot as a child— people in the garden, the scent of water, colored light around her Nana's body. When two hands part the tall grass and tiger lilies, Bay gasps.

"Are you all right, honey?"

"Ruthie?" Bay stands, a sudden giant among the lilies. "What are you doing here?"

Ruthie, her bathrobe buttoned all the way to the lace collar, her hair in pin curls, looks up at the moon. "Well, I guess I had the same idea as you, dear. It's such a lovely night, isn't it? Why, I remember—"

"Quick. Hide."

Ruthie gives up her attempt at squatting behind the wild flowers in favor of sitting with her legs splayed out in front of her, her sneakers white beacons in the dark.

The headlights brighten as the car approaches too fast, so fast Bay worries that rather than being kidnapped, they are in danger of being crushed, though the car holds the curve as it speeds past.

"Well," says Ruthie, picking bits of weed and grass off her robe, "is this how you entertain yourself out here?"

Which makes Bay laugh. Ruthie laughs too, her stick-out teeth accentuating her horsey look.

"The same car keeps going by," Bay says. "Once with his headlights off. I think he was looking for me."

"Oh, my," Ruthie says. "One can't be too careful these days. He turned his headlights off? That does sound suspicious. Do you think it's safe now?"

Bay listens carefully, noting a new, strange sound that takes a moment to identify as Ruthie's breathing, slightly labored as if she had been running. "We can get up, but we should probably stick close to the side of the road."

"Well, will you look at that? You just pop up like a sunflower, like it's no effort at all." Ruthie, struggling to stand, accepts Bay's assistance. She is surprised by how big Ruthie's hand is, how firm her grasp.

"What in the world is that?" Ruthie asks, peering into the woods.

"Oh, that's just the old witch's place."

"What old witch?"

Bay can't believe she called it that. "Nobody," she says. "No one lives there. It's just something people say."

Ruthie leans forward to get a good look. "I wonder who the new witch is."

"No one lives there. No one has lived there my whole life. It's just a rundown cabin."

Ruthie squints down at Bay. "Let's have a look."

Bay points to her bare feet. She can't walk through the woods like this.

"You're not wearing shoes? Why would you do such a thing?"

Bay would like to say that Ruthie isn't exactly a model of practical dress herself, but doesn't want to be rude.

Ruthie turns her back, palms braced above her slightly bent knees.

"Did you lose something?"

"Goodness, what do I have to lose? Hop on."

"Hop on what?"

"My back, silly."

Bay doesn't say that Ruthie is too old, but that she herself is. "What if someone sees us?"

"Oh, who's going to see us out here? I know you're afraid you're going to break the old lady's back, but I'm stronger than I look."

Bay shakes her head.

"Now listen to me. A person doesn't get to be my age by making foolish choices. Well, actually, I've made plenty of foolish choices, but if I couldn't carry you, I wouldn't offer. You're insulting me. Do you think I'm senile?"

"No, it's just—"

"All right then. The only hiccup is that I can't bend very far. Put your arms around my neck, not too tight, lean onto me, closer, Bay. Press more like I was a boy you think you are in love with. Now this is the tricky part, when I say, well what should I say? Obsidian! I'm going to stand, and you're going to make a little jump to bring your legs up around my waist. Ready?"

"I don't want to hurt you."

"Well, I should hope not. One. Two. Obsidian."

Ruthie wavers, the tiger lilies tremble, the tall grass ripples, the moon glow shivers like water, but Bay holds tight, remembering the sensation of almost drowning, determined not to fall.

"Are you all right?"

"Just give me a minute, dear. I have to get my earrings."

"Your earrings?"

"Bearings, I mean. All right, hiccup yourself a bit more. Yes, that's it. Now, where is it? Oh, yes, there it is."

"I'm not too heavy for you?"

"I should have made another course for dinner, that's what I think. Put some fat on those bones of yours. You're as light as a cupcake."

Bay, her arms already around Ruthie's neck, presses her face close, inhaling the clean scent of lemon. It's weird to be fifteen and getting a piggyback ride, but now that she is no longer in danger of crashing to the ground and squashing Ruthie, Bay remembers how her Nana used to give rides like this when they came out here to look for fiddleheads. Back then, Bay had to be carried because her little feet got tangled in the weeds. "I think the forest wants to take you back," her Nana would say.

"Are you having goose pimples? Did someone just walk on your grave? Isn't it just the sweetest place? Can't you just picture it with a little garden of daffodils? Deer won't eat daffodils, you know, but they love tulips. And some rocking chairs and wind chimes?"

Bay looks past Ruthie's bobby-pinned hair at the old cabin, the door dangling on a hinge, the crooked porch littered with stones, the windows, black hollows edged with glass like a jack-o'-lantern's smile. Ruthie picks her way across the forest floor's uncertain terrain, talking about decorating, a little picket fence, lace curtains, pottery. For just a moment, Bay pictures it that way, as though it's been obvious all along, but a slivered glint catches her eye and breaks the spell. "Be careful of broken glass," she says.

"You are an extraordinarily cautious child."

"Sorry."

"No need to apologize. I wish my son would have been more careful. You're right to worry. Cut your foot out here, and you would turn into a fairy-tale character for sure, you know the one. Look at that stone chimney. Bay, do you think there's a fireplace?"

"Oh, it has a big fireplace, but it's falling apart."

"Can't you just imagine a nice bowl of stew cooked over the fire? And bread? Can't you just smell it?"

Bay inhales the scent of dirt, skunk cabbage (a musky scent more pleasant than it sounds), grass, and—could it be?—she closes her eyes: the yeasty scent of fresh bread, quickly replaced by Ruthie's lemon perfume.

"'Whose woods these are I think I know,'" Ruthie says.

"You do?"

"Robert Frost. You're familiar with the poem, aren't you?"

"No."

"Well, my goodness, what kind of education are you getting? Isn't it just the sweetest little cabin? A person could be really happy out here, I think."

"Ruthie?"

"Yes?"

"How do you... I mean it seems like you know my Nana really well."

"Is that a question, dear?"

"This is kind of hard to say. But I mean, like, do you think... is my Nana a witch?"

"What did you say? My hearing isn't what it used to be."

Bay leans close to Ruthie's ear. "Is my Nana a witch?"

Ruthie's body stiffens. "We'll come back in daylight," she says, turning toward the road, "when you are wearing proper shoes."

Bay bites her lip. Should she not have asked? Apparently she should not have. The silence, which previously felt so companionable, now feels thorny. When they return to the side of the road, Bay slides carefully down Ruthie's back, trying to think of something to say, something pleasant to restore the good feeling they'd shared all evening, but she can't think what that would be. They walk down the road in silence, staying close to the bank in case they need to dive for cover. Bay stops to brush off the tiny stones that stick to the soles of her feet, but Ruthie continues walking, as though she doesn't even care if Bay falls behind, vulnerable to kidnappers, or "turns into a fairy-tale character," whatever that means.

Ruthie is humming. Bay has no idea what song it's supposed to be; it barely sounds like music at all, more like a slightly melodic throat clearing. Bay realizes she's hurrying to keep up with an old woman wearing sneakers and a robe, her hair in pin curls. *There's more than one reason*, Bay thinks, *to hide if a car approaches*. She'll never live it down if anyone from school sees her.

"Well, there's nothing like a summer's night walk," Ruthie says. "Though obviously one must be aware of the usual dangers. It's been ages since I've done anything like this! Where I live the streets are not nearly so pleasant. And my husband was overprotective."

"Did he really try to poison you?"

"Oh my, yes. Why would anyone make up such a horrible story?"

"Well, like I said, I understand why you would want to kill him."

Bay worries that Ruthie is having a heart attack or something, because she stops suddenly with her hands clutched over her chest. Before Bay can even remember what she learned in health class, Ruthie says, "Don't," in a terrible voice.

"Don't what?"

Ruthie shakes her head, the glittering copper bobby pins like starlight in her hair. "Don't ever understand the urge to kill." Still clutching her hands over her heart, she leans down to look directly into Bay's eyes. "No one should understand such a thing. You must do whatever it takes so you don't understand, do you hear me?"

Bay finds herself momentarily caught in the stare of Ruthie's small blue eyes, too close to her narrow nose. *Killer eyes*, isn't that what Stella called them?

"Yes," Bay says. "I hear you, and I hear Stella. There's

nothing wrong with my hearing." It's a moment of rudeness she immediately regrets.

"I got over the urge for murder a long time ago. You never want to feel that way, Bay. It's a terrible, terrible way to feel, and it will destroy you and ruin your life." With an abrupt nod, Ruthie turns and continues on her way, leaving Bay at the side of the road.

Wait? What? Bay doesn't know if she wants to catch up or run in the other direction. She watches Ruthie walking slowly up the road in her sneakers and bathrobe. Where else can Bay go? Nowhere can be safer than home. She pries a sharp stone out of her foot; it leaves a drop of blood shaped like a tear. When she looks up, Ruthie is standing by the side of the road, watching. *What is it about the light tonight?* Bay wonders. Ruthie, in her pink robe, moonlit pin curls, and bright white sneakers looks like she is glowing. Not sure what else to do, or where else to go, Bay walks toward her.

PARSLEY *Transporting parsley is bad luck, and transplanting it will result in death. Wearing parsley increases cheerfulness. Only witches can grow parsley.*

⁀◯

Nan looks past the moonflowers, beyond the road to the droop of weeds lining the drainage ditch while the memories swirl around her like a little tornado. Her parents, laughing on the porch swing; why has she forgotten how they used to laugh? She remembers a lavender ribbon and her mother saying, "Here, Nanolan. You have such pretty hair." Why? Why has she forgotten that for so long, and why does this memory return tonight?

Mavis says it is time they get started on the ceremony. She scoots across the chair accompanied by that clank of bracelets. When she stands, both she and the chair rock precariously.

Nan peers up at Mavis. Old now. Dying. At a distance, as if in a dream. What is she saying? Nan can't be sure; the taste of ash overwhelms everything else; she is filled with it as though on fire.

"I'll be right there," Nan says, though her words sound strange, distorted, distant. "I need a few minutes alone."

Mavis grunts, waving her hand in that way she has, as though every time Nan opens her mouth, gnats swarm the air between them.

◯⁀

Even though it was December, Nan sat on the porch swing, staring at the black night, searching for stars in the dark embrace of winter chill. She had taken to doing this in the past week, donning coat and mittens to sit outside. Earlier, when she went in to use the bathroom, Nan heard her parents arguing. "It isn't normal," her mother said. "I am afraid there's something not right about her, and it's been getting worse. We never should have let her develop a relationship with that woman."

Nan sighed, glancing at "that woman's" house. Miss Winter, recently returned from visiting her sister, with violet jelly and potted parsley as a thank you to Nan for changing Fairy's water and filling her bowl with cat food, never suspecting, Nan hopes, that she was the sort of girl who took advantage of trust.

"It's a sign of larger developments," her mother said. "A young lady does not sit on the porch in the middle of winter."

"It's her birthday." Her father sighed, sharply interrupted by something inaudible from Nan's mother, he continued. "Well, all right, tomorrow. Let her be. She's a thoughtful child."

"But she's not a child. That's what you don't seem to realize. She's a young woman now."

Lately, it seemed to Nan, there was no safe thing to think about. Everything was infected by what happened to Eve. Nan stood so suddenly, the porch swing rocked behind her as if with a ghost. She opened the front door and called into the house, "I'm going."

Her mother came on noisy heels to look at Nan as though she had turned into something grisly.

"To Mavis's," Nan said, pretending to be cheerful. "To sleep over. Remember?"

"Where are your things?"

Nan was afraid of entering her own house, even for her nightgown and pillow. She didn't trust herself, afraid she'd say the wrong thing, afraid she'd tell the truth.

"I took my bag over earlier. I'll be back tomorrow," she said, not waiting for a response.

Her mother hated it when she ran but Nan loved the cold

air on her face, the feel of her hair blowing back. She ran the whole way to Mavis's house. Mrs. Hearn, used to this sort of wild behavior from her own daughter, only said, "Mavis asked me to tell you there's been a change of plans. The sleepover is at Eve's house tonight."

But Eve never had sleepovers. The feeling started to creep up on Nan that something wasn't right. Something wasn't right. It went through her head, over and over again, like a playground chant or camp song. Nan tried to shake it away, but something wasn't right.

Mr. Leary answered the door, chewing on his tongue, but not acting like anything unusual had happened. He pointed his chin toward the back of the house, where Eve's bedroom was. Nan walked down the narrow hall. Maybe they were having a surprise party for her! They were waiting with balloons and cake! When Nan opened the door, she saw Eve in bed and Mavis on the other side of the room, signaling to shut the door, which Nan did, revealing Ruthie in the corner, her round cheeks flushed.

"What's happen—"

"Shhh, not so loud," Mavis hissed. "We can't let anyone hear."

Nan looked at Eve's face, glowing white. "Is it the flu?"

"Don't be ignorant. You know what it is."

"We have to tell someone," Nan said.

"No, we don't. We promised."

"We can't," Ruthie whispered. "He'll kill her if—"

"Don't fight." Eve didn't open her eyes to speak. She didn't move her head. "I just need…"

What? Eve never said what she needed, but they tried to find it for her. At some point Ruthie produced a damp washcloth, which they took turns administering, patting Eve's forehead, her chin, her cheeks, her neck, until the cloth was clammy and pointless. Not daring to disturb her head, they brushed the exposed pillowcase until she asked to be left alone. They went to separate corners, watching Eve as though their lives were tied to hers, and when she stirred, they stirred too, returned to the patting and cooing, the useless gestures they employed. *It's like all of a sudden we are mothers*, Nan thought. Eve moaned, a low sound, almost a growl. *But we aren't very good at it.*

When footsteps creaked through the carpeted floor, evidence of someone walking down the narrow hallway, they stared at one another with wide eyes. The footsteps stopped just outside the room and Ruthie gasped but stifled herself with her hand pressed across her mouth.

"You girls need anything?" he asked.

"Not a thing at all," Mavis called brightly, so cheerful that, for a moment, Nan felt she misread the situation and everything was fine.

"Eve?"

They turned to look at her, a still figure on the twin bed, her lips white; she opened her eyes wide—*frightened*, Nan thought—and said, "Good night, Dad," in a shockingly normal voice.

"You girls need to keep it down in there. I have early shift."

"Okay, Dad."

Nan was once again struck by the horrible realization that as good of an actress as Mavis was, Eve was better. She fooled all of them for a very long time.

Who are you anyway? Nan thought. With everything else going on, she hadn't realized—she was angry at Eve! And in just that moment, their eyes locked across the room cast in a pea-green glow. *Liar*, Nan thought and Eve closed her eyes.

No, I take it back. I don't mean it. I'm not angry. But why didn't you tell us? Why didn't you...

Nan could hear Mr. Leary send the boys to bed. Sound traveled through the walls as if there were no walls at all, and Nan wondered if they have already been too loud. How could he not be suspicious?

"We need to call a doctor," Nan said. "She needs—"

"No," Mavis hissed. "We promised. No one else can know. They said she might have cramping. They said she would be tired."

How long the night! How the hours spilled like sand through Nan's bones while she brushed Eve's hair, tried to make her drink water, waited for her to open those eyes and smile! Nan longed to see Eve smile, even if it was a lie.

Finally, unable to keep her own eyes open any longer, Nan curled into an uncomfortable compromise in the chair and slept. She must have slept, because she awoke to hear Mavis apologizing to Eve. But Nan couldn't rouse herself; she was heavy with the black night drifting through her bones, sleeping again, until at last she awoke out of her paralytic state to blink in the dim morning light at the sound of Ruthie sobbing.

"Stop it," Mavis hissed, "or I swear I'll kick you out of the house, and I won't let you back in."

Nan almost smiled at Mavis's power. One second Ruthie was weeping, and the next she was not. Maybe it would be like that for Eve. Mavis would tell her to sit up, shake it off, get over it, and she would. But Eve's complexion was a terrible white; her skin shimmered like a naked lightbulb.

The footsteps again came down the hall, knuckles tapped the door though he continued walking.

"He always does that," Ruthie whispered.

Nan did not go to Eve, but instead turned away to part the dismal curtain and stare out the window at the cold morning. *My birthday*, she thought. She jumped at the sound of the back door pulled shut and watched Mr. Leary, lunch pail in hand, saunter down the walk, stopping at the curb as though he forgot something. *Yes*, Nan thought. *Turn around. Save her. Save us.*

Who would ever guess that Mr. Leary, of all people, could be the one? *What are you waiting for?* Nan thought. *Here's your chance to make things right.* But whatever caused him to pause—watching the road as if waiting for a bus—passed, and with a hitch of his shoulder, he continued down the walk.

Eve murmured, was it something about blood?

Nan turned from the window to hear better.

"The boys," she croaked.

"What about boys?" Mavis asked, her voice at normal volume, a shock.

"School," Ruthie squeaked. "She gets them ready."

"You do it," Mavis said.

Nan volunteered to help, happy for an excuse to leave the tiny room.

"Where's Eve?" little Danny asked.

"Oh, she's sleeping in," Ruthie said, her voice ringing with false cheer. "Every mother needs a day of rest."

"She ain't our mother," Danny said as Petey nodded.

"Well, she sure acts like it." Ruthie pulled off T-shirts, washed faces, buttered toast, and made sandwiches while Nan followed like a lost child, finally stopping to stare out the kitchen window at the gray sky, remembering summer, how persistent it seemed, the green days, the sweet flavor of strawberries.

Nan didn't even realize she was crying until Danny said, "What's wrong with her?" and Ruthie said, "Oh that's just Nan. She's full of emotion."

"I'm about sick of girls crying all the time."

"Well, then, why don't you just get out of here?" Ruthie softened her voice before she continued. "You don't want to be late for school now, do you?"

"What about Sissy?"

"I already said, didn't I? She's sleeping this morning. Everyone deserves a rest, and today is Eve's turn."

"I don't know about that," Petey said, but Danny told him to hurry.

I should help, Nan thought, standing at the kitchen window, watching through the dirty glass. Petey and Danny, dressed for snow, hurried down the sidewalk, almost as if they knew this was a house to run away from.

Nan didn't notice when Ruthie joined her, only realized that she had. They stood side by side, staring out the window, watching the snow drift slowly past the orb of morning's streetlight. The children walked past: boys with big ears, girls with braids. The children walked to school, sticking out pink tongues and mittened hands to catch the flakes, while Nan and Ruthie stood frozen as though trapped in ice.

Ruthie finally turned away and Nan followed like a child more interested in daydreams than reality. *When they open Eve's bedroom door, Mavis will be asleep in that chair, and Eve will be sleeping too, her color returned, the long night vanquished*, Nan thought. But Mavis stood by the side of the bed, blood on her hands, a streak of red on her face, the blanket and sheet pulled down, Eve's brown dress blossomed in red.

"They said there might be blood," Mavis said, but Nan was already spinning out of the room, stumbling down the hall, opening the door, stepping into a world of white, shocked by the cold and the apple blossom scent of snow.

ROSES *Rose petals, steeped in oil, are a remedy for diseases of the uterus. Seeing rose petals fall is a sign of death, though this might be countered by burning them. A symbol of secrecy and silence, roses are a common funeral flower.*

⁓

Bay and Ruthie walk back to the house in silence. Bay wants to make things right between them but doesn't know where to begin. Ruthie walks up the sidewalk leading to the front door, but Bay stays on the grass, which is soft beneath her sore feet. Nan and Mavis are no longer on the porch, though a chair gently rocks there as though someone just departed.

They both start to speak, then stop. It would be funny in other circumstances. Ruthie looks down her long nose at Bay. "What does Nan say about this witch business?"

"I never really asked. Not right out."

Ruthie, her lips pursed, nods. "Well, dear, it has been my experience that when you have a question, the best thing to do is to ask it."

Bay has the funny feeling they are talking about more than it seems. Does Bay want to ask Ruthie what she meant earlier about having gotten over the urge for murder years ago? Does Bay really want to know?

"You're not planning on taking any more midnight strolls, are you, dear?"

Bay shakes her head. Where did she think she was going anyway? What did she expect to find out there?

"That's good. 'Cause I'm as worn out as galoshes."

"What are gal…thank you," Bay says, surprised to find herself pressing the side of her face into Ruthie's soft robe, inhaling the scent of lemons.

At first Ruthie hugs Bay as though she might break, but then she squeezes back until, for just a moment, Bay thinks she can't breathe, and right then, Ruthie opens her arms wide and says, "You have been the top light of my visit, you know."

"Me too. I'm so glad you came. Dinner tonight was the best meal of my entire life."

Ruthie opens her mouth, but snaps her lips shut without speaking. She nods abruptly and walks up the front steps at a surprisingly brisk pace, into the house.

The white moonflowers have blossomed from the heart-shaped leaves all the way along the porch railing and up the drainpipe. Bay can't remember when she's seen so many blooms in one night. All these flowers will be dead soon; poor moonflower! She leans forward to inhale the intoxicating scent. Other summers when she had the bedroom next to her Nana's, right over the porch, Bay drifted to sleep on a cloud of moonflower perfume. Is that why dreams were sweeter then?

"Bay, where have you been? We've been looking for you."

Bay is not used to thinking of her Nana as pretty. She wears that old dress almost all summer, often with that stupid walnut wreath and her clogs. In winter she wears the green dress with various colored cardigans that strain across her chest. Bay can't remember a time Nan has dressed differently before tonight. She stands there in her blue velvet, with her white hair hanging down, the silver strands catching the light. *She looks sparkly, not like a witch at all,* Bay thinks, *more like a fairy.*

"Do you think we could plant a moonflower next year beneath my window?"

"We could do that," Nan says. "I'm sure we could."

On any other night, Nan would have heard the car pull over to the side of the road. She would have heard it even if she were all the way in the back of the house in the kitchen, singing at the top of her lungs. She would have heard it with all the windows closed in the depth of winter. She would have heard it even if she was at the high school, sitting on the hard bench with all the screaming people, watching Bay's swim meet—so attuned has Nan been for just this moment, she would have said nothing could stop her from noting its arrival; and yet, when she hears the sound of the car door close, her first response is pleasant anticipation, smiling as she turns.

"Sheriff Henry," she gasps.

"Did you call him about Karl?" Bay asks.

Nan watches the sheriff come slowly up the walk, by all appearances enjoying the shoe garden, not noticing them at all. It occurs to her to send Bay away. Instead, Nan pulls her close.

"Mz. Singer. I didn't see you."

"Sheriff Henry."

He's aged, though he still isn't old. Somehow, in spite of his profession, he's maintained an amiable countenance, as though he is everyone's favorite visitor.

"I'm sorry to just show up like this but—" He looks at Bay, actually startling, which Nan assumes is meant to be cute. "Is this…" He glances at Nan, turns back to Bay. "Are you?"

"You remember Bay, don't you, sheriff?" Nan says.

"Last time I saw you, you were the size of a loaf of bread."

This makes Bay smile, as if her birth size was some kind of accomplishment, and Nan squeezes tighter. *No need to grin at wolves.*

"I'm sorry to drop in like this. I tried to call, but we got disconnected. I wanted to—"

"Warn me? I think you said."

He nods. "In case there was a time you preferred."

"It's late now," says Nan. "And I have guests."

"I'm sorry, it's just, I found the whole case, and I don't know if you heard? I'm moving?"

"Where to?" Bay asks.

"What are you now? Twelve? Thirteen?"

"Fifteen."

"Fifteen?" He shakes his head. "This big," he says, his hands before him, holding the imaginary loaf.

At least he isn't being mean, Nan thinks. *Maybe he'll even let me steer Bay away so she doesn't have to see the handcuffs.* Nan doesn't feel she deserves special treatment, of course, but Bay does. And maybe the timing isn't horrible after all. At least with Ruthie and Mavis here, Bay will be taken care of.

"I can bring it up to the porch or into the house, if you like. It's heavy."

Nan can't believe how her mind wanders. How, at this pivotal time in her life, it has wandered again.

"You all right, Mz. Singer?"

"Nana?"

"It's just…" She shakes her head. "What are you doing here?"

Sheriff Henry stares at Nan a moment, and in that small space of time she feels herself sinking, as though swallowed by the earth, buried alive.

"Orange blossom honey," he says. "I don't eat it myself, and now that I'm moving out of state…"

"Honey?"

"I remember my mother saying how much you loved her honey. She told me…" He glances at Bay. "She told me how you helped her. Before I was born. My mother was…"

Incredibly, standing there in his impressive uniform, Sheriff Henry's voice quivers.

"We love honey," Bay says.

Nan wishes she could remember what she did for his mother, but she can't. There were so many for a while there, and then, when the law changed, there were less and less until she was no longer needed. There were stragglers, of course; those who didn't want a doctor. And there were always the others. Nan sometimes forgets about them. Her garden worked both ways, didn't it? Some women came to her with a desperation for birth, didn't they? She looks at Sheriff Henry's kind face and wonders if she sees a bit of hollyhock there.

"Ma'am?"

"Yes," Nan says. "We love honey. You can just bring it to the porch. Orange blossom, you say?"

Nan wonders, briefly if it is some kind of trick, but he walks to the car with a generous man's gait, swinging his arms, taking broad strides. He unlocks the trunk and reaches in for a large box. Why he didn't just leave it, the way people do, Nan has no idea, but decides she is not one to judge others' eccentricities. Still, it isn't until Sheriff Henry passes and she gets a whiff of the musky sweet blossom that Nan releases her hold of Bay, who is still standing there when the sheriff drives away, promising he'll send them a postcard.

Nan can't believe it. Has she really avoided the worst?

"Wow," Bay says. "You must have done something really nice for his mom. I thought he was going to cry."

"Oh, well," Nan says, "just being neighborly."

"Nana, are you a witch?" She hadn't meant to ask like this, though in a way it's a relief to have it out.

"Why? Whatever gave you that idea? Did Ruthie say something?"

Bay nods. After all, it was Ruthie who said that the best thing to do with a question is ask it. "Are you?"

Nan blinks against the question. *What am I?* She is stunned by the simplicity of it. For so long everything seemed complicated.

"I'm going to tell you now." Nan looks closely at Bay, trying to stay focused. It's strange how this weekend has wound up time, how one minute she is an old woman and the next she is young again.

Bay thinks, *Well, here it comes.* She isn't sure she wants to know. What if she could go back in time to just a year ago, to when the nights were scented with moonflower and not the loamy scent of river water? Bay hears the others in the backyard, their voices a distant murmur. Nan must hear them too, because she turns in that direction for a moment with a longing look.

"Do I fly through the sky at night?" Nan asks. "You know I don't. Do I disappear and walk through rooms like a ghost? Of course not. Do I make terrible things happen?" Nan is startled by her own question, arrived at unexpectedly. She nods slowly. "Yes, sometimes I do. Sometimes I do."

Bay regrets asking. Why, her Nana never did a bad thing in her life, and this whole matter is just incredibly "stupid."

"Yes," Nan says, nodding. "I've been stupid. I should have learned. I should have learned a long time ago. Don't you see, Bay? Don't you see?"

Bay not only doesn't see, but is entirely confused.

"What I'm trying to say, Bay, is that the only thing that matters now is what you believe."

"What I believe?" Bay likes the feel of the words, as if what she believes is actually important. What she believes is that her life would be a whole lot easier if her Nana were a whole lot different, but Bay doesn't say that, of course.

"I just want to be normal," she says.

Nan nods, pretending she is not in the middle of an epiphany. But of course! Of course Bay wants to be normal. Why has Nan considered this a problem when she, herself, has longed for, well, if not normalcy, something of what her life would have been had it not been so tragically altered?

"Everyone's waiting," she says. "Let's finish this conversation later."

The front yard's flowers, while in their shoes, are strangely out of place, growing crooked and broken, and Bay realizes the garden damage was more thorough than she had previously understood. The hollyhocks, bent with the weight of summer, appear to be in despair. Who put them there anyway, where the sun will never find them? *Everything is wrong*, Bay thinks.

Torn flowers planted with roots exposed in dirty shoes, sun plants in the shade, shade plants in the sun.

As they walk along the side of the house, Nan blinks against the memory of smoke. How strange life is, one minute to be a young woman watching Miss Winter's house burn down, knowing that those who lit the match would set it to Nan herself if they knew the truth, and the next to be an old woman who has lived a long life, walking with her daughter to the backyard where Mavis, Howard, Thalia, and Stella sit in a small circle beneath the moon-bright sky. No wild flames and acrid smoke, just the night garden, the scent of summer: pennyroyal, parsley, angel roses, and mint, with only the vaguest odor of death emanating from beyond the lilacs and pampas grass.

"Oh," Bay says. "You changed again."

Stella, sitting in the grass in her party dress, looks puzzled. "What?"

"From before."

Stella glances at Howard and shrugs.

Nan, who has a great deal of sympathy for the vagaries of memory, reminds Bay, "Everyone changed for the party. You remember, don't you?"

They are all looking at Bay as though she has suddenly grown as old as Nan. "Of course I remember, but she was wearing a different dress afterward. That's what I'm talking about." To be polite, Bay turns her face away from the group and whispers, "She's pretty drunk, actually."

Nan, who's been looking for this sort of thing for a while, asks Bay to describe the other dress.

"It was brown, with red roses on the skirt."

"I don't know what you're talking about," Stella says. "I don't own anything like that."

"Nana? Are you all right?"

"Let's start this thing," Mavis says with a great deal of

grumbling as she struggles to stand, and Howard comes to his knees to assist her.

"What thing?" Stella leans back on her elbows as though tanning beneath the moon.

"Hey, what happened to your curls?" says Bay.

"Stop." Nan puts out her hand like a crossing guard.

Mavis, who is massaging her hair in such a vigorous manner that it appears to slide like a tectonic plate, sighs. "In Africa," she starts.

"Oh, stop with Africa. You don't know anything about it." Nan feels bad, talking to Mavis this way, until she remembers how pity would bury her alive. She turns to Bay. "Don't worry, dear, it's all going to make sense soon enough."

"It is?"

"Well, not all of it, of course," Nan says, turning back toward the house.

The kitchen, lit by the stove-top light, is cloying with the mingled sweet and savory scents of dinner. Flowers droop like exhausted girls in ball gowns shedding petals to the floor, creating the lovely illusion of a garden carpet Nan hates to tread on. Nicholas, curled on a kitchen chair, opens one eye to watch her pass. Walking up the creaking stairs, Nan notices a single red petal stuck to her big toe. She has lived in this house for a long time; there is nothing in the dark that frightens her, not the twisted stairs or sharp corners, and not the ghosts. She always hoped they'd speak and tell her what to do. What frightens Nan is the way the past sneaks up on the present, consuming all in its path. *Like I am the flower*, Nan thinks, *and life is the feast.*

She pushes open her bedroom door, mumbling, a bad habit, bad enough for her, but she's noticed Bay has acquired it as well, which can't be good. She pulls the dresser drawer open; it groans, sticking the way it does. She should have done this weeks ago. She should have had the courage. She finds the narrow box beneath the underwear, slips, bras, and socks, pulling it through the flutter of silk and cotton, the narrow box, once used, years ago, for handkerchiefs embroidered with posies. The light through the bedroom window makes Nan feel like she's in a dream, though she's sure she's not sleeping. She sits on the bed, the box in her lap. Her hands shake as she lifts the lid and sets it to the side. Why has she resisted doing this before? She pulls the pink tissue apart and for just a moment, Nan feels the excitement of opening a present; there it is, the caul, looking like one of the fake webs people put up for Halloween. Nan holds it between finger and thumb at either end, hoping it will lend some of its magic to her, but all she sees is the other side of her room, the image blurry, as though already just a memory.

The future, with all its nasty implications, is as easy to destroy as lace. Who needs a silly ceremony? *Rip it apart*, she tells her trembling hands, *and Bay will no longer see ghosts.* Well, she might see them, but it would be the way Nan sees them, vague and distant. Tear it apart, and Bay will no longer have a natural affinity for healing. But didn't she specifically say she had no interest in medicine? Hadn't she said something about wanting to be a chef? Tear it apart, and Bay can be whatever she wants to be. She will no longer predict the weather, but there's much worse in life than having to carry an umbrella when it doesn't rain, or getting wet when it does. Tear it, and Bay will no longer seem so strange to other kids her age. Tear it, and she will no longer be safe from drowning, but the girl swims like a fish anyway. *Rip it*, Nan tells her hands, *and Bay can have the normal life she's always wanted.*

Nan feels the tear roll down her cheek. *I don't want her to hate me,* she thinks. *I don't want her to know.*

Mavis, Howard, Stella, and Thalia form a small circle on the grass, talking about what, Bay has no idea. She's restless and tired, out of sorts around all these people. Her heart feels weird. When she wanders away from the little group, they don't seem to notice. If they do, they certainly aren't bothering her about it, which on the one hand she appreciates, while on the other, she resents; why is she so easily forgotten?

What is it about this night, she wonders, weaving toward the shoe flowers and away from them, meandering the way Nicholas does, that makes her feel like everything matters so much, as though her life teeters in some kind of balance? Maybe it's just that she's not used to having so many people around. It's been fun, sort of, but also weirdly exhausting. She's glad everyone's leaving in the morning. What is happening? Is this what growing older feels like?

Bay presses her palms against her chest and confirms what she already knows, the strange feeling there, like a butterfly beating its wings, trapped, but seeking flight. Without thinking about it, she has wandered to her secret place. She lies down, first on her back, staring at the moon and then rolls to her side, closing her weary eyes.

JASMINE *Jasmine, a night-blooming vine, is a relaxant for nerves, a sedative, and an aphrodisiac. The flowers are a symbol of compassion and love. In olden days, the petals were used to depict snow during summer celebrations.*

⌒

"Nan, are you awake?"

"Ruthie?"

"Oh, good."

When Ruthie enters the room, looking quite bright-eyed, Nan tries to hide the caul, but her quick gesture only attracts attention.

"What on earth is that?"

"Oh, just some old fabric I was thinking of using in a quilt," Nan says.

Ruthie, her expression pinched as the pin curls tight around her head, watches Nan carefully return the caul to its pink nest. "I've had such a nice time," Ruthie says. "I can't believe I have to leave tomorrow." She sits beside Nan on the edge of the bed. "I was thinking, why didn't we do this sooner? Of course I know the answer, but why didn't we try? Thank you, Nan, for bringing us together."

Nan, who loves a compliment as much as anyone, refuses to be lulled into a pleasant feeling by Ruthie's false ways. After all, didn't she just say…something to Bay? Come to think of it, Nan realizes, she never did determine what exactly Ruthie said, but whatever it was, it prompted Bay to ask about witches. It alarmed her, and that's the point.

"Nan, why are you looking at me this way? Are you all right?"

Well, you aren't the only one who can wear a sweet mask. "You worked so hard. I hope you aren't exhausted."

Ruthie shakes her head. "Oh, stuffy nonsense. I enjoyed

myself immensely. I didn't realize until this weekend how lonely I've been."

Nan thought she'd grown out of the need for companionship decades ago, but she agrees it has been nice to be with friends again. She doesn't say how worn out she feels. After all, Ruthie is the one who did all the work while Nan took a ridiculously long nap and had a bubble bath.

"I have a confession," Ruthie says.

Nan has to hold back the urge to scold. If this is an apology, she hopes she can be gracious about it. Bay was upset, but certainly she's heard this sort of witch business from people far more threatening than Ruthie.

"Here we are, with the weekend over, and I still haven't said what I came to say." Ruthie stares straight ahead, her profile sharp, toothy, surprisingly stern. She takes a deep breath, the air suddenly flooded with the scent of mint toothpaste. "We should have listened to you. We should have taken her to Miss Winter, and not that horrible doctor. All through my entire life, when I remember that conversation we had, I always try to change it. I agreed with you, you know, but I was afraid to say so. No. Wait. I want to say this now. I was supposed to be her best friend. I was supposed to protect her. Not just do whatever Mavis said."

"You were trying to do the right thing. We all were. Even Mavis."

"Well, yes, but that's not why I agreed. I agreed with Mavis because she was, well, Mavis, and you know how it was back then. How I was too. I did whatever Mavis said to do. But that's not what I want to tell you. I came to say you were right. You were right that we should have consulted Grace Winter in the first place, and you were right again when we should have gotten help much, much sooner. Obviously."

Nan has believed, for a long time, that nothing could free her criminal heart, so she is surprised by the feelings in her chest, a fluttering she hopes is less symptomatic of biological problems than of forgiveness.

"You know," says Ruthie, "I worried that you might be bringing us here to...oh, I don't know, scold us, chastise us? I suffer from poster stress disorder, that's what it's called. Ever since my husband poisoned me, I've been afraid of the damage people do."

"You have?"

"Oh my goodness, yes. Of course he was a bastard—"

"Ruthie!"

"Well, he was, that's the simple truth. I married a bad man, Nan, and I stayed married to him for a long time. There are many reasons for this, it turns out, but at least part of it was I figured I deserved the bad things that happened to me. I really felt—"

"Nan, are you in here?" Mavis doesn't wait for a response; she comes in like an invasion, with her noisy bracelets and her boa shedding tiny orange feathers. "Oh. Ruthie. I thought you were in bed."

"Isn't this fun," Ruthie says. "Come. Sit."

Mavis frowns at Nan. "What about—" she starts, but stops, darting quick eyes at Ruthie.

"Oh, sit," Nan says. "There's time enough for everything."

"Easy for you to say," Mavis grumbles.

They sit, perched on the edge of the bed in uncomfortable silence until Nan suggests they scoot back, which they do with a great deal of effort, the tiny orange feathers wisping around them. *As though we are in here plucking baby chicks*, Nan thinks.

"What's in the box?" Mavis asks.

Nan taps the lid. "This? Just some material."

"Material?" Mavis, who is so close Nan can smell the burnt scent of the cancer (she blames the busyness of the last couple of days for not having noticed sooner) looks skeptical.

Ruthie leans across Nan to speak. "We were talking about

Eve. I was just saying how I always thought it would have made a difference if we'd taken her to Miss Winter, if we'd gotten help sooner."

Nan, pressed between Mavis and Ruthie, holds still, trying not to let her body betray her distress. How bitterly will this weekend, their friendship, and their lives end?

"Yes," Mavis sighs. "But what's the point?"

"What's the point?" Nan asks.

"The unchosen path is always perfect, isn't it?"

Nan shudders.

"Are you cold?"

When she turns to face Ruthie, Nan almost gasps. She should be used to it by now, but every time it's a shock. Where are the girls they'd been? What happened to them? How has time turned like this, not a spool, but a sharp stone, a piece of glass, nothing that can be unraveled or rewound?

Yet, it's wonderful, isn't it, to be here now, pressing shoulder to shoulder, hip to hip with these old friends? All the wasted hours! So much unshared and unknown!

"Think of girls today," Mavis says. "Basil and Tammy down there, and Sonya."

Nan glances at Ruthie, but this is too somber a subject to fall into giggling at Mavis's trouble with names.

"Generations of girls," she continues, "who will never know."

"Never know what?" Ruthie asks.

"The terror of choice," Mavis says. "The terror of getting it wrong."

"Oh, I don't know about that," Nan says. "Girls today still have to choose. They still suffer consequences. Bay's mother had to make a choice. I had to choose as well, after Bay's arrival. I had to make a very difficult choice that I've never told anyone about." Nan stops abruptly. It is a tremendous word burp, but haven't they been good at keeping each other's secrets? In spite of everything else, haven't they been good at that?

"You know you can tell us anything," Ruthie says.

"Yes. We'll be dead soon."

Was Mavis trying to be funny? Nan can't even summon a polite grin of support. What is she doing? Is she really going to confess now? After all these years?

Mavis and Ruthie wait expectantly, their eyes tired but kind. In all the wide world, who else would Nan ever share this secret with, but them?

"If you don't want to tell," Ruthie starts, but Nan shakes her head.

"I'm not sure where to begin."

"What about with Bay's arrival?"

"It was one of those mornings," Nan says. "Those misty summer mornings, when you might expect to find a rainbow in the garden, not a baby on the porch. But there she was. In a shoe box, if you can imagine. Do you know, for a while I considered naming her Adidas?" Nan shakes her head. "I don't know what I was thinking."

"Adidas?" Ruthie asks. "Isn't that a boy's name?"

"Well, I don't really know." Nan tries to recall what made her reject the preposterous moniker all those years ago. "I don't think that occurred to me. I just remember being certain she should be named after a shoe. I rejected several choices before—"

"As charming as this is," Mavis says. "I suspect you've gone off track already."

Cutting her eyes at Mavis, Nan leans toward Ruthie. "Why, do you know at one point I tried so many shoe names on the child I considered calling her Cinderella?"

Nan leans back, a smug smile on her face, as Ruthie chortles. Even Mavis, Nan notices, can't suppress a grin. "Well, I eventually moved away from shoes into herbs and made the obvious choice. Bay. The baby I thought I'd never have. We needed each other, and I do believe we loved each other immediately.

I know it doesn't always work like that, but it worked that way with us, and then…and then…"

"Her mother came back?" Ruthie offers.

"What? No." Nan shakes her head. "Not really."

"Not really?" Mavis asks. "What does that mean?"

"It means she didn't really come back," Ruthie says, turning to Nan as Mavis rolls her eyes. "Go on."

"We had the rest of July, all of August, and much of September. I was happy. I was the happiest I'd ever been, I think. I think I really was. I was also exhausted, of course. Well, you understand. You both had children. Imagine a newborn! At my age."

"I shudder at the thought," Mavis says, and Ruthie nods vigorously.

"I was just stepping out onto the porch with my cup of tea, planning to sit in the rocker and watch fall's arrival. I had already put Bay down upstairs and set the baby monitor out there. Well, you know how it is with babies. It takes twenty tasks to do one thing. I was worn out, and there he was, walking up to the house. I thought he was about fourteen."

"Who? Who?" Ruthie asks. "Did I miss something?"

"Just listen," Mavis says. "She hasn't gotten to that part yet."

It is a moment of reprieve, Nan thinks, an opportunity to take it back, make something up entirely, but even as she considers more lies, she continues with the truth.

"I thought he was fourteen, but it turns out he was two years older. He nodded and called me ma'am, like a man about to tip his hat. He was trying to use his best manners, I suspect, but right away I had that voice in my head that made me pretend with him. So I pretended he didn't frighten me, though he did.

"His car was in front of the house. A boy's car, you know. A teenage boy's car, parked on the side of the road squarely in front of the house. Anyway, I thought maybe he'd come for a remedy. I used to do that for a while, though I hadn't recently, and even then it had been mostly girls."

"A remedy?" Ruthie asks.

"Never mind," Mavis says.

"You know." Nan shrugs, not sure that Ruthie will ever understand. "Herbs and such. For colds, and unwanted…things."

"Unwanted things? But what do herbs have to do with… oh…"

Nan watches Ruthie's blue eyes widen in the dim light. "Oh," she says. "You mean babies?"

"Fetuses," Mavis snaps.

Nan expects to see disapproval register on Ruthie's face, but she tilts her head slightly and, after a moment, nods. "Of course," she says softly. "That makes sense."

"I couldn't fathom what he wanted, even as I sensed the danger. I was distracted by fear. One minute he was talking about his sister, and the next he was saying he'd come to take the baby. He had a right, he said."

Ruthie gasps. "Bay's father?"

"Her uncle."

"Dear God," Mavis says.

"He just sat right down in the porch rocker, as though we were friendly that way. He said his sister told him she left her baby here. I don't know how that conversation came about. I like to think they were close. I like to believe she confided in him because he was good, and that the things he said to me were because he was overwhelmed. Just the way I like to believe I am a better person than I was to him, generally."

"Oh, you are a wonderful person," Ruthie says. "Whatever would make you think otherwise?"

Nan appreciates the comment, but who knows what Ruthie will think by the end of this conversation? Why, it might even be too much for Mavis.

"She told him she spoke to me once when she dropped off a shoe donation. I am sorry to say I have no memory of that. While he was talking, all the time rocking and flicking that hair off his face and shrugging his shoulder the way he did, just one shoulder going up, like he couldn't make the effort for both, I realized I wasn't going to be able to fight it. Bay wasn't really mine. No matter how much I loved her, and I love her a lot."

"Oh, we know you do," Ruthie says.

"Without a doubt," adds Mavis.

"My whole life I felt like I didn't deserve happiness. You girls understand, don't you?"

Ruthie nods vigorously. Mavis clears her throat and then, with a quick gesture, pats Nan's knee, one tap, like a bird on a hot wire. They understand. Of course they do.

"I asked why he had shown up without his sister, and while his answer was circuitous, I came to comprehend she had not wanted him to interfere. Naturally, I wasn't going to hand Bay over to some random stranger just because he said he had a right, but as he talked and rocked and twitched, shrugging his shoulder, as though it was all nothing more than cute circumstance, I knew I wouldn't be able to put him off forever. Then I heard him say it. He couldn't have said that! I asked him to repeat it.

"He'd heard the rumors that Bay was some sort of 'freak.' He said"—Nan pauses, hardly able to formulate the words—"he had plans. A baby like her, a 'freak,' he said, could make money.

"He must have seen how horrified I was, because he told me it could all be done over the Internet. 'It's not like I'm talking about selling her to the circus or nothing like that,' he said, and actually laughed as if he was being funny."

"Not funny at all," says Ruthie, closing her lips in a tight line of disapproval.

"I didn't know what to do. I sat there, staring at my yard filled with shoes and dying flowers, the autumn grass and those odd spears that stand after the tiger lilies die. I looked at my elm tree, the leaves just turning gold, and thought how I had imagined someday Bay would climb those branches and lie under them for shade. I looked at the purple aster, the late sunflower, the unfathomable rose, and the foxgloves. I looked at the foxgloves while I listened to Bay breathing peacefully, with no idea of what had come for her, and I thought how love is like a monster, you know?"

"Yes I do," Ruthie says, so emphatically that for a moment Nan and Mavis both study their friend before Nan continues.

"I told him he looked thirsty, as if I could see such a thing in his freckled complexion.

"'As a matter of fact,' he said, 'I am.'

"'Just a minute,' I told him. 'Wait right here.' I went inside and locked the door while he continued rocking like he thought he could take that chair into space. I think he was feeling proud of himself for conducting business the way he was. As far as I know he did not hear the lock turn or suspect I considered him an enemy. I did not want him to follow me inside my house, our home.

"I walked right to the kitchen—straight to the glass of fox-gloves on the windowsill there and plucked them out. I did take the time to fill a different glass with water for the innocent flow-ers, just so you know. The old foxglove water was warm, and also had pieces of plant matter floating in it. I picked them out the best I could. Then I dropped in a few ice cubes and stirred in some sugar, and I sliced a lemon too.

"It's funny, isn't it, the things we do for love? What we did for Eve, what I did for Bay. Who knows? Who knows what his reason was? He never mentioned love, but who knows? People don't always say. I don't think he was evil. He was just a boy, really. In way over his head.

"When I brought him the drink, he smiled as he reached for it. He smiled in a way that made me hold back. His eyes were rather narrow, which initially made me think he was shrewd, but they widened when he saw the lemon, and I could see the boy he was.

"When his hand reached for that glass, I observed that he had thin, long fingers, sensitive, just like Bay.

"I thrust the glass at him. He took it without appearing to notice the shift in my attitude. I had a feeling he was used to rough exchange, and not much experienced with gifts. Even one as simple as sugar water with a twist of lemon and a faintly odd flavor, vaguely flowered, which he apparently enjoyed. He drank it right up.

"I sat down, rocking against any regret. I listened to the faint purr of Bay breathing while he talked. He told me how her mother used to drive up and down the road, trying to decide what to do. She'd heard how I helped girls, a long time ago. Eventually, she got the idea it would be a wonderful thing for a child to grow up in a big house with her own room, and a garden. She liked the shoe garden, especially. She was driving past when her water broke. She pulled over up the road a bit. She told her brother, and he told me that in spite of everything, she felt safe out here. She felt like this house provided protection. She'd been thinking about it all along, but until that night she wasn't sure what she would do. She took it as a sign. She said, he told me, she said, 'I know people say she's a witch, like that's a bad thing, but I think she's good.'

"He stopped talking and rocking all of a sudden. He just stopped. Like he'd seen a ghost. He was holding the empty glass and staring into space.

"You all right?" I asked.

"'Might have the flu,' he said. 'I guess I'll take her now.'

"That's when I said that there was no way I would ever let him near my girl. I told him to get off the porch. I didn't raise my voice. I didn't think there was a need. He looked surprised for just a second, and then he looked like he was used to adults turning on him. I got up and went into the house.

"Until that evening, I thought I was somebody who had once, years ago, made a terrible choice. I thought it was an exception, not a personality trait. I couldn't bear to look at that freckled face, turning pale right before my eyes. I went into the house and locked the door. I locked the back door too, just in case. I sure didn't want him coming into the kitchen and making a big mess that would have been difficult to explain. It was only moments later when I heard the crash. I knew right away what it was."

"He broke in?" Ruthie asks.

"No," Nan says. "Later they said he'd taken the corner too fast and hit the tree. The car was a misshapen mass, smoke snaking out, the front door open. It looked like a spaceship crash-landed on the road. I prepared myself to see something horrible, but he was lying there with his head back, his mouth agape, his eyes open. He looked, for all the world, astonished. Only one trickle of blood, here." Nan taps her forehead.

"Oh," Ruthie gasps. "Thank the stars he was all right."

Nan shakes her head. "They said he never knew what hit him, or what he hit. No one called for an autopsy. The cause of death was obvious. They said the impact was so hard his shoes flew off. One shoe did, and I didn't find it until much later, but I took the other one right off his foot. I don't know why. I can't always explain myself. I guess I thought I would plant it, you know, as a memorial, but I never managed to do so."

"That's understandable," Ruthie says.

Nan takes a deep breath. "It was quite the event. Covered at some length by the local paper, the way the death of someone young usually is. I saw her at the funeral, and I saw her a few times around town, afterward. She looked like Bay but with brown hair, a pretty girl who had sadness all around her like it was her own atmosphere. I hope never to see Bay so clouded like that. Anyway, they weren't from here. They were the kind of family that moves around a lot, and they did just that about a year later. I never told anyone what I did, and I never said anything to her. She knew who I was. If she wanted to talk, she knew where to find me."

In the silence that follows her confession, Nan finds herself remembering her summer garden: the vivacious display of opened blossoms, the murmur of bees, the flutter of butterflies and birds, the cacophony of her haunted season.

"Well, that certainly is a dramatic story," Ruthie says, shaking her coppery head.

I should be pleased, Nan thinks. *I should be happy to be misunderstood,* and she almost is before she is reminded of Mavis, clearing her throat.

"You can't be serious," she rasps.

"My goodness, of course she is," Ruthie says. "Why would she make such a story up?"

"You don't believe you killed the boy, do you?"

"What in the world makes you say a thing like that?" Ruthie asks. "You heard her. It was a car accident. You know how boys are, why my own—"

"Really, Nan, you can be so dramatic."

"Me, dramatic?" Nan would almost find this funny in another circumstance, but to be so accused by Mavis, of all people!

"You do have a bit of that streak in you," Ruthie says. "I have noticed."

Nan is stunned by the confluence of emotions; the release of having confessed, the pleasure of not being understood by Ruthie, the shame of Mavis's comprehension, the annoyance— the annoyance—of Mavis's impervious attitude.

"Foxgloves," Nan says, "are poisonous."

"Poison?" Ruthie squeaks.

Nan narrows her eyes at Ruthie. "You know that. You must know that. You made that entire flower feast without my help. I know Mavis is ignorant, but certainly you know about foxgloves."

"Well, yes but—"

"You don't need to insult me," Mavis says.

"Insult you?" Nan covers her mouth, surprised by the sudden arrival of tears.

"Are you crying?" Ruthie asks. "Is she crying? Why are you crying?"

"She thinks she murdered him," Mavis says.

"No. She's shaking her head no. See. You always read people wrong," Ruthie scolds Mavis. "Why are you crying, Nan? You can tell us."

"I did," Nan says behind the muffling hand, which she removes for clarity. "I killed him. I gave him foxglove water, and he went into cardiac arrest, and I killed him. I did."

She isn't sure what her two old friends are thinking, though neither turns away. Ruthie produces from some magic pocket a square of folded tissues, which Nan applies to her nose, while Mavis pokes at Nan's back in a gesture she assumes is meant as a reassuring pat.

"Now listen here," Ruthie says. "You need to stop this. I do know a thing or two about poison, and there wouldn't have been enough time for it to work. Even the Ebola virus takes a week."

"Well, I—"

"And I don't even know, I really don't, if water would work in any case. I've heard of the flowers and leaves being dangerous, but the water?"

"There wasn't time," Mavis says. "That's the point. You had nothing to do with that boy's death."

Nan remembers the look on his face when she ran to the car, feeling as if she had just swallowed a rose, thorns and all. He was dead already, but that look—that look of astonishment—she feels mirrored on her own face now. Is it possible? Could it be?

"But don't you understand?" Nan asks. "Does it even matter whether it worked or not? I meant to kill him. That's the point."

"Well, we'd certainly all be criminals if we were condemned for our murderous thoughts," Ruthie says.

"But it wasn't just a thought, I—"

"What?" Mavis raises her arms in that gesture of supplication.

"You destroyed the world? Is that it, Nan? Is everyone's death your fault?"

"I wanted him to die."

Ruthie snickers as she swats the air. "Oh, that's nothing."

"Let it go, Nan," Mavis says. "Quit blaming yourself for everything."

Nan opens her mouth, then snaps it shut. Is it possible they are right? Is it possible it wasn't her fault?

"Are we done?" Mavis asks. "I'm exhausted."

Imagine, Nan thinks, *just imagine for now that it was only a horrible accident.* She can't believe how tired she feels. *Imagine*, she thinks as she lets her head rest on the pillow between Mavis already breathing deeply and Ruthie yawning a peppermint scent. *Imagine.*

As Nan's eyes close, she thinks of *Sleeping Beauty*, though she's far past the age for that comparison. She remembers the description of everyone in the castle falling asleep, the entire household cast under a slumber spell, even a fly in the pantry. Perhaps that is why, at the border between awake and dreaming, she finds the boy leaning over to kiss her forehead with lips like ice. She opens her eyes but must still be sleeping, because he is dropping petals over her body; they drift slowly from his narrow fingers, like a flower snow.

BAY *Bay is a protection against witches, the devil, thunder, and lightning. The withering of a bay tree is a sign of death, but a healthy bay tree is a symbol of resurrection. Bay leaves placed under your pillow ensure pleasant dreams.*

B ay dreams all night of people she has never known and will never meet. They say words she won't remember in the morning, present her with tokens she cannot keep. It sounds disturbing, but it isn't. Karl drifts by, sullen; he pauses long enough to whisper in her ear. Bay, in her sleep, wipes at the mosquito buzzing there. She'll remember the strange dream of Karl pouring words into her as though she were a cup, but she'll never remember what he said. This will be all right upon waking, as it is in sleep. He treads softly in his bare feet, not letting the ground shake her awake, as if he cares. Stella appears as well. "Don't forget to tell them," she says, which Bay remembers, waking with the strange sensation that the words have been spoken and it was the voice that awoke her in the small clearing, her special place. But it's one of those awakenings that is still a dream; for an old woman stands there, not Mavis or Ruthie or Nan, the other one; she disappears like a drop of water in the sun.

Bay sits in the grass damp with dew, a few blades stuck to her face; she scratches her ear. One has to be careful of deer ticks, though she hasn't been careful so far. She inspects her arms, her legs, her feet, picking off the squashed blades of grass, wondering if she has ruined Ruthie's beautiful dress. Upon inspection, Bay is pleased that in one of life's little miracles, the dress has survived the careless night undamaged.

What is that smell, anyway? Bay can't believe her solution for dealing with the stink most of the summer has been to basically ignore it. Her feet hurt when she walks across the weeds with their toothy leaves guarding the forest's perimeter, but she doesn't have to go far into the forbidden wood before she sees the deer carcass, mostly bones now, interlocked like a sculpture with bits of dangling pelt.

Bay bites her lip and blinks, stepping away from the stench, backing right into the sharp point of a branch, which causes her to feel trapped in a fairy tale, the kind where trees attack, but that notion is quickly replaced by the scent of something sweet, which she investigates by simply turning around to discover the August-ripe apples, plump and red.

How can summer be over so soon? She has not gone to the river often enough, she has not eaten enough s'mores, she has not gotten tired of sitting on the rocker, watching fireflies, she has not grown weary of the hot days and short nights.

Bay feels sad at the thought of returning to school, but she's made no other plans, and besides, she can't abandon Thalia. Truth be told, she actually likes some of her classes. This year she's taking a course in cake decorating ("We didn't have classes like that when I was a girl," her Nana said). She also likes other things about fall: wearing sweaters, making squash soup and apple pie. She even likes Halloween, though when she was young, Bay hated the way she woke the next morning to find her jack-o'-lantern smashed, the porch decorations torn. Now she enjoys thinking of ways to trick the tricksters, watching through dark windows as the smashed pumpkins explode with water, or how, when they bend to write mean words on the sidewalk, they discover their own names written in chalk. Sometimes she gets them wrong, but she likes to watch them run. She likes to watch them squeal away in the dark. She likes to make them afraid. It's not very nice, but she puts up with them all year, and she deserves one night for revenge.

Using the skirt of her dress as a bowl for the apples, Bay blinks against the sun to watch a cardinal flit past, a flash of red, quickly gone. She squints, spying Stella, Thalia, and Howard, like strange flowers in the grass. Bay walks over to them, thinking they look so peaceful she is tempted to lie down beside them, to share their dreams. She turns to survey the yard. What is she looking for? Does she think her Nana, Mavis, and Ruthie were visited by the same strange compulsion to sleep on the ground like wild animals? Was there something in the air last night that enchanted everyone?

"What time is it?" Stella asks in a sleepy voice.

Bay looks at the sky, pretending she can read time there. "I don't know. Early, I think."

Stella brushes her dress, inspecting it for damage the way Bay inspected hers. "We have to talk."

"You already told me," Bay says. "I know."

"You do?"

"You forgive them all. You were never angry at any of them. You were glad they were there in your dark hour."

"I have no idea what you're talking about. I guess I freaked you out. I'm sorry, Bay. I was trying to do the right thing, okay? But I never said I forgave them."

Bay shrugs. What's the point?

"I mean, they're nice old ladies, but they can't just get away with it. You understand, don't you, Bay? I'm sorry to tell you this. I'm sorry, but I'm really beginning to suspect they had something to do with Eve's death."

Bay rolls her eyes. Stella is plain crazy, not in the mentally ill, needs-compassion-and-medication way, but in the she-says-stuff-that-doesn't-make-sense-and-there's-no-reasoning-with-her way.

Bay turns on her bare heels in the damp grass. She is suddenly consumed with an overwhelming need to make pie. She hopes there's enough butter.

"Bay? Bay, you understand, don't you?"

Why do you care? Bay wonders. *Why is it so important to you that I believe your lies?* She walks up the lawn to the back stairs and opens the door into the sunny kitchen. *I don't care if my Nana is a witch,* she thinks. *I'm going to make a pie. After everyone leaves, we'll sit on the porch to eat it, and everything will get back to normal around here. Stella's lies can't ruin the sweet truth of apple pie.*

APPLE *Apple blossoms are symbols of love, youth, beauty, and happiness. The apple, which has cancer-fighting properties, is associated with immortality.*

⌒

Apple pie, apple crumb cake, apple strudel, apple cider, and in the back of Nan's china cupboard, the apple wine she bought last fall at the Harvest Festival, subtly flavored with cloves and cinnamon, she was told. It's going to be either wonderful or nasty. Maybe that's why she still hasn't opened it. It's rather nice to recall something hidden in her cupboard that might be pleasant. Much better than remembering something that wasn't.

Nan opens her eyes, surprised to find herself lying on top of the bed, still wearing the velvet dress. She wonders how that happened, then remembers Ruthie and Mavis interrupting her dark plan. What had Nan been thinking? Clearly she'd lost her mind for a while.

Ruthie is no longer in the room, but Mavis is curled on her side, making a pillow of her folded hands. At some point she must have grown tired of the wig, because it's no longer on her head, which is bald and much smaller than Nan would have imagined, surprisingly smooth but spotted, like a quail's egg. The box rests in the center of the bed. Nan opens it in a hurry and pulls back the tissue, relieved to see Bay's caul safely nestled there. She refolds the tissue, smoothing it as she does, and puts the lid back on, absentmindedly tapping it with her fingers. How frightened she has been of the truth. For so long! How she's let this fear rule her.

"Are you practicing for the drum corps?"

"Oh, Mavis! Did I wake you?"

"I suppose you want me to lie."

"What? Oh, no." Nan giggles, feeling almost like a child again, caught in some innocent transgression.

"What time is it? I have a plane to catch."

Nan is surprised by the arrival of sorrow. Well, what did she expect, that this would go on forever? Wasn't she just yesterday counting the hours until everyone would leave and things could get back to normal? That is, if normal ever comes again. Who knows what Bay will think when Nan tells her everything.

"I find I have reached a time in my life," Mavis says, "where I must, in all seriousness ask, do you know where my hair is?"

Nan looks from the messy bedside table to the messy dresser to Nicholas lying curled on the floor. He rarely sleeps on the hard wood, and he is not sleeping on it now; lavender hair pokes out around him. Nan has to admit it's a very pretty combination, his white fur against the purple.

Still holding the box, she slides off the bed, prattling about how the wig must be around somewhere, making enough noise to wake Nicholas, who she nudges with her foot. He lowers his brow at her but stands to arch his back. Nan scoops up the wig, holding it close as she walks to the dresser. "Here it is," she says, pretending to find it there even as she opens the drawer and returns the box to its nest of underwear and slips.

"Is that clock working?"

Nan frowns at the red numbers. "I think so."

Mavis sits up slowly, stretches her arm toward Nan, who understands she is expected to hand over the wig. "I'm going to have to borrow your phone. I had an early flight. I should have brought another one of these with me." Mavis brushes and plucks the wig littered with dust and cat hair.

"Why don't you stay?" Nan says. It's a word burp. She doesn't know where it came from. She can't believe she's said it.

"Stay?"

"Don't you feel like we've only just got started? Don't you think it's too soon to go?"

"It feels sudden," Mavis says, "though I always knew it would come."

Nan realizes the conversation has veered, and the thought of where it has veered to makes her sad. She sits on the edge of the bed. "We have doctors too, of course," she says, and when Mavis starts to speak: "I understand you are done with all that. I'm just saying. If you changed your mind, there are doctors in town and a hospital in the city. If you changed your mind, Mavis. I wouldn't do anything against your wishes."

"My family—"

"Would always be welcome."

There is a silence during which, Nan notes, Mavis does not insist on leaving, but only picks at her wig, the morning sun shining on her bald head.

"Do you smell apples?" How Nan loves the seasons! "Stay. You can sit on the porch and watch the leaves change color. I'll make apple butter, and we'll have apple toast, apple muffins, and apple pancakes. We'll decorate the house for Halloween and eat all the candy we want, and make pumpkin soup." Nan claps her hands, one quick clap. She can't believe how excited she feels. "Stay."

"You paint a lovely picture," Mavis says, turning the wig in her hands as though it is something strange she's found. "But we both know death is a messy process."

"Stay," Nan says. "I'm not saying you have to be neat about it."

There is a soft knock on the door. "Nana, are you up?"

"Bay?"

Mavis hurriedly puts on the wig; there is no time to make adjustments. Bay steps into the room, wearing an apron over the butterfly dress. She looks from her Nana to Mavis on the bed. Are her Nana and Mavis girlfriend-girlfriends? This is all right, of course. Of course! People love who they love; Bay is certain she'd feel equally odd about the situation if it were a man in her Nana's bed.

"You look quite befuddled. Are you all right?"

Bay feels her eyes slide toward Mavis. She knows it's rude to stare, but what is going on with her hair?

"I have to tell you something," Bay says. They both nod, Mavis's hair sliding oddly.

"Do you know," says Nan, "that you smell like apples this morning?"

"I made a pie."

"Well, that's just lovely. What a lovely thing for you to do."

They are both looking at Bay, their eyes hooded but kind. Even Mavis.

"Bay, do you need to speak to me alone?"

"Don't mind me," Mavis says and begins to work her way across the bed. "I'll just disappear."

"No. Stay. You should probably hear this too."

Mavis scoots back, propping a pillow against the wall. Nan starts to help, but Mavis glares and says she's not an invalid.

"There's something I have to tell you," Bay says, struggling to begin. "You know how some people say you are a witch and how that always made me so mad?"

"I suspected that's bothered you."

"Well, I've thought about it a lot, and I want you to know I wouldn't change anything about you."

Nan folds her hands over her heart, as though it is in danger of floating away.

Bay parts her lips to say more, but the door opens, and Ruthie steps into the room. "Water is leaving." She wiggles her fingers beside her head. "I just had a brain wave, I guess. Not Water. Who would name their daughter Water? I meant to say Thalia."

"What about Thalia?" Bay asks, but even as she speaks, she hears the car pulling up in front of the house. She walks across the room to watch Thalia running in her bare feet, clutching her backpack, sleeping bag, and shoes.

"She has to leave," Ruthie says. "They're going somewhere today, and she has to go."

Thalia opens the car door, then looks up at the house. Bay waves. Luckily, Thalia sees her and waves back.

"Ruthie, she's still wearing your dress."

"Oh, do you think I could fit into that little thing? I told her to keep it."

Thalia ducks into the car. The door barely closed, Mrs. Desarti peels away.

"She seems like she's in a big hurry," Bay muses, not realizing she spoke out loud until Ruthie says that Thalia had asked her to deliver a message to Bay. Something about being "sorry she had to leave so early, but she had to go, she had to go…well, I'm afraid I don't remember where or why," Ruthie says. "I'm sorry, Bay, I know messages are important."

Bay turns from the window. Her Nana sits on the bed, still wearing the blue velvet. Mavis sits against the pillows, looking— what word should Bay use? Why Mavis, Bay is surprised to discover, looks quite loving, as does Ruthie, standing by the door, smiling, even her killer eyes, too close to the narrow nose, are filled with kindness.

"I didn't mean to interrupt," Ruthie says, turning to go.

"No, wait," says Bay. "I have to tell you something. All of you." She takes a deep breath. "I think you should know. Stella thinks you are all involved in murder."

"Murder?"

"I told her she's wrong, of course." Bay is interrupted by Mavis, grumbling as she inches across the bed, saying something about writers and secrets and how they should have sent Stella away as soon as she arrived. Nan says they need to set the record straight, and it's all just a horrible mix-up. Ruthie breaks into the noise without even raising her voice.

"He didn't die," she says. "I didn't actually kill him."

What is that expression her Nana uses? You could hear a petal drop? Yes, in the hot silence, Bay thinks she can hear moon-flower petals falling to the ground below the bedroom window.

"Who didn't die? Your husband?" Nan asks.

"No, not him. Why does everyone keep saying that? My husband is alive and…well, whatever he is. I grew out of all that years ago, don't you see?"

"Not really," says Nan. She starts to inch across the bed but finds her butt against Mavis's bony knee. "Move over. I have a feeling this is going to take a while."

Mavis scoots back, and Nan follows, stopping every few inches to adjust the skirt of her velvet dress, which twists beneath her in a most uncomfortable manner. Once situated, she signals Bay to join them, and she more or less throws herself across the bed, which emits a grunt from Mavis and a murmured apology from Bay. All three of them look up at Ruthie, who remains standing in front of the closed door, blinking teary eyes at them.

"I never told anyone," she says.

Bay nods. She wants to believe in Ruthie, she really does. She wants to believe there's a good explanation, though she can't imagine what it would be.

"I came back the summer after I got married," Ruthie says. "I already knew I'd made a mistake with my husband. I kept thinking about Eve, how if she'd been alive she never would have let me make such a bad choice. She would have protected me, even though I did such a poor job of protecting her. I aimed for his heart but hit his leg instead."

"Who? Who?" Mavis squawks.

"Mr. Leary," Ruthie says, shaking her head sorrowfully. "Eve's father."

"You shot him?"

Ruthie nods and brings a fist to her mouth, blocking her lips just as they turn up at the corner.

"I remember," Nan says. "I remember hearing how he'd been cleaning his gun. Everyone said that family just couldn't get a break, first his wife, then Eve, and—Ruthie—you shot him?"

"He couldn't tell anyone. I said if he did, I would tell everyone about what he did to Eve. He pretended like he didn't know what I was talking about. He called me a fat, silly girl, and then I shot him."

Ruthie blinks rapidly as they stare at her. "I had too much wine," she says. "It was just a graze. I didn't kill him." She looks directly at Bay. "I never drank again after that night. I felt miserable when I discovered Danny was home. Remember how he was? Always spying on us?"

Mavis and Nan nod solemnly, but Bay shakes her head, shocked that no one asks the obvious question. "Why? Why would you shoot Eve's father?"

Mavis, usually so direct, is suddenly unreasonably focused on picking feathers off her dress. Ruthie's eyes widen beneath the arch of raised brows, her lips pinched. Only Nan returns Bay's questioning look with a steady gaze as she says, "I think Bay and I need some time alone."

The bed groans, and Mavis does too as she slides across the mattress. Ruthie walks in her sensible, quiet shoes to wait by the bed, an easy arm for Mavis when it comes time to stand. Mavis, apparently noticing Bay looking at the crooked hair, reaches up and straightens it, winking as she does. A wig! Mavis and Ruthie walk out of the room arm in arm. Mavis isn't exactly leaning on Ruthie, but she does lean toward her.

"Didn't you have an early flight?" Ruthie asks. Nicholas makes it out just as the door closes behind them.

Nan isn't sure where to begin. *The silence is so expectant you could hear a petal drop,* she thinks. "Remember when I used to tell you fairy tales?"

Bay nods, though it's embarrassing to think of her love of fairy tales when she is well beyond the age for that sort of thing.

She hates to admit she still enjoys them. *I really must be some kind of freak.*

"What did you say?" Nan asks.

Had she spoken out loud? Bay takes a deep breath. "Why does it always smell like lavender in here?" She remembers the scent from since she was a little girl sitting in the bed, the big book of stories in her lap, watching Nan brush her long silver hair in the moonlight.

I have lied to you about making soap, Nan thinks. But isn't that a silly way to begin this serious subject? Won't she be in danger of getting completely off track with such a start? Why did she feel she had to keep up such a foolish pretense, anyway? Is Bay really going to care that the soap has been store-bought?

"Lavender oil," Nan says. "I sprinkle it in the closet."

Which is true. It hasn't all been lies.

Suddenly, and for no reason she can think of, Bay isn't sure she wants to know. She feels both thrilled and frightened, as though she is on a carnival ride, suddenly spinning in a new direction.

"This is a hard story to tell," Nan says.

"You don't have to."

"When I was young," Nan says. "When we were young, we were raised to believe that the best thing we could do with our lives was get married and have babies."

Nan stands so suddenly she worries for a moment she's had a stroke. How has she gone so quickly from the downy cushion of feather bed to the wooden floor? She turns to the window to draw the drapes, hoping to keep the heat out. Just the way, all those years ago, they shut the curtains in Eve's room, as though that could shelter her from the damage already done.

"Now, where was I?" Nan asks.

"Everyone wanted to get married and have babies."

"Well, not exactly." Nan flits about the room, lightly touching things: the curtain, the painting of trees, the dresser where she pauses to pick up a mug with the film of tea at the bottom, staring into it as though she could read the mold for guidance. "Not everyone wanted babies, but we were told we should. I, however, was privy to a different, secret world, and I never even had to leave my front porch to find it."

Nan sits on the edge of the bed. She would much rather talk about anything else, but Bay looks up at her, waiting. "The women came," Nan says, "in gloves and hats as though for a tea party, but they came at all hours. One night my father discovered me watching. He asked what I thought they came for. 'Well, it's obvious,' that's what I said. 'They're witches.'

"He didn't say I was wrong. He only said that if my mother saw me it could cause trouble, and if the women saw me, it could cause harm. 'Some secrets are meant to remain so,' he said. I understood. I knew about the burnings, of course."

Bay has heard about these things too, but what does this have to do with Ruthie shooting Eve's father? Bay looks at her Nana, sitting beside her so close now that it is hard to pretend any longer. She is so old she's not making sense.

"I loved Miss Winter's garden, but my mother, and the women she spent time with, thought it was a disgrace. It was all out of order, you see, wild. Miss Winter grew chives with her roses, well before it was popular to do so. Her cabbage nestled between the daisies. Her strawberries grew up the side of her house. My mother said it was a typical witch's garden. She wasn't evil, you know, your grandmother. Women back then didn't have power the way they do now. Well, they had it of course, but they weren't encouraged to use it. Anyway, she believed in a certain kind of reality and was terrified of anything that didn't conform to it.

"She's the one who sent me into our yard with pruning shears, sun hat, and gloves. I'm sure she later regretted it. While I was cutting back, Miss Winter was planting bulbs in the middle of the grass. When spring arrived, tulips and crocuses appeared in her yard as though they'd grown wild there. This probably sounds quite ordinary to you, lots of people garden like this now, but back then it was radical.

"Eventually, my mother realized I had formed a friendship with Miss Winter, who was not initially eager to chat with me, as I went about our yard cutting things, but by that time it was too late. Mother didn't want me to watch Miss Winter's cat when she went away, but I had already promised, and Mother had standards."

Poor Nana, Bay thinks. *What will we do if she has Alzheimer's?* But just in the time Bay let her own mind wander, Nan has made a big leap. Now she's talking about working at summer camp with Eve, Ruthie, and Mavis, how much fun they had, how free they felt, wild even. It was only through the intervention of the ladies from church that Eve was allowed to work at the camp, since after her mother died, she was needed at home.

"They told Mr. Leary that the money she earned would be a boon for the family. We earned very little really; most of it went for room and board. Everyone in town knew Eve needed a break. It took me years to realize how culpable they all were. Like everyone else, her father was interested in appearances, so he agreed. On the condition that she come home for the occasional weekend, 'to take care of things.' That's what he said."

Nan catches her breath. Here she is, doing nothing more than sitting on her comfortable bed, telling her daughter a story. Why does she feel like she's been running for a long time? *Are you listening? Are you here? Do you know how sorry I am?*

"Nana? Are you all right?"

"Eve was not a bad girl. Eve was a very, very good girl. She never wanted to cause any trouble."

Wasn't I just a girl myself? Nan thinks. *Wasn't I just running through the snow?*

"Nana, you don't have to—"

"No, Bay, I really do. I should have done this a long time ago. Eve was pregnant."

Bay shakes her head. "But I still don't understand why Ruthie shot Eve's father."

Even after all these years, Nan finds the words too bitter to speak. She simply looks at Bay and thinks, *Why, you are only a few years younger than we were then.*

"Wait," Bay says, "did Eve's father...did he molest her?"

Nan pats Bay's knee. "You young people know so much more about these things than we did. It is a terrible bit of calculation. None of us had heard of such a thing, and it took me far too long to figure it out."

Bay wonders how she has arrived here. Wasn't she just a little girl listening to fairy tales in this very bed? Wasn't she just in the kitchen making apple pie? Wasn't she feeling, only an hour ago, that everything would get back to normal soon? How has she come to this place where the terrible stories are true?

"Can you imagine? Can you believe such a thing? Her own father... We were trying to help her. We were trying to save her. We weren't murderers, but what if we had taken her to someone else? What if we had taken her to Miss Winter, which is where everyone assumed she went? What if we had taken her there instead of to the so-called doctor in the city? And what if, when things turned bad, we had not waited so long?"

Bay shakes her head. Poor Nana, poor Eve, poor Mavis and Ruthie!

"My neighbor, old Miss Winter, with her crazy garden and weird-smelling herbs, helped girls in trouble, you know. It was quite illegal, of course. It was all illegal back then. But Eve didn't go to her. Oh no, we had to do the 'right thing.' In the midst of committing this crime, we became provincial. We took her to a doctor. Or so he said. Who knows what he was? He was bad at it.

"Then later, when Eve was dying, we fooled ourselves into

believing she wasn't. That's why I say don't fool yourself about reality, Bay, it's never worth it. In the morning, I came to my senses, that's what it felt like, as though I had been cast under a spell. For a long time I blamed Mavis for it, as though she had power over me. But all of us were just muddling through, even her.

"People saw us running down the street in the snow. People saw me and Miss Winter, and they assumed they knew what they had seen. The night of Eve's funeral, someone burned down Grace Winter's house. Her poor cat, Fairy, died. Miss Winter wasn't hurt, physically that is. She left town before the cinders burned out."

"But, Nana, you were so young, and you were afraid, and—"

"This was a terrible thing, Bay. I watched my friend die in her bed, and then I let the whole town think Grace Winter killed her. I am sorry to tell you this about me, but it's time you know.

"When I left after my parents died, I thought I could leave that part of me in the empty lot where Grace Winter's house once stood. I was a weak person, Bay, I am sorry to say. All I did was take some pennyroyal from the wild garden that grew where her house had been while Ruthie, our Ruthie, of all people, did what no one else had the courage to do. She shot Eve's father. Our Ruthie did that, and even after all these years, I only wish she had better aim."

Bay stares at her Nana, sitting in bed in the velvet dress, her white hair hanging around her wrinkled face. Who would ever guess that this sweet old woman had such a secret?

"We always said we'd be friends forever, but we didn't get along after Eve's funeral. I believe my father suspected; maybe not everything, but some of the truth. He couldn't talk to me about it, though. I'm not sure it would have helped if he tried. We girls blamed one another, you see, and we blamed ourselves. I'm not sure anyone could have saved us from what we did and didn't do.

"I never thought I'd be happy again, and then you came along, and I was. Happy, I mean. I didn't want you to struggle the way I have, and because of that I am afraid I overprotected you. Everyone has power. We weren't entirely helpless. We had power, and we did the wrong thing with it. Which brings me to you."

The room is too warm. Whatever made Bay think autumn was near? Why is her Nana looking at her like this? Bay doesn't even realize she's shaking her head, until Nan says, "Yes. It's time. Don't interrupt. You have to listen, Bay. You've lived in fantasy long enough."

"I've lived in fantasy?"

"Being born with a caul is perfectly natural. I know you think it's disturbing, but it isn't. It's amniotic membrane, that's all, formed over your face. You don't need to make that sour-lemon expression, Bay. Some people call it being born behind the veil. It's not a veil of obstruction; it's the veil that separates you from the obstructions most of us suffer. As long as your caul is safe, your gifts are too. You can't drown. You'll be able to predict the weather. You have a talent for healing."

"I really don't want to talk about this," Bay says. She wants to get off the bed, leave the room, and rewind time. She remembers how happy she felt, just this morning, cutting apples for the pie.

"You have a talent for healing, and—"

"Please, Nana, stop."

"You will see ghosts."

"Not if I don't want to, right?"

"You will see them whether you want to or not."

"But I don't want to see ghosts. I don't want to be scared all the time. I just want to be normal."

"Who said anything about being scared all the time? You really don't need to make a big production out of this, Bay. Plenty of people see ghosts. It's just that most of us see them from a great distance until we are close to death ourselves. Your gift is really a matter of focus."

Bay is sorry that Thalia left. Today would be a good day for a friend. "Will they hurt me?"

"Oh, no," says Nan. "We're not talking horror movies here. Look at me. I've had a ghost or three following me for years."

Bay closes her eyes. This is too much to absorb. "Are you saying you're almost dead?"

"What?" Nan shakes her head, trying to compute backward to understand how Bay came to this conclusion. "You mean my ghosts? No, no, you have to pay attention. They are very far away, barely visible. Even that started happening only after I moved here, and I was still quite young then. It's because of this house."

"This house? But...wait. Who would...Eve? And Miss Winter? Was she an old lady? I think I saw her."

"Yes, Bay. I do too. I can only guess how much she hates me. I have to live with that. But, Bay, it would break my heart if you hated me too."

"Oh, Nana, who could ever hate you? You were trying to do the right thing. You were just... Nana, wait, I wanted to tell you! Last night, I had this dream. I fell asleep in my special place, and I dreamt that all these people passed through. Most of them just walked past, but one stopped to talk to me. Karl! Karl whispered something in my ear, but I don't know what he said. And I saw her, Miss Winter, I think. Actually, I thought I was awake, but I must have still been asleep, because she disappeared. She didn't say anything, Nana. I don't know what she wants. I'm sorry."

"But you see, Bay, even that is some help to me. Maybe she's more at peace than I thought. It's bad enough that I ruined her life. I have always feared I ruined her death as well. Have you seen anyone else?"

Bay shakes her head. "Sorry."

"Are you sure?"

"Sorry." What's the good of seeing ghosts if she can't do

anything about it? *Here I am*, Bay thinks, just accepting it. *Like, well, okay, I see ghosts.*

"It's all right, dear."

"I wish I could help."

"Don't give it another thought. Do you want it? The caul, I mean? It is yours and—"

"No, Nana. You keep it for now, okay? I know it'll be safe with you."

Nan nods vehemently, as if there's never been any doubt. "Oh, I hope you don't mind. I invited Mavis to stay with us."

Bay pretends she doesn't mind, though she's been harboring the pleasant thought of sharing apple pie with her Nana after everyone has gone, sitting in the rockers on the porch, just the two of them again, everything back to normal.

Nan smells the salt, but it doesn't bother her. She is feeling so relieved, pleased at how well everything went, that she almost forgets the rest. Bay is standing by the bed, leaning over to kiss Nan on her cheek when she says, "Wait. There's more."

More? Bay can't imagine. What? Unicorns? Fairies? Vampires?

"Your birth mother," Nan says. "I know her name."

CINNAMON *Cinnamon is derived from the inner bark of a tree of the laurel family. It is used as a perfume and anointing oil. In early times, it ranked in value with gold and frankincense. Cinnamon is said to possess excellent properties for immunity against disease.*

⌒

Nan thinks that went fairly well, actually. The big secrets she's been afraid of telling are told. The house still stands. The garden, it is assumed, still blossoms and dies, doing the business of gardens, more or less. The world still spins. The sun still shines and, Nan suspects, darkness will fall at the expected hour.

Thank goodness the dress has a side zipper; she can't wait to get out of it. What a lovely dinner they had! It's been a good weekend, a strange weekend, but good. Nan brings the garment to her nose, smelling it to determine if it goes to the dry cleaner or back on the hanger. She is distressed to discover how over-whelming the scent is. It is not the sweaty smell of her youth, but a sour odor underneath the scent of camphor. Has she been walking around smelling like something rotting in mothballs? She drops the dress to the closet floor. She hasn't taken anything to the dry cleaner in years. She wonders if she'll bother to take the dress; after all, when will she ever wear it again? On second thought, she determines to attend to it. Nan has tried to give Bay a good life, a carefree childhood, but knows that ever since Bay was a little girl, she has worried about death. Bay thinks this is her secret, but it isn't.

There's no getting around it, Nan thinks as she changes into her favorite housedress, so old the cotton is tissue-soft and unfortunately easy to tear, as evidenced by the small holes throughout. She can't live forever. The least she can do is not leave extra laundry for Bay to deal with.

Nan brushes her hair, a few deft strokes and she is done. How distressing it was, all those years ago when her hair began falling out. How stubbornly she has clung to what remains and the idea that pulled into a bun, as she is doing now, her hair looks fuller. And yet, how fortunate she is to not have suffered hair loss the way Mavis did.

Nan resists the temptation to step into Bay's bedroom to check on her. One of the hardest things about mothering teenagers is learning that sometimes you just have to leave them alone with their misery. Bay's door is closed, but Nan thinks she hears crying. What Nan wouldn't give to take it all away. Why, she'd give everything. Last night, she almost gave more than it is her right to give. It breaks Nan's heart, it really does, to think of Bay hurting like this. But at least she knows what she's dealing with. At least she knows what is real.

Nan slowly descends the stairs. She is tired, experiencing a new pain in her bones, and she is weary, though happy that the headache that's been plaguing her is gone. She must have been a little crazy last night to consider tearing Bay's caul like an old dust rag. Whatever came over her? She decides to blame the wine.

The kitchen is bright with morning sun, scented by the apple pie resting on the cooling rack at the center of the small table where Mavis and Ruthie sit, arguing.

"We have to make sure it's set out long enough," Ruthie says, "or it'll be running."

"Who cares?" Mavis says. "I'll eat it with a spoon."

"You can't eat pie with a spoon."

"Oh, for goodness sake," Nan says by way of salutation. "Let's not turn apple pie into a debate."

"All right," Mavis says, "we cut it, and those of us who want to eat it can, and those who don't want to, don't."

"But if you cut it before it sets—"

"Here's the knife," Nan says, "and the server. Who wants milk?"

The three of them are sitting crouched around the small table, murmuring how good the pie is, when Stella enters the kitchen, showered and changed, her short hair in damp spikes around her face like an angry porcupine.

As if they'd come to some agreement, though they had not; as if they were all suddenly fourteen again, they simply ignore her. Nan is aware of how rude this is, how immature, how futile, but she is savoring the power the three of them create when they are in agreement.

"Okay, I get it," Stella says. "Bay told you. But I'm giving you an opportunity to explain yourselves and tell your side of the story."

"If you're so interested in our side, why didn't you contact us before you'd made up your mind about it?" Nan asks.

Stella doesn't move her head, but glances sideways. Nan follows her focus to Ruthie, who is using her pinky finger to tuck an errant pie crumb into her mouth. "Oh, didn't I mention? I invited Stella here this weekend," she says.

"Well, aren't you turning out to be Miss Devious?" Mavis asks.

"She already had her ideas. I thought this would give her a chance to get to know us better. To see how we really are."

Nan waits for Mavis to say something smart and cruel, but instead she attacks the pie with her spoon, entirely focused on the task. Ruthie appears to be concentrating on finding crumbs so small Nan can't see them, jabbing the table with the point of her index finger.

"I'm here," Stella says. "This is your chance. Though I can see why you wouldn't want to talk about it. What can you possibly say?"

Mavis looks up from the pie, a juice-dripping spoon poised in her hand. She looks at Nan; they turn to Ruthie, who stops jabbing crumbs with her finger to return their gaze, her thin eyebrows raised.

"You better get your recording device," Mavis says.

"You'll talk to me?"

"You might want to bring in a chair from the dining room," says Nan. "This is going to take some time."

The morning light fills the room as they talk, so bright that for a while no eye contact can be made. It reminds Nan of something like the lingering feeling of a dream, like being caught between time and space, memory and absence.

How easy this is, Nan thinks as she listens and adds details—*after all these years, how easy it is to tell the story, which is not a scandal after all.* "We were so young," she blurts out at one point, and a cinnamon-scented hush settles over the room.

"Yes," Mavis says. "And now look at us."

"We're like soldiers," Ruthie says.

"Whatever do you mean?" Nan asks.

"Well, you know," says Ruthie. "Home at last."

MARIGOLD *Marigold blossoms are used in broths as a tonic against winter's wind and chill. The flower, rubbed on a bee sting, is said to bring relief. Marigold is known as a death flower.*

～○

B ay sits at the edge of her bed, horrified. Karl, her uncle? That, in itself, is enough to make her want to puke, and thinking he is dead doesn't exactly make her feel better. What kind of uncle would he have been? She doesn't think she'd like him. She doesn't like him. It was sweet though, wasn't it, the way he came to introduce himself, bringing a pot of marigolds for Nan? How horrible that he died right afterward. *Who knows,* Bay thinks, *maybe he would be different if he lived. Maybe dying made him strange. Maybe he would have been a wonderful uncle.* Bay tries to believe this, but finds it difficult. Karl? Dead? Her uncle? Wonderful?

She looks around the room, afraid of what she'll see, though it's just her room with its slanted ceiling. She walks over to look out the little window into the backyard at the shoe garden shimmering in the August sun. When she sees the shadowed figure near the lilacs, her heart beats rapidly. She is trapped in her life, this ghost-filled world. She leans closer to get a better look.

Oh, Howard.

As soon as Bay opens her bedroom door, she hears their voices rising from the kitchen and is surprised to discover that she is happy they haven't left yet. She tries to decide how to act. It isn't that she means to be deceptive, it's just that she is feeling so many things; it's hard to know what she feels most.

Nan, Mavis, Ruthie, and Stella sit crowded around the kitchen table, the pie Bay had baked earlier reduced to crumbs. They are laughing. Bay doesn't know what's going on. The laughter is a good sign, though she is annoyed that no one thought to leave a slice for her. They don't even notice as she walks through the kitchen and out the back door.

How strange, Bay thinks, *as if I am invisible, though apparently the pie wasn't.* It's annoying that they ate the whole thing, but also, she feels sort of proud. "Bay's Pies," she thinks, imagining the name of her website, or "Pies by Bay," but will pies be enough? She might need cakes. After all, as hard as it is to believe, not everyone loves pie.

Howard, sitting in the grass with his back toward Bay, turns at her approach.

"What's up?" Bay asks, dropping to the ground like a puppet severed of her strings.

Howard is still wearing last night's pants, the tie and jacket abandoned, the white shirt unbuttoned with the sleeves rolled up. He shakes his head like he can't believe what he's saying. "I'm going to Africa. With Mavis."

"What do you mean? Mavis is staying here."

"Don't say anything to Nan until Mavis tells her. We talked this morning. She says she's always wanted to go, and she figures it's now or never. I'm going to be her companion, you know, to carry the heavy stuff, and when things get bad, I'll stay with her."

"What do you mean when things get bad?" Bay asks. "Are you dropping out of school? What about your parents?"

"They're not going to be happy, but I have to live my life, you know? Things are going to get bad because of Mavis dying."

Everything is changing, Bay thinks. The lavender looks leggy, like a giant spider blossomed with occasional purple. There is a scattering of leaves at the base of the lilacs, not autumn-colored yet. This morning she made an apple pie, learned what happened to Eve, found out the name of her birth mother, and that Karl is her uncle. And now this: Mavis is dying. Why didn't Bay realize? It seems so obvious. She wonders how she missed it. It makes no sense. How could she see ghosts (supposedly) and not see what was happening right in front of her?

They sit together like two old friends. In a few weeks, Howard will be in Africa; they already have their passports. "She's been renewing hers for years," he says. "She always meant to go." Mavis and Howard will be in Africa. Bay will be back at school.

Bay is surprised she didn't immediately look her mother up on Facebook. For now, at least, it seems enough to know that she can. "Truth waits," Nan said earlier. Bay realizes she's glad it does. She's curious, of course, but she doesn't have to know right away. She's almost positive she will look, eventually, but maybe not. It's enough, for now, to know she can; she has a choice, unlike with the ghosts. Bay isn't happy about them. She resents it even, but in the bright afternoon it seems more an inconvenience than a disaster. Maybe they'll go away if she just ignores them. Maybe that's what they've already done. After all, the not-drowning thing is good, and it is nice to be certain of the weather, she never gets caught unprepared. Finally, she sort of likes the idea of healing with cake or pie, though she is uncertain of the recipe.

Bay lies back on the grass. After a moment, Howard joins her. Together they lie side by side, not speaking, watching the clouds drift overhead, like two old friends who no longer need to fill the silence.

ELM *The elm tree is a symbol of communication, love, letting go, and freedom. Don't stand under elm trees; they have a habit of dropping heavy branches without warning. An elm tree marks the crossroads leading to the fairy world. Elm wood was traditionally used for coffins.*

⟳

Because Halloween falls on a weekend this year, Bay has an entire day free of the distractions of school to think about what the night might bring. Ever since she's found out about her talent, she's expected the haunting to begin, though it still hasn't. Strangely, she is surprised to discover that mixed with her fear is a vague feeling of excitement. Hope, even. Maybe it won't be horrible. Is it possible it would even be kind of fun, as Thalia (sworn to secrecy) says it will be?

The only experience Bay can claim so far is poor old Miss Winter, who didn't say a thing when Bay saw her, and Karl, who she hasn't seen since the night of the Flower Feast when he whispered to her while she was asleep. She still isn't sure she believes he's the same boy who died in front of her house. After all, there certainly can be more than one person named Karl in the world. Sometimes she thinks that the Karl she knew just moved on to wherever he was going. In fact, she thinks there's a good chance that's what he told her. Though that was a dream and probably doesn't count.

The Halloween ghosts made of old sheets, tissue paper, and webby fabric, dangling from porch railings and tree branches, mock Bay with black eyes and gaped mouths. "You want us," they seem to say. "Are you sure?"

She is not. Yet, there is something exciting, Bay thinks, in believing she will be able to communicate with the dead. Weird? Yes, but maybe weird in a good way. She doesn't know. How can she know?

She goes into town with her Nana for chocolate chips, eggs and butter, gummy worms (though Bay has outgrown her taste for them years ago, they seem to give Nan such pleasure), M&M's, red licorice (another favorite of Nan's), and the ingredients for beef stew. Bay is thinking about becoming a vegetarian but decides not to say anything about it yet, because she loves beef stew.

On the drive home from the store, they point out vibrant leaf displays to each other, as though the season's change is street art. After the groceries are brought into the house and put away, Bay announces she's going to take a nap. Nan, who is sitting at the computer table in the kitchen, says they've gotten an email from Mavis and Howard, with a photograph attached.

They stand in front of a split-rail fence, the sky blossomed behind them. Mavis is wearing one of her turbans, bright orange, pinned at the front with something that looks like glass. She is wrapped in a purple shawl that covers much of her dress, which is long and reminds Bay of the leaves, dyed as it is with all the shades of fire, including the faint bit of blue at the center of a flame.

"She looks good," Bay says. "I think she's getting better."

Beside Mavis stands Howard, handsome in a simple T-shirt and khakis.

"What's it say?" Bay asks.

"Eat. Play. Drink. Sleep. Repeat," says Nan.

"That's it?"

Nan nods.

Bay laughs. "Mavis must have written that one; Howard would say more," she says, yawning loudly as she goes up the stairs.

"How are you?" Nan types, then backstrokes out the words. If Mavis wanted to spend her last weeks recording every aspect of dying, she would have done so. Instead, Nan writes a cheery account of the Halloween preparations, the carved pumpkins perched on the porch, the bowls filled with candy.

How dark the afternoons are; it isn't too early to light the candles, and she better get the stew started, or they'll be eating at midnight. With a grand gesture, a sweep of her hand as though conducting a symphony, Nan clicks the cursor and sends her response to Africa.

"Yoo-hoodle, anyone home?"

Before Nan can respond, Ruthie pushes through the kitchen door, bringing with her the scent of stew rising from the large cast-iron pot she carries in her hot-pad-gloved hands.

"There you are! I hope you can help," Ruthie says. "I got carried away and made an enormous amount of beef stew. Enough to feed an entire… Nan, are you all right?"

Nan wonders why it has taken her so long to realize the truth about Ruthie. At first there was just all the business with Bay, and the past that existed between Mavis, Ruthie, and Nan; after all that was straightened out, there was so much activity, first with Mavis and Howard going to Africa, then with Ruthie announcing her plans to buy the old cabin down the road. "For a melody," as Ruthie said over and over again because, seriously, who would ever want to live in such a run-down little place? Though it fixed up very well. Nan was kept so busy she almost didn't get the bulbs in before the ground froze. It must have been all the distraction that prevented her from seeing clearly.

"I'm just going to set it on your stove. I'll turn the heat on low. That should keep it simmering. You and Bay can eat whenever you're ready."

"Don't you want to stay?" Nan asks, hoping Ruthie will decline.

"Oh, I couldn't possibly. There's so much to do. You know, for the little monsters and the like."

"They don't really come out this far," Nan says. "I thought Bay would have told you."

"Oh, well." Ruthie looks up at where the wall meets the ceiling, then out the window over the sink. "I left the fire going. I didn't plan to be gone long. Besides, I still have to carve my turnip."

Her turnip? Nan is tempted to ask, but determines not to be distracted. "Ruthie, I'm surprised you celebrate Halloween. Isn't it, you know, against your beliefs?"

Ruthie can't seem to help herself. She giggles, a light, airy sound like bells.

"Why did you say all that?" Nan asks. "When you first came in August? Why did you say all that stuff about exorcists for witches?"

Ruthie reaches into the bowl of gummy worms for a long red one with green, blue, and yellow markings.

"Why did you lie?"

Ruthie acts like she hasn't been caught at all. She sucks on the gummy worm, letting it dangle from her mouth, lifting the lid off the kettle with one hand and reaching for a wooden spoon with the other.

"Ruthie," Nan says, using the tone she used to employ with Bay when she was younger and had done something wrong.

Ruthie looks sideways at Nan. Then, apparently seeing something definitive in her expression, sets the spoon on the spoon rest, puts the lid back on the pot, and removes the remains of the gummy worm from her mouth. "Nan, you know how it is. We can't just go around revealing what we are. It upsets people. It causes trouble. Why do you think my husband tried to poison me? And at first I wasn't sure. You understand, don't you? I wasn't sure what you and Mavis believed, and then, after a while it was just kind of fun to see what I could get away with."

Nan sits back with a gasp. Of course. It all makes so much sense now, except—"I could never tell you were lying. That's the thing I do best."

"Oh, well," Ruthie says, "a little kitchen magic is a remedy for that. Didn't you notice all the lemon?"

"But—"

"I'm sorry, Nan, I know you have lots to talk about, but I have to get going. This is a big holiday for me."

"Well, yes, of course," Nan says, but she is so stunned she doesn't even wonder what Ruthie's plans are, exactly, until she has already kissed Nan on the cheek and walked, humming, out of the kitchen.

The simmering stew fills the room with an enticing, earthy aroma. Nan decides to have just a little taste, but after dipping the spoon into the large pot several times, she ladles a small bowl for herself. Why is this so delicious? Potatoes, sweet onions, carrots, hunks of tender meat, salt and pepper, of course, but what is the secret ingredient? She can't figure it out.

Of course! Of course Ruthie would use kitchen magic to cover her lies. Nan wonders what all those lies might have been. How could Ruthie not realize how much soup she was making? How can she not have noticed all the potatoes being peeled, the carrots scraped, and the rest? *No*, Nan thinks, spooning stew into her mouth, savoring the flavor, *the fact is that Ruthie got away with so much because she let everyone believe she was simple. What a clever disguise.*

Nan places the empty bowl in the sink, resolving to save her appetite for later. It's time to mix together the batter for the chocolate chip cookies so they'll be ready for baking tonight when she and Bay sit around the kitchen table, pretending someone might actually come for treats this year, and not just for tricks.

Though it is only afternoon, it is almost November, and the gloaming comes early. Nan likes the cast of light that others find uncomfortable. She creams the butter with the sugar, adds the vanilla and the eggs, stirs in the dry ingredients. She pours in extra chocolate chips. "You can't have too much chocolate," she says, wondering if anyone is listening.

She hasn't tasted ash since the weekend of the Flower Feast. Bay says there aren't any ghosts around, but Bay is still learning to manage her talent. Nan doesn't think she can give much credit, at this time, to Bay's assessment of the spirit population. An hour ago, Nan might have found this odd, but that was before she discovered her own weakness in assessment.

She puts the cookie dough into the refrigerator, and places the dirty dishes in the sink beside the soup bowl. She'll do the dishes later. Now she's going to light the candles. They keep the front light on, a signal for trick-or-treaters to come, though they never do. Well, the tricksters come, of course. Nan turns the kitchen light off. The flames flicker for a moment and settle back. She goes throughout the rooms, Nicholas weaving between her feet, which slows her considerably.

When the downstairs glows with golden light and the shadows move across the walls, Nan returns to the kitchen, happy to find Bay sitting at the table with her legs tucked beneath her, holding her own small bowl of stew.

"I'm just having a little," she says. "This is the best ever."

"Ruthie made it. She made too much and brought over the extra."

"Ruthie was here?"

Bay has developed a deep affection for Ruthie that Nan is happy she no longer has to monitor.

"When did Stella get here? Are we having another party?"

"Not Stella. Ruthie."

Bay looks into her small bowl and sets it, too hard, on the table. Nan is worried for a moment that Bay is upset, but her expression is completely placid. The girl just hasn't learned her own strength yet.

"No, Nana," Bay says. "I know Ruthie made the stew, but I'm asking about Stella. Where is she?"

"I imagine in the city," says Nan. "Working on her book."

"But she was just in my bedroom. I was talking to her."

"You were…" Nan sits down so suddenly, she thinks it was only lucky she landed in a chair. "What did she say?"

Bay shrugs, that old one-shoulder shrug of hers. "I was half-asleep. She was saying the same things she said that night. She said to make sure to tell you and Ruthie and Mavis that she never blamed you. All of you were a light in her darkest hour. I guess she's happy rewriting her book."

"You never told me she said that."

"I did, Nana. Didn't I? I meant to, at least. Nana! Do you think Stella's got multiple personality disorder or something?"

"No," Nan says. Where does the child get such ideas? "Think, Bay. Did she say anything else?"

"Where'd she go, anyway?" Bay peers around the room as if expecting to find Stella hidden in the shadows. She lowers her voice. "I know you guys made up and everything, but she still makes me kind of nervous."

"How did she look? What was she wearing?"

"She looked, well, you know, how she usually has such cute clothes but sometimes wears that big old dress for some reason. She was wearing that. I'm really surprised she likes it so much. It doesn't look good on her at all, it's so old-fashioned and—" Bay stops in midsentence, looking up at Nan, wide-eyed.

Nan hesitates; how will Bay react? It would be easy enough to lie. Well, not entirely easy, it would have to be quite a good lie. Nan reminds herself that she has already rejected any notion of interfering with Bay's power.

For some reason, Bay can't say the word, ghost. She can barely think it. It's like it has suddenly grown claws, or something. "She didn't look like…she didn't look dead," Bay says.

Nan nods, but clearly she is distracted. "She said she never blamed us? Did she really say that?"

"Yes," Bay says, feeling not the horrible fear she had worried about, but happy to deliver this message.

If anyone had asked Nan how she would respond if, through magic or circumstance, she would learn that Eve forgave them a long time ago, she would have thought she'd hardly respond at all. It's one thing to be forgiven by someone else, another to forgive yourself, she might have said. But now that it's happened, she has placed her hands over her face, as though shielding her eyes from a terrible brightness.

"Nana, Nana?"

"I'm all right."

"But Nana, look."

Nan doesn't know what to expect. Eve? Grace Winter? Ghosts? Angels? Or something worse?

Bay points behind Nan's shoulder. "Look."

With slight trepidation, Nan turns.

"Nana," Bay whispers. "It's snowing."

Nan rises slowly, shuffling across the kitchen to look out the window, past the pinecones that litter the sill, barely noting the glass of foxglove with its silent bells. *How funny it is,* Nan thinks, *that in some system of counterbalance she has never understood, the more snow that falls, the more she feels released.* The snow falls on the brown grass and on the shoe garden of October flowers with its stalky stems and dried blossoms. The snow falls, and Nan feels strangely light. She might at any moment rise out of her clogs and fly above her house and garden, like a sparrow. The snow falls, and Nan covers her mouth with one hand, as though to prevent the exhalation that will release her from the gravity of a world more beautiful than anything she deserves.

NANA HOLLY *Nana is a compact species of the holly plant, which is known to protect homes from malevolent fairies or allow good fairies to take shelter. It is used for decoration at the feast of Saturnalia, the festival of light. Holly symbolizes hope in the midst of despair.*

⟡

There is salt snow and wet snow, hard snow and crystalline snow, as though fake and part of a giant snow globe. There is graupel, the snow skiers love because it acts like ball bearings beneath fluffy snow, perfect for gliding across. There is wild snow, the kind that swirls across the sky like an angry child's scribble. And there is lace snow, which falls delicately, revealing to any close observer the various patterns of flakes. The snow Nan gets for her birthday that December is a combination of all these types, and it has been falling all day.

Nan is glad no one she knows is traveling. The road conditions can't be good. She turned off the radio hours ago, after reading the email from Howard. She shut everything off, the computer, the radio, even the lights. The stove is on, and the oven, of course. The dining room table is set. She used the lace tablecloth and pink china. The candles are lit. She stands at the front door in her blue velvet dress, looking out the window, waiting.

In spite of everything, when she sees them coming, and she is certain it is them—who else would it be?—she claps her hands, one happy clap, causing the candles throughout the house to tremble.

They come up the snowy hill, passing beneath the great elm with its yearning branches, the lacy flakes doing nothing to dampen the little flames flickering on the cake. *Only Ruthie*, Nan thinks, *would carry a lit birthday cake through the snow*. Bay, wearing her coat unbuttoned, as though it were a warm spring evening, sees Nan and waves an ungloved hand at her.

She's going to catch cold, Nan thinks, opening the door. Ruthie, also apparently unaffected by the weather, her back straight, head erect, smiles beneath the close-set blue eyes. She insists they can't come inside until the candles are blown out. Bay starts to explain how they don't do that, but Nan leans into the falling snow to make her wish, enjoying the flakes on her face, the cold sting. (*Snow bees*, that's what Andersen called them.) The cake's beautifully feathered white frosting glitters with snow. "Bay did it herself," Ruthie says in response to Nan's compliment as they shrug off their coats. When Bay takes the wet things to hang in the bathroom, Ruthie leans close to Nan to whisper, "She's quite overcome me with her talent, you know. All I can do is teach her the basics and watch what she does."

Ruthie carries the cake into the dining room. When Bay joins them, they take a vote, and it is unanimous: they will eat cake first, because, as Ruthie says, they don't want to ruin their appetites. Nan is about to slice into it, the gleaming knife hovering above the perfect terrain of frosting, when the doorbell rings.

"Well, who could that be?" Ruthie asks.

Nan shakes her head, though she thinks she knows. She goes to the door and takes a deep breath before opening it, Ruthie and Bay peering over her shoulder. In all the excitement, Nan's tears are mistaken for joy.

"What? You going to leave me out here like an old boot?"

She's not dressed properly, of course. Bay takes the purple shawl into the bathroom, and Ruthie offers Nan's slippers, but stops midsentence to peer suspiciously at Mavis.

"Don't you have any luggage?" Bay asks.

Mavis waves a bracelet-clanking wrist, the question an unreasonable distraction as she walks past them into the dining room, which shimmers with candlelight. She says she isn't hungry; she's eaten enough "for an entire lifetime," she says. "Don't mind me," she insists. "I'm on a completely different schedule now. What are you doing here?" she asks Ruthie.

Nan cuts the cake while Ruthie explains how she fell in love with the little house in the woods. "They call it the witch's cabin." She laughs, as though this is the funniest thing. "It needed work, but we fixed it."

"Oh, wait until you see," Bay says. "There's a stone fireplace and a front porch. Today, while we were baking, a deer stood right outside the window, watching."

The frosting, Nan thinks, is so light it melts in her mouth, barely sweet, the vaguest taste of rosewater, a confectionery dream. When she wipes a tear, the others look at her, but no one demands she explain herself, which she appreciates.

After dessert, they eat their dinner while Mavis regales them with tales of Africa. Nan feels a little shy about serving Ruthie and Bay, who are the better cooks, but she has kept it simple, no fancy tricks. Goulash. Warm rolls. A good merlot.

"Don't you even want wine?" Bay asks Mavis. "Wait! Where's Howard? Is he with his parents?"

"He stayed in Africa," Mavis says, "taking care of business."

Bay puzzles over this as she clears the dishes. She comes in and out of the room a few times to complete her task, and all the while, Nan stares at Mavis; what to say, how to say it? Ruthie seems struck by the same sort of reverie, for she, too, is uncharacteristically silent.

Bay takes extra long to return after the table is cleared. When she does, she brings with her the scent and chill of cold air, the glisten of snowflakes in her hair.

"Come on, Nana," she says.

Nan stands slowly, accepting Bay's hand, which is quite cold but exceptionally soft, letting her lead the way, looking back to see Ruthie pushing her chair in, patting her tight curls as though some damage could come to them. Mavis remains seated, flickering in the shadows. With a gentle squeeze of Bay's hand, Nan stops.

"Are you coming?" she asks.

Mavis shakes her head.

"I'm glad you were here," Nan says. Bay gently pulls, but Nan can be surprisingly strong when she needs to be. "Do you hear me? I'm glad you were here."

Mavis, who has been staring at the candles as though mesmerized by them, turns to Nan and smiles.

Nan dons her coat, gloves, scarf, and boots, resisting the temptation to look out the kitchen window. Bay steps from foot to foot like an excited child, while Ruthie smiles thinly, distracted, figuring things out. When Nan is finally ready, Bay opens the back door, waving her hand with a flourish.

Nan steps into the snow-fresh world, walking carefully down the stairs into the yard (one can never know about ice) toward her candles. Blinking against the pelting flakes, she takes a deep breath that fills her lungs until she gasps. "Why, look at all that light," she says, pressing her hands over her heart.

Bay stands at the window, watching Nan in her red boots, her long black coat, the old knit scarf wrapped around her head, the snow swirling, like a figure in one of those globes, solid in the midst of a shaken world. *Forever*, Bay thinks, her fingers hovering near, but not touching, the glass. "Forever," she whispers, reaching toward the small flames swollen to golden auras like the hundred magic moons of a fairy-tale garden.

Forever

Acknowledgments

"Sometimes our inner light goes out, but it is blown again into flame by an encounter with another human being. Each of us owes the deepest thanks to those who have rekindled this inner light."
—Albert Schweitzer

With gratitude to: Lori Alberts, Cathy Barber, Kristen Barrows, Bill Bauerband, Christopher Barzak (first reader, patient friend and guide), Rick Bowes, Dr. Brugaletta, Tom Canty, Haddayr Copley-Woods, Basha Cord, Karen Crandall, Shana Drehs, Dr. Richard Dunham, Jeff Ford, Connie May Fowler, Meg Galarza, Douglas Glover, Marcia Gorra-Patek, Anna Klenke, Joshilyn Jackson, Ellen Lesser, the Lyons family, Howard Morhaim (your affection for this work has meant a great deal to me), Beth Phelan, all the folks at the Howard Morhaim Literary Agency, my family, Terry Schuster, Sourcebooks, Jonathan Strahan (here's your witch's story!), Thomas Tunney (words can never say...), Gordon Van Gelder (special thanks for opening the door), Vermont College of Fine Arts, Karen Wiederholt, and Gary K. Wolfe.

Reading Group Guide

1. Discuss the meanings of the plant descriptions at the beginning of each chapter. How does each plant relate to the events of the chapter, and why do you think the author chose each one? Are there certain plants, herbs, or flowers that have special meaning to you?

2. Nan's unusual garden is a constant presence in the novel, acting almost as a character itself. How does the garden setting affect the mood of the novel? What are some other examples of gardens used in literature?

3. At the beginning of the novel, Nan is seventy-nine years old and Bay is fourteen. How do you think their relationship has been affected by Nan being a significantly older mother?

4. What secrets does Nan keep from Bay? What secrets does Bay keep from Nan? Nan, Ruthie, and Mavis are all very aware of their age and status as older women. How do age and the passing of time play into the novel?

5. Nan tells Mavis that she especially hates being called "cute." Do you agree? Has your relationship to the word changed over the years?

6. Nan reveals herself to be a complex person—overall, do you think she's a good person?

7. Nan, Mavis, and Ruthie each had potential that went largely unrealized in their lifetimes. Is this because of what happened with Eve, or simply what happens with age?

8. Nan, Mavis, and Ruthie took Eve to the city for an abortion given by a man who said he was a real doctor. What if they had made a different choice? What if they had gone to Miss Winter instead? Would things necessarily have turned out differently? What if Eve didn't have the abortion? What would her life have been like? Would the four of them have remained friends?

9. At the time of Eve's abortion, there was no legal option for one. Nonetheless, Mavis insisted they go to a "real" doctor. Discuss why she thought this was a better option.

10. Discuss the characters in the story. Who behaved criminally? Who behaved heroically?

11. Is a criminal act defined by conscience or law?

12. Why does Ruthie respond so passionately to Bay's comment that she understands how it feels to want to murder someone? Could Bay ever have been an actual threat to anyone?

13. In some ways, this novel is about how people don't see one another. Discuss how this is explored in all the characters. Have you ever had an experience where you later realized you had not "seen" someone?

14. Although much material is written about broken romance, broken friendships are given less attention and yet can be just as difficult. Have you ever lost a friendship you wish you had maintained?

15. Ruthie and Mavis convince Nan that she had nothing to do with Karl's death. Were they right to do so?

16. How does Nan's guilty conscience affect her life and the decisions she makes?

17. During the feast, Stella says that forgiveness is done for the self, rather than for the one who has done the damage. Do you agree or disagree?

18. When Mavis asks Nan if she has forgiven Eve's father, Nan indicates that she has her limits. Is forgiveness a duty? Should someone who has been harmed always feel responsible to give forgiveness? By the end of the novel, who has been forgiven and who hasn't?

19. Discuss the way food is used in this novel—Nan's birthday breakfast, the sandwiches Bay leaves for Karl, her birthday dinner, Ruthie's pancakes, the flower feast, the apple pie—and what different foods mean to you. Have you ever had a meal or dish that carried a strong emotional impact either while you were eating it or later as a memory?

20. By the end of the novel, we realize Ruthie identifies as a witch. Discuss all the ways she used her secret power for good.

21. How is each person changed by the end of the novel?

22. How does the fact that Bay sees ghosts affect her future with Nan, Mavis, and Ruthie?

23. At the end of the novel, who is dead and who is alive?

24. What might Bay's life be like in the future?

A Note from the Author

When people ask what my novel is about, I often find myself chewing air until I sputter "a garden" or "memory" or "death." I might add, "But it's sweet." I try the *elevator pitch*, a term writers use to describe the summation of an entire novel into the space of time it might take to pique the interest of a publishing type miraculously riding the same elevator as the author.

I, however, live in a town not only not frequented by publishing types (alas, there isn't even a bookstore), but also, as far as I know, there is not a single elevator. Perhaps that is the reason I am so bad at the infamous pitch.

"It's about old women," I say. "Friends who haven't seen each other since the bad thing happened. It's about mothers and daughters, forgiveness. Here." I awkwardly thrust a small packet of forget-me-not seeds at the inquisitor. "It's about gardens."

Almost never do I say it's about witches, so wary am I of the reduction that often arrives with the archetype because, I learned, many people have formed an idea of what a witch is and can be, or what a witch story is about.

I am not the sort of writer who knows where I am going. Only later, as I pull the disparate elements together, do I ask what their reasons might be.

Why witches, I wondered. *Why tell this story with witches?*

In many ways, this is a tale of hidden things and illusions—secrets, masks, and that oldest trick of all, hiding in plain sight. In fact, in spite of the sweet tone, this is a story about one of the greatest hiding-in-plain-sight manifestations of all—death. The challenge was how to write about this aspect without diminishing its potency or allowing it to overwhelm life's tendency toward regeneration. The tradition of the witch's garden, with its uncertain seasons, seemed a fine way to address both the fetid and fertile elements, while witches revealed themselves to be perfect figures to stand at the border. Who better suited to traverse the feminine power of creation and its opposite than a witch?

While writing this novel, I was a student at the MFA program of Vermont College of Fine Arts, where I was fortunate enough to work with author Joshilyn Jackson. Early in our acquaintance, she asked what food my story would be, which is not, actually, the typical writing teacher question.

"It's a dark chocolate truffle," I said in a gleeful rush, knowing I had found my perfect mentor, "with a hint of cayenne that sneaks up on you."

Most of us live lives of half memory and illusion. For most of us, death is the shock that overwhelms the sweet. "Wait, what's this?" we might ask, slowly recalling the ingredients. After all, it's not like we haven't been *warned*.

I'm afraid we've gotten into a terrible habit of separating our tastes as if sweet and bitter not only shouldn't associate, but can actually be kept apart. Why is it we insist forgiveness is sweet but forget how bitter it is to produce? How can it be that, at this late date, we still look at old women as if the only stories they might have to tell are about baking cookies and raising children? Why is it that even in the mythic landscape, the very definition of borderless space, we tend to confine witches, the symbol of malleability, within narrow parameters? What are we so afraid of?

I guess I don't tell people this is a story about witches because it seems to diminish more than to inform, which is kind of the point. Yes, this is a story about witches, but this is also the story of the way women are reduced by society's expectations for their behavior; the way people look at old women and think they are cute, or regard young girls as insubstantial.

I am happy to applaud the old men who march in our Fourth of July parade, the veterans in their uniforms and medals; I cannot imagine the battles they fought, but I also wonder about the old woman applauding beside me who likely fought some battles of her own for which there is little recognition because, even now, women's stories are often lost to misconception.

It is October as I compose this, sitting at my desk before the same window I looked out during the years it took to tell this story. A giant spider fashioned from some sort of weatherproof material crawls across my neighbor's house, while a gauzy creature with a ghoulish face dangles from the oak tree's branches. I am having a difficult time finishing this rumination, and I recognize that this is a result of some reluctance to let go. On a shelf next to my desk is the stack of books I have read as research for my next novel, and tucked into the drawer are its first pages. Yes, it is definitely time for me to move on, yet, as I look at the house which served to ground me in the space of Nan and Bay's garden home, I like to think these characters I came to love will always exist in the space they lived in, a place Bay calls *Forever*. I like to believe this is what life is about—an untamed garden, a spiral of light, seasons of creation and destruction and yes, bitterness. Too often we forget the power we all possess. What could be more wondrous than forgiveness, that alchemy that produces from its dark root the bright flower? What could be a better trick than the one many of us struggle with—the ability to hang on even as we let go?

I just saw this season's first snowflakes drifting outside my window. I have forty daffodil bulbs to plant; alliums and tulips, as well. *The seasons don't wonder*, as Ruthie would say. *They just move along.*

And so must I, but not without first taking this moment to

thank you for sharing this magical place. Please join me in a toast (or raise a chocolate toad). To the cut flowers! We are the living and the dead.

Mary Rickert
October 28, 2013

About the Author

Before earning her MFA from Vermont College of Fine Arts, Mary Rickert worked as a kindergarten teacher, coffee shop barista, balloon vendor at Disneyland, and in the personnel department at Sequoia National Park, where she spent her free time hiking the wilderness. She now lives in Cedarburg, Wisconsin, a

PHOTO BY WILL BAUER

small city of candy shops and beautiful gardens. This is her first novel. There are, of course, mysterious gaps in this account of her life, and that is where the truly interesting stuff happened. www.maryrickert.net